Black Hearts Golden Wings

By

Leon E. Emo

PublishAmerica
Baltimore

© 2002 by Leon E. Emo.

All rights reserved. No part of this book may be reproduced in any form without written permission from the publishers, except by a reviewer who may quote brief passages in a review to be printed in a newspaper or magazine.

First printing

ISBN: 1-59129-337-5
PUBLISHED BY PUBLISHAMERICA BOOK PUBLISHERS
www.publishamerica.com
Baltimore

Printed in the United States of America

To

My Father
An Adventurer Through Life

To BOBBY KAHN

A GREAT MADERAN BUT, MOST OF ALL, A LONGTIME n CHERISHED FRIEND

ACKNOWLEDGMENTS

I wish to thank the people who aided in the creation of this novel. Without their help and encouragement the text would not have been accurate or interesting.

It began, over a couple of beers, at the Paso Robles Inn. I proposed the idea of this book to my best friend Keith Davis. Together, over a few more brews, we tweaked my concept into the basic plot. Through the months it has changed, but without his help and optimism the concept would not have been placed into words.

Mario Gonzales, an extraordinary mechanic, was a valuable source in describing the operations of a crop dusting business and the intricacies of the World War II Stearman Trainer that was used for agricultural spraying and dusting throughout the San Joaquin Valley from the late forties into the seventies.

The pilots, both living and dead, were a great resource. Thanks to venerable ag-pilot Ray Pool for letting me sit in one of the last fully operational Stearmans in order to get a feel of the controls and what the pilots had to operate while flying low over the crops, dodging standpipes, wires and power poles. My appreciation could not leave out current pilot Andy Haynes. His valuable insight into the actual flying technique and feel of the aircraft while in the air and during maneuvers added much to this story. Also my gratefulness goes out to my own flight instructor and friend, Vern Lund. He managed to get me in the "left seat" and to even "solo." Something not accomplished except by my own father when I was a teenager.

As I completed the text, I would ask two ladies to read each chapter. Their reading and always encouraging remarks kept me punching the keys. At the counter of her little store, I would anxiously await the verdict of Marie Bunch as she read each chapter. Then I would rush it to my sister Paula Garner in hopes of her approval. Finally, Genevieve Frede was the first I trusted to be left alone with the entire manuscript. She returned it, delighted, and with continued encouragement.

I could not even have attempted to try to publish the work without the perusal and respected words of educator and mentor Art Davis. Mr. Davis' words of constructive criticism were a boon to the finished project. One of his students, my own son Michael, has never read the text but he continually harped to his father to finish the effort. His "hurry up" remarks were ceaseless and, now I realize, a necessity.

Of course, my wife Viola helped in the completion of this volume in ways she would never understand. Always encouraging. Always willing to leave me alone in "my room" to work while she sat alone in the living room. Then, without a moments notice, she would be asked to drop whatever she was doing to come an listen while I read aloud each chapter as I made changes to the text. She never complained when I would suddenly leave the house in the mornings to drive the city streets, backcountry roads, or sit alone in my vehicle at a lonely, forgotten airfield in search of inspiration.

CHAPTER ONE

The alarm sounded at three thirty in the morning. Young Jack rolled out of bed and onto all fours after just a few hours of sleep. He felt sick. If he could just get up he knew it would get better. He grabbed the side of the bed and pulled himself to one knee. Then, pushing on the mattress, he rose to the normal human standing position. It was a Saturday in the summer of '62 and a day off for most. But for Jack it was the beginning of a long day of helping operate his father's crop dusting business. It was the busiest of times. He had done it each summer since he was in seventh grade. Learning to spin the props, taxi and load the aging World War II Stearman trainers that were converted to agricultural purposes after the war.

The night before, he had gone to Sheila's high school senior prom. Jack was two years older but they had begun secretly dating after meeting her while she worked as a carhop at a drive-in. After the dance they had copped a six-pack of beer and a bottle of sloe gin and headed for Millerton Lake to watch the "submarine races." Known by teenagers in the community as an excuse for love making at vista point, the "races" never took place. Their parents were clueless as to its meaning along with the fact that Jack and Sheila were dating. By midnight, they were headed back to town and to her house. The wind blowing in their hair as he drove his first car, a '58 Ford Convertible, fast but confident down the two-lane highway toward home. Sheila was feeling no pain. Mixing the sloe gin and Coca-Cola during the night she was giggling at every turn and swerve that Jack made cruising madly down the road from the foothills to the valley floor. A block from her home he turned off the lights and engine. The Ford coasted silently down the street. At her driveway he stopped and she stepped out leaving the door open. She straightened her skirt and sweater and walked slowly to the door. He waited in the darkness for her to enter the house and then a few more minutes. He saw the light come on in her bedroom and wished he were there. Jack turned the key. The engine roared to life and when he slammed the accelerator pedal down the open passenger door swung closed as he sped off down the street.

But morning had come early. "Damn that shit," Jack muttered to himself as he went slowly to the bathroom. The kidneys had done their job and the bladder was screaming for relief. He took a long time to piss. He leaned over the sink and turned on the faucet. The cold water on his face gave relief and had an instant sobering effect. A half-hour earlier his father had left for breakfast at a truck stop before heading to the airfield. Jack had to at least be at the field when Pop arrived. He was careful not to wake his stepmother who had probably gotten in late also. But not as late as he had, for once. He quietly closed the front door, climbed in his car and headed for the airfield.

The "field" was an old Army Air Corps training facility smack in the middle of the San Joaquin Valley, the world's richest agricultural region. The tarmac the military had used had been removed and replaced with concrete and asphalt. The field was now the town's Municipal Airport with a few private planes, mostly Pipers and Cessna's, but the biggest businesses there was Jack's father's Cal-Ag and a competing company, Western Dusters, owned by Sheila's father. Jack raced north a few miles on old highway 99. Entering the left turn lane he looked for oncoming traffic. No lights, so he coasted through the stop and across the southbound lanes onto Airport Drive. As he passed the café on his left, he saw his dad's truck parked outside. He still had time to get to the field and get the planes warmed up. A mile farther he slowed and was on the airfield. To his right there were two hangers and the old officers club which was used as the airport manager's office and doubled as a pilots' and mechanics' lounge. Inside, candy and soft drinks were sold over a small counter with a glass top. Several tables and chairs for card playing were in the middle of the room. Next to the walls, a few old sofas were used for resting and since the place was never locked, sleeping off hangovers. The walls were decorated with photos of the airfield's military days and early history. He drove past the office and parked next to the first hanger. This large metal building was home to Cal-Ag. It could hold up to three planes and had an office with a couple of wooden desks and metal file cabinets. Outside was his father's air force. Seven Stearman biplanes, three equipped for spraying and four for dusting, were parked in their respective rows facing each other. Each had been painted with a black fuselage with gold wings and tail section. Parked next to the three spray rigs were a Piper Comanche and a V-tailed Beech Bonanza that were used for a charter service by the three pilots of Cal-Ag when the need arose. Jack turned the Ford's motor off, jumped over the door of the convertible and ran to the first duster.

It was still dark as the mechanic found the cockpit edge and climbed up onto the lower wing of the old Stearman. He raised one leg over and pulling the other in lowered himself into the rear pilot's seat of the former army trainer. The front seat had been removed and a "hopper" for chemicals had been inserted down into the fuselage. He leaned his head over the edge of the cockpit to catch a glimpse of Jack slowly turning the propeller blade to push oil up into the cylinders. After several rotations Jack yelled, "Contact," and the mechanic switched the magneto to on and answered, "Contact." Jack grabbed the left side of the propeller blade with both hands. He swung his right leg upward for leverage and pulled down as hard as he could while at the same time backing away. The prop spun counter clockwise twice and then stopped. "Shit," muttered Jack. He again approached the blade. "Off," he yelled to the mechanic in the cockpit. "Off," came the reply. Jack reached up and turned the prop parallel to the ground. "Contact," Jack cried again. "Contact," said the mechanic. "Come on," Jack muttered as he once again whipped his leg upward and then back down. Pulling hard with his hands and arms he swung the blade to his right. Like a ghost from the past the big Pratt and Whitney engine roared to life. In the twinkling between darkness and sunrise Jack could see the orange hot flame belching from the exhaust like a huge Roman candle on the fourth of July. Flames that would render the engine cowling and right fuselage a sooty black. As the engine slowly warmed to operating temperature the flame would become a brilliant blue. Brownie, the mechanic, climbed out of the duster cockpit and made sure the chocks that kept the wheels from rolling were secure.

"Just made it again, hey kid," Brownie said, kidding his boss's son.

"Yea, too much partying, you won't tell Dad will ya Brownie?" Jack pleaded.

Brownie laughed. "Not if you wash and lube ol' 93 after we're through."

"Ah, come on Brownie not today. I have to meet Sheila for lunch."

"Now that's something you wouldn't want me to tell the old man about," Brownie said laughing again. He was referring to Jack's dad, the chief pilot of Cal-Ag.

"Come on kid, let's get three-seven and seven-one warm. We got all three aces working this morning." Brownie pushed Jack in the back toward three-seven. The crew, in place of names on the aircraft, used the last two digits of the federal aviation identification number painted on the vertical tail section. Today, besides Jack's dad Alan, and second pilot Gary Wilson, his young cousin Pat would be flying low over the fields of the valley killing bugs. Pat was Jack's Uncle Dan's oldest boy. At 24 he already had three years of experience in crop dusting. Jack, four years younger, admired Pat. Jack could fly also and was learning quickly the low level flying skill it took to be a good Ag pilot. Gary, like Jack's father, was a former bomber commander in World War II and now was the number two pilot and airport manager.

The planes were warming up and the pilots were in the hanger office going over notes on fields they would have to fly today. Checking the location of irrigation standpipes and power lines at each field. Today they would be using a county road out on the west side for loading the spray rigs of Gary and Pat. Two men jumped in a big water tanker and headed for the road where the chemical company had already unloaded the 55-gallon drums of Malathion. Jack climbed in a black and gold painted pick-up truck, stopped to pick up Brownie at the hanger and headed toward the Stage Ranch. There a landing strip, paid for by the county, had been built for use by anyone who got there first. Sometimes, both Cal-Ag and Western Dusters used it. Whoever arrived first took the prime loading area. As Jack left the warm up area and headed toward the airport road, the sun was just cresting the mountains to the east. He looked across the airfield to the south end and saw the scarlet and white Stearmans of Western Dusters warming up. Someday, somehow, Sheila's father would have to learn about the two of them.

"Step on it Jack," Brownie demanded. "You know how your old man hates to be number two."

"We'll make it if this jalopy will do seventy," Jack answered, pondering if he shouldn't let his passenger drive. Ten miles in ten minutes is all we need he thought.

CHAPTER TWO

The roads in the county were spaced a mile apart and formed a checkerboard on a map. Within a mile of the landing strip, the sun was now rising above the towering Sierra mountains to the east and Jack could see the outline of a Stearman already being loaded with sulfur.

"What'd these sons of bitches do, spend the night?" Jack growled.

"Must've brought breakfast and coffee with 'em," answered Brownie.

As Jack turned onto the short dirt road that led to the paved strip, he could see the glimmering metal blades of the prop spinning. The two loaders from Western almost had the plane ready for take off. He drove past the biplane and parked a hundred yards farther down the strip and the next stack of fifty pound sulfur bags. This meant that after loading his father's plane Alan would have to taxi back to the east end, turn the plane around and point it upwind before taking off.

Western Dusters' aircraft was ready now. There was no taxiing or turning. Just full on the throttle and head into the wind. As the plane roared past, Jack and Brownie could see the scarlet helmet of the pilot. It was Sheila's father, Harry, at the controls. He lifted the biplane into the morning haze. The wings banked gently left and the plane, still gaining altitude, was soon headed south to the pilot's assigned field. As that Stearman disappeared another appeared from the north. This one, painted black and gold, was just a couple of minutes away.

"Jack, got your grape knife?" Brownie asked as he donned his goggles and gloves.

"Right here, close to my heart," Jack replied, pulling the curved blade from the hip pocket of his jeans.

Brownie tossed Jack's goggles toward him. "Let's be ready when the ol' man gets here. You take the cockpit. I want to see the way he looks at you when he climbs out."

The Cal-Ag plane approached from the east. It formed a black silhouette against the rising sun. Brownie and Jack watched as both the front wheels and tail wheel touched down at the same time.

Another three point landing. The Stearman whizzed by, stopped and turned one hundred and eighty degrees and taxied back to where the two loaders and the stacks of sulfur were waiting. Alan, the pilot, glided the lower left wing over the top of the bags and stopped. Brownie set the chocks in front of the tires as Jack approached the cockpit. His father, leaving the engine and prop turning on idle, climbed out of his seat and onto the lower wing. Jack waited. The pilot jumped down off the lower wing. Passing Jack without speaking or nodding, he walked to the outer edge of the wing. Leaning on the lower airfoil he lit a cigarette and looked at the crew from Western waiting for their plane to return. Jack quickly jumped onto the wing and climbed into the cockpit. Standing on the pilot's seat, he leaned forward and flipped the two latches that held the hopper door closed. Placing his fingers under the edge, he opened the door exposing the hole of the tank deep inside the fuselage. Brownie threw the first fifty-pound bag up and onto the space between the hopper and cockpit. Jack, grape knife in hand, sliced an opening right down the middle. Flipping the bag over, he emptied its contents into the hole and tossed the bag off the opposite side. The prop wash blew it backwards ten or so yards behind the plane. Again and again Brownie heaved the bags perfectly to the middle where Jack would rip, flip, empty and throw. Thirty-six times they would perform this routine until eighteen hundred pounds of the yellow bug killer filled the hopper to the maximum. Jack closed and latched the hopper door and stepped out of the cockpit and jumped from the lower wing to the ground. The "ol' man" had finished his cigarette and walked behind the rear of the lower wing to return to his pilot's seat. He passed his son Jack as he was dusting the sulfur off his clothes using the turbulence from the prop. No gestures, expressions or conversation was exchanged. As Alan pulled his goggles down and buckled his safety harness over his shoulders and lap, Brownie pulled the chocks from the wheels. Alan gave the Stearman some throttle and taxied toward the end of the strip to turn around yet again. He passed the Western loaders and waved once with his left hand. The loaders, still sitting on their sulfur bags gave him a thumbs up. Turning into the wind, Alan gave the plane full throttle and the big Pratt and Whitney engine roared loudly as it again passed the loaders. Now, with its heavy load, it lifted off the strip almost at the end and headed toward its first low level passes over a cotton field.

"Well, he didn't say much," Brownie mused as he and Jack picked up the empty bags.

"Didn't say shit, didn't even look at me." He must be pissed, Jack feared.

"Aw, don't worry about it Jack. It wasn't your fault they got here first."

Jack, an arm full of bags, carried them to the pile Brownie had already started well away from the prop wash.

Brownie, the senior mechanic and chief loader, thought a lot of young Jack and tried to ease his worry.

"By the time this morning is through he'll be over it," he told Jack.

"I hope you're right Brownie. You know he's not mean to me or anything but he has a way of letting me know what he thinks that makes me feel really bad."

"It's supposed to and besides, sure as hell beats gettin' whipped or grounded doesn't it?" asked Brownie.

"Don't even mention grounded," Jack answered.

"What'sa matter? Wouldn't be able to see little Sheila?"

"Well, that and other things," Jack again answered

"Other things!" exclaimed Brownie. "She's the only thing. At least that's the way it looks to me."

"Yea, I think a lot of her Brownie, so what."

"So keep your mouth shut. You're starting to drool," Brownie kidded.

Young Jack didn't say anything more but wanted to. Brownie opened his thermos and held out an empty cup.

"Want some coffee kid?" he asked.

"No thanks, don't drink much of that stuff."

"I'm going over to shoot the shit with those guys," Brownie said, nodding toward the two loaders from Western. "Wanna come?"

"Nah, just going to sit and think," answered Jack.

"Well, don't think about her too much, you might embarrass yourself with those tight jeans you kids wear nowadays." Brownie laughed as he walked away.

Jack could see his friend chatting and laughing with the competition's loaders. Even though both companies battled each other constantly to dust and spray the farmer's crops, he knew there was a certain camaraderie between the crews. Even the pilots sometimes would share drinks together at a local nightspot and talk of war years and flying adventures. The two people you would not see socializing were Alan Lawrence, Jack's dad and Harry Gebhardt, owner of Western Dusters. These two did not share much in common other than they were both pilots. Alan had been a former bomber pilot in the war and afterwards raced midgets and motorcycles in southern California. By 1948, he and his brother Dan had discovered that central California needed a crop dusting business. With just two renovated army trainers they had started spraying and dusting the farmers' fields. Alan was the pilot and Dan the loader, manager and bookkeeper. Soon the business was growing. More planes were added and a charter flight service was also offered. Brownie had been hired as a loader but soon with his mechanical ability was promoted to head mechanic. Three years later, Harry Gebhardt arrived with two dusters and two sprayers. Harry was younger and had missed the war. He had just finished navy flight training school when the conflict ended. He bought himself a Navy N3N biplane and started a small outfit in Arizona. But with crops sparse in the desert in 1952, he and his family decided to move to the San Joaquin Valley of California. Harry's wife, Debbie and only daughter, Sheila had become comfortable with the community after almost ten years.

Jack heard the roar of an engine and saw the Western plane approaching. Brownie finished his conversation and returned to sit down a few feet away from Jack.

Together they watched Harry Gebhardt touch the front wheels to the strip and then lower the tail wheel to the ground. Soon the plane was being loaded. This went on for most of the early morning, the planes alternately landing, loading, and leaving. Toward the end of the loading session the Western Dusters plane turned off its engine. Time for refueling. One of the loaders climbed into the cockpit and placed his feet on the pilot's seat. Stepping up to the center of the fuselage, he then climbed on top of the center of the top wing. This is where the fuel tank was located. The other loader handed him the fuel hose and began pumping the gas as the man on the top wing held the nozzle in place. This all took an extra five minutes. But that is all it took for the planes to be at the same landing strip at the same time.

After fueling, Harry Gebhardt climbed in and eased his plane out on to the strip. Checking to make sure everything was clear, he noticed his chief loader pointing upward and behind him. Harry turned and looked over his shoulder. It was the Cal-Ag plane on his final for landing. "Damn it," Harry muttered to himself knowing the landing plane has the right of way. "I can make him go around if I just ease a little farther down the strip," he thought. His hand pushed the throttle ever so slightly forward. The plane rolled slowly down the strip. By now the Cal-Ag duster was fifty feet off the ground and descending at a speed of eighty miles per hour. Both Jack and Brownie could see the ol' man was not going to abort his landing.

"Hell he's gonna try it," Brownie yelled, jumping off the sulfur bags to watch.

"Shit, Dad," Jack said as he stood up on the bags for a better look.

Everyone was quiet as the Cal-Ag plane crossed the end of the strip. Harry Gebhardt was revving his engine and just about to release the breaks when a giant black shadow passed directly over him. The wheels of Alan's aircraft barely missed the center section of the top wing where the fuel tank had just been topped off. A hundred feet more and the same wheels hit the ground. Alan was standing on the breaks now as the plane neared the canal that marked the end of the runway. With expert agility he alternated the brakes back and forth and brought the biplane to a stop ten yards from the ditch. Just enough space to turn around and taxi back. The two groups of loaders just looked at each other. Brownie slapped Jack, still standing on the sulfur bags, on the back of the leg.

"Yep, that's your ol' man, kid. Not too many could have done that."

"Yea, I know," Jack replied. Thinking that his dad wouldn't have had to do it if he would have got to the strip first.

Alan stopped his plane at the remaining bags, leaving enough room for Harry's duster to take off. It roared past at full throttle and was soon headed toward another field. Now it was time to fuel his dad's plane. Alan shut off the engine and climbed out.

"Nice landing, Dad," Jack announced as his father removed his helmet.

"Thanks, Son. Coulda been a three pointer though," replied his father, lighting another cigarette. Brownie and Jack followed the same procedure as the other two loaders had in filling the Cal-Ag plane. The Stearman was loaded and gassed up but Alan was waiting, slowly finishing his cigarette.

"Hey Pappy, you want me to start her up for ya?" Brownie asked, holding an arm full of empty bags.

"No thanks, Brownie. Almost done."

Alan, his helmet sitting on the wing, heard the faint sound of a Pratt and Whitney engine. He put out his cigarette on the sole of his boot and put his helmet on.

"Grab the prop, Son," he told Jack as he climbed into the cockpit. Jack grabbed the blade. "Contact," he yelled.

"Contact," came the reply from his father.

Jack spun the prop and the still warm engine roared to life. Alan Lawrence looked toward the east and saw a faint black spot in the sky getting larger. He rolled the plane out and maneuvered the duster to the end of the strip. Pointing its nose and wheels down the runway for take off, he looked behind him and saw the scarlet and white biplane of Harry Gebhardt approaching fast. Brownie, Jack and the two other loaders knew what was going to happen.

"Ya gonna see a repeat performance," yelled one of the Western loaders.

Brownie whispered to Jack, "We will see who the better 'short lander' is now, hey kid?"

"But he does have more room than what he gave Dad," answered Jack, noticing his father's plane at the very edge of the runway.

The Western biplane came in a little high. Missing the top wing of Pappy's plane by ten feet. As it passed Jack and Brownie, again standing, the plane was still airborne.

"He's too late, he'll never have enough room," yelled Brownie over the roar.

Halfway down the strip the duster touched earth. But the tail wheel never hit the runway as Harry tried to slow the plane by putting all his weight on the top of the rudder pedals. Nearing the end of the strip he pushed hard with his back against the seat. He could feel the balls of his feet pressing through his boots against the pedals. Almost at the same spot that Pappy had stopped the Stearman of Harry raised its tail wheel ever upward. The propeller bit into the ground, spraying dirt and gravel for hundreds of feet. By now the fuselage was perpendicular with the earth. The tail was straight up and teetering ever forward. Harry closed his eyes and crossing his arms, grabbed his shoulder harness. He felt himself turning upside down and heard the crushing of the tail section as the vertical stabilizer hit the ground splintering wood and tearing fabric. All was quiet now. Harry looked up and saw the ground. He would have to wait for help. If he unbuckled his harness he might plunge to the ground head first breaking his neck.

At once, the Western loaders jumped in their truck and headed toward the wreckage. Brownie and Jack, being closer had got there first.

"Let me help you Harry," offered Brownie.

"Get outta here, assholes," hollered Harry.

"Are you okay?" Brownie asked.

"What do you think? Just get out of here, now!" screamed Harry.

The Western loaders were now at the scene and Brownie backed away. Looking down at the far end of the runway Brownie could see dust rising in the air behind Pappy's aircraft.

"Oh shit kid, the ol' man is gonna take off," Brownie said, looking back at the loaders helping Harry out of his plane.

"He could wait a little doncha think?" asked Jack. "He waited to finish his cigarette."

"That was for a purpose."

"What purpose?" ask Jack.

Pointing to the wrecked Stearman on its back Brownie answered, "That purpose."

Harry was out of the aircraft now. Brushing the dust off his clothing he heard the roar of the engine at the far end. Everyone was looking at the sun reflecting off the metal prop spinning toward them. The biplane was nearly on them when it lifted off into the air. Everyone ducked or hit the ground on all fours as the wheels and wings swooped pass them just over their heads and roared off to the fields. It was quiet now.

"Well, I guess someone is through for the day," Jack touted as Brownie nudged him.

"Listen you son of a bitch, your old man better watch it or I'll turn him in," scolded Harry.

Jack started toward Harry. "Let it go kid," advised Brownie

grabbing him by the arm.

"Remember your lunch date," he reminded him, "wouldn't want to go all dirty and busted up would you?"

In two groups they headed back toward the loading area. The Western Dusters truck headed onto the main road and back to the airport. Later that day they would have to hire a flat bed truck and crane to lift their badly damaged plane and haul it back to the airfield. Alan Lawrence, Jack and Brownie would finish a couple of more loads, landing and taking off around the wreckage and then head home.

CHAPTER THREE

He was late. The dusting, because of the accident, had taken longer than usual. Then Brownie still made him wash the sulfur off his father's airplane. "No favors for the boss's son," he said when they had returned to the airfield. Jack had gone straight to the drive-in after work. His clothes still reeked of the odor of the yellow dust. As he pulled into the parking area, he could see Sheila sitting in a booth with her back to him. The long strands of her blond hair lying gently on her shoulders reached to the middle of her back. He walked quickly to the inside dining area of the few tables and booths. A jukebox in the corner was playing Buddy Holly's "That'll Be The Day." There was a small dance floor in front of the music machine. Jack sat down opposite her in the booth and clasped her hands in his own.

"Hi babe, sorry I'm late."

"It's okay, I figured something happened," she said in a forgiving tone.

"Did you order yet?" Jack asked. "Are you hungry?"

"Not yet, just waitin' for you," she answered.

Jack signaled for a waitress and one slowly walked to their table. "Like to order?"

"Two cheeseburgers with fries and...what do you want to drink babe?" asked Jack.

"Cherry Lime Ricky," answered Sheila. "Cherry Coke for me," said Jack.

The waitress left to place the order.

"So what'cha been doing this morning while I've been working my butt off?"

"At school, helping plan the decorations for our graduation dance," Sheila answered.

"Two weeks from yesterday, right?" Jack wanted to make sure.

"Yes, finally finished," responded Sheila, "where are you going to take me after the dance? Dad said I could stay out 'till the sun comes up."

"Not with me, I bet," Jack said rather sarcastically.

"Of course not, silly. But what he doesn't know won't hurt him."

Jack wondered if she had found out what had happened earlier that morning.

"Have you seen your dad today?" he asked.

"No, but he has some paper work for me in the office this afternoon. That's where I'm headed after we eat."

Jack took a chance. "Then you don't know what happened this morning?"

"No! What happened?" Sheila asked, pulling her hands away from Jack.

The waitress brought their lunches and seemed to stand at their table for an insufferable amount of time. Jack, famished, took a bite of his cheeseburger and washed it down with his cherry coke. Sheila didn't touch her meal. The waitress finally left.

"What happened Jack?" she demanded.

"Well," he swallowed hard, "I don't know if I should be the one to tell you."

"Then you shouldn't have said anything," Sheila demanded again. "What happened?"

"Your dad got in a little accident and flipped his Stearman."

"Oh shit, is he hurt, did you see it, Jack. What happened, what happened?" Her voice rising and quivering at the same time.

"Well, he just ran out of runway and flipped it," he answered. "He's alright, nothing hurt but a little pilot pride."

"I've never seen Dad make an error like that. Something must've been wrong with the plane."

Jack saw his reprieve. "Yea, must've been the brakes. Musta just locked up. Aren't you gonna eat. It's getting cold." He wanted this to end with the usual kiss.

Sheila took a bite and sat a few minutes slowly eating her lunch. Finally she spoke.

"That's the first time I think, for Dad...a wreck I mean."

"It happens to the best of us," Jack said. Thinking that in the less than a hundred hours of low level practice flying and landing on short strips he hadn't come close.

"Honey, I don't want you crop dusting. It's too dangerous."

Jack finishing off the last of his French fries mumbled, "Do you think my dad would let me try it if I wasn't ready? Come on now, finish your burger and let's go."

Sheila took one more bite and emptied her drink. "Okay, let's go. Where're you parked?"

"Right out front, I didn't see your wheels," Jack said paying the bill with no tip.

"I got a ride from a girlfriend. Give me a lift back to school or maybe you just want to take me right up to the airport office and drop me off?" Sheila chuckled.

"Very funny, you know babe, I could make you walk."

Sheila turned her body slightly and flipped her long hair back over her shoulder. "I wouldn't be walking very long, I bet."

"Okay, let's go. And don't be doing that to anyone else."

Jack opened the car door for Sheila and she slid into the seat, tucking her knee length dress under her. Jack got in and started up his car and headed the few blocks to the high school. He pulled up beside Sheila's car and let his hotrod idle in neutral.

"Aren't you going to let me out?" Sheila asked.

"What! Jeez, such demands," Jack said as he went around to open her door.

"Just getting you in practice for our special night after graduation."

"Okay, you happy?" He said closing her door. "And no flirting."

"You can't be jealous of a relationship that nobody's supposed to know about?"

He grabbed her around the waist and locking his fingers together behind her pulled her body close to his. "Yes, I'm jealous and I would say this is becoming more of a relationship, wouldn't you?"

Sheila was silent. She pressed the middle of her body against Jack's. He looked into her blue eyes. She tilted her head slightly backward and parted her lips. They kissed for a long time. Jack could smell her fragrant aroma. Like spring flowers, he thought, hoping the smell of sulfur was not emanating towards her. "See you tonight, call me," he whispered as their lips parted.

"I love you Jack," Sheila admitted, getting in her car. He blew her a kiss and drove off with a squeal of his tires.

He was headed back to the field. In the afternoon it was easier work. Mainly he just hung around and handed Brownie wrenches and sockets as he worked on a plane. Sometimes he would get to do some minor maintenance or ride on a short charter flight to a valley destination. If his dad was pilot, Jack would get to sit in the left seat on the return trip and fly the plane home. He already had his private license and soon he hoped he would be dusting and spraying the crops as his dad and cousin did every morning. But for now he was content on just being around the airplanes and people that worked for his dad and Uncle Dan. Brownie was the head honcho on the field. He knew a Stearman trainer from front to rear, every nut, bolt and rivet. He was well respected as a mechanic and just a couple of years older than Jack's cousin Pat. Together they were a pair to draw to. In the evenings after work they would go out carousing the town and looking for girls or just a good time. And usually they found both. They were athletically built. Brownie was a former professional boxer and Pat had been a star athlete in high school. They liked what little nightlife the small valley town had to offer and if that wasn't enough there was always Fresno just a half-hour away. Jack pulled up to the hanger. Brownie and his assistant, Lew, were playing ping-pong with Pat challenging the winner.

"How's it going guys?" Jack said after a point was made by Brownie, "Who's ahead?"

"Who do you think," said Lew, "I'll never beat this guy."

"Shit Lew, you have trouble beating me," said Jack

The game went on with Brownie winning easily. Pat's turn at the table and Jack watched the spirited play between the two. "I win and you drive tonight, right Patty?" Brownie smiled.

"Hope you got plenty of gas in your rig," Pat answered, slamming Brownie's serve back past him for a winner. Jack watched a little longer then wandered outside the hanger. He looked south toward the office of Western Dusters. He saw Sheila's car parked outside and wondered if she and her father were discussing what had happened that morning. Guess he would find out later.

"Hey kid, you wanna ride with us tonight? We got plenty of room. Goin' to Fresno."

It was Pat yelling from inside the hanger. Jack walked back inside.

"Come on kid, we'll set you up," his cousin joked. "About time you lost your virginity."

"No thanks cous'. I got a hot date of my own and I don't have to go looking for it."

"If you keep dating her the only thing you'll be remembered for is looking for trouble," Pat announced.

"Don't worry, I can take care of myself," Jack assured his cousin.

"Well, just be careful and don't get caught." Pat pulled out his wallet and produced a condom. "Here take this. Just in case. You do know how to use one of these don't you?" laughed his cousin.

"Yes, and I don't need yours. I have my own," Jack replied, getting angry.

Brownie interrupted. "Let's get back to work guys. Come on Jack, I need some help mounting this new boom on three-seven." Jack grabbed an end of the long metal spray device and held it while Brownie bolted it in place under the wing. By 4:30 that afternoon the hanger doors were being closed and the crews heading home. Jack arrived at his house and jumped in the shower. The hot water rinsed the sweat, sulfur and frustration off his body and out of his mind. This night with Sheila was going to be good.

Later, Jack was sitting in the front room watching television. As the opening music for "Have Gun Will Travel" played he was thinking of just one thing.

His dad and stepmother were getting ready for a dinner engagement with some friends at the Town House. It was their favorite restaurant and one of only two in town that you could get a good steak with all the trimmings. They would usually end up in the bar afterwards and Alan, having to fly in the morning, would call it a night by ten. His stepmother would sometimes stay out later and take a cab home.

The phone rang. It was Sheila with directions. She would leave her car at the drive-in where she worked and Jack could pick her up there. They talked a little. But when Sheila's mother walked into the room she said goodbye and hung up. Alan, already dressed for dinner, came into the room.

"Going out tonight, Son?" he asked.

"Yep, but I'll be home by midnight. Gotta work tomorrow, right?"

"That's right," his father confirmed. "If I don't see you later, I'll see you in the morning. By the way, can I ask who she is?"

"You know, Dad. That high school senior I've been dating,"

answered Jack.

"Let me tell you something, Son. I know who she is and who her parents are and I really don't care if you date her. If you have feelings for her."

"I know dad. And I appreciate it," Jack paused. "And I do have feelings for her."

"Just be careful and don't get caught. There won't be much your old Dad can do about it, you know."

"Jeez Dad, you sound just like Brownie and Pat this afternoon."

"Well, it's nice to know someone else around here is watching out for you," Alan said as he opened the front door for his wife and they left for dinner.

Shortly after his parents had driven away, Jack was in his Ford convertible headed for the drive-in and Sheila. When he arrived she was sitting in the same booth as before. Except this time she had company. It was male company. Jack approached and said hello to Sheila.

"Hi honey, I'd like you to meet Carter O'Kane. He's on summer vacation from college and working for Dad." Jack shook hands with Carter and sat down next to Sheila.

Carter was slightly taller than Jack. He had curly blond hair and light blue eyes. A thin, lightly colored mustache occupied the space between a well-formed mouth and his angular Romanesque nose. Jack was immediately jealous, but kept the emotion hidden deep inside.

"So, what school you attending Carter?" Jack asked.

"Berkeley, I'm majoring in poli-sci," answered his newfound competition.

"Poli-sci," Jack repeated not quite sure of that field of study.

"Yes, I should have a degree by this time next year," Carter bragged as he looked across at Sheila sitting quietly beside Jack.

"That's great Carter. You ready to go babe?" Jack asked grabbing Sheila by the hand and standing up.

"Well, I guess so," answered Jack's girl as she was being pulled out of the booth.

Carter also stood up and faced the pair.

Without extending his hand Jack offered a simple, "Nice meeting you, see you later."

"Yea, see you at the field, and you too, Sheila," Carter said, smiling at the both of them. His mustache rising at each corner of his mouth, exposing an almost perfect set of glistening white teeth. Turning his eyes toward her he added, "See you, in the office."

The couple left and Jack opened his car door for Sheila and soon they were headed down the main street of town.

"Where do you wanna go tonight babe," asked Jack.

"Oh, I don't care Jack," Sheila said looking out her side at the small houses passing slowly by. "What did you think of Carter?"

Jack, the rage again rising inside, "Does it matter? Besides he's just summer help right?"

Sheila, sensing his resentment answered carefully. "That's right, by September he'll be back in college. Let's go to Fresno and eat at Mars."

"Mars?" Jack questioned her choice of drive-ins, "that's the same food we can get here."

"I know, but we can drag the strip a little and see what's going on," Sheila pleaded.

"Okay, anything you want." Jack turned onto the highway and headed south toward the biggest city in the valley. Bright lights and adventure.

They ate at Mars Drive-in and drove up and down Blackstone Avenue for over an hour. Top down and listening to Presley, Holly, Fats and others singing what Sheila's mom called "the devil's music," rock and roll.

By the time they cruised back into town it was near midnight. Jack, sensing his manhood stirring between his legs, asked if Sheila wanted to go to the field.

"Why, we're there all day as it is?" Sheila answered.

"We could sit on the couch in the officers club," Jack said.

"I don't think so Jack, I'd feel funny. Besides, I better get home."

Jack's manhood went limp. "Okay, I'll take you back."

When he arrived at her car the drive-in was closed and dark. Jack pulled his car up to Sheila's and pointed the headlights toward the vehicle.

"How about I come by in the morning on the way to work?" Jack asked hopefully.

"Are you crazy?" wondered his girl.

"Yes, I am, for you," Jack said, proud of his stab at romanticism.

"But where and how?" Sheila queried.

"Leave your bedroom window open. I'll park a block away and walk."

"But Jack, the screen."

"I can take that off from the outside and put it back when I leave. Nobody'll know."

Sheila worried how she would look that early in the morning and asked, "What time?"

"I'll be there at four. That'll give us a half hour together, beautiful," Jack answered. Caressing the back of his girl's head and then pulling her toward him, he moved his hand around to her far breast. He gently squeezed her nipple through her bra and then slid his palm downward and cupped the same area of womanhood in his hand. They kissed a long time, Sheila's supple tongue exploring the inside of Jack's vocal orifice.

Sheila got out of the car. "I'll be waiting honey, but please be quiet," she pleaded.

"I will. Just have the window open," said Jack as he watched his girl get in her car.

They both drove off in opposite directions. That night as he lay in bed, Jack would hear his father come in and go into the master bedroom. An hour later his stepmom came in and quietly closed the door of their room behind her. Jack would spend a restless few hours trying to get some sleep.

CHAPTER FOUR

Jack drove slowly. A block from Sheila's house he turned off the engine and coasted around the corner. This morning he had taken the Cal-Ag truck that his dad had driven home the night before. Getting out of the truck Jack eased the door closed. Holding in the knob of the handle, he pushed gently until he heard the latch click against the post. He quickly walked the block to the house and crouched behind a neighbor's hedge. He could see the window to the bedroom where Sheila was waiting. He jumped the hedge and approached the house. The damp grass kept his footsteps silent. At the window, he found the screen unlatched from the inside. Jack pulled the bottom out and slid the screen off the two hooks above the window frame. Putting both hands on the bottom frame he pushed down and jumped, simultaneously catapulting his body into the opening. It was dark inside. Suddenly he felt something soft and tender grab his hand. His eyes, adjusting to the darkness, could see Sheila's disrobed body draped only in a transparent baby doll nightgown of the sheerest nylon. She held his one hand as he completed his covert entrance and stood in front of her. She held one finger up to her lips, but just for a moment. Jack gently took her hand and placed the same finger on his lips. Jack removed his shirt. Leaving his belt on, he unzipped his pants. Sheila came closer. He felt her hands move up his back. She caressed his shirtless shoulders. He pulled his manhood through the opening in his pants. He wasn't wearing underwear this morning. Still standing, Sheila lowered one hand to Jack's member, spread her legs and placed it between them.

"Kiss me," she whispered.

Jack being taller, kissed her hair, her ear, her now closed eyelids and then finally her waiting lips. Still embraced they took short steps to the bed. Sheila lay back and looked up at the only lover she had ever known. He raised the baby doll nightgown and stroked her small soft breasts. He felt her nipples swell and harden when he squeezed them tenderly between his fingers.

She held Jack's testicles in her hand. Gently rubbing them together and then, grabbing his cock, she softly rubbed the taut skin.

Moving her hand up and down. On each downward stroke she would push against the base and hold it. Jack was now massaging her other breast.

"Kiss them Jack," his lover asked. "Suck them honey," Sheila pleaded. Jack slid downward on her body. Careful not to put any weight on her smaller frame he placed his mouth over her nipple and gently sucked. He manipulated his rough tongue over and around the areola and distended teat. He could feel her body quivering under him. He moved his hand to her thigh and her legs parted slowly. His hand moved between them.

"Yes, there. Oh Jack, yes, yes...."

She was as soft and smooth as velvet when he slipped a finger into her.

"Oh Jack, don't stop."

Jack was busy trying to unbuckle his belt with his free hand. The young body beside him was in ecstasy.

"Oh Jack, Oh God, Oh Jesus," Sheila murmured.

His pants finally free he pushed them down from his waist. They fell to his lower legs now hanging off the edge of the bed. He pulled his finger from between her legs and reached down for his wallet and a condom.

"Hurry Jack, I'm hot, I want you," said the girl arching her back up from the bed.

Jack, now standing, his pants on the floor, ripped the rubber from its package. Suddenly, he heard an alarm clock sounding in the house.

"Shit what's that?" he said to Sheila. She opened her eyes wide and raising up turned to sit on the edge of her bed.

"Dad's getting up to go to work. Just be quiet," she whispered.

"I better go," said Jack bending down to kiss her.

"You can't leave now he might see you," Sheila warned. "And shut-up for Christ's sake."

Sheila stood up. Her nightgown, falling over her beating bosom, returned to its normal position. Just as she was checking the door to make sure it was locked she could see the knob try to turn.

"Sheila! You okay in there?" The concerned voice of her father sent Jack scurrying for his clothes.

"Yes Daddy, just a bad dream." Jack could see Sheila pointing to the closet. Holding all his clothes in his arms and the unwrapped but unused condom in his hand he squeezed his nude body through the double door opening and quietly closed them in front of him. Sheila unlocked and opened the door.

"I don't know how the door got locked Daddy, but everything is fine."

"Okay honey, I just usually like to check on you before I leave for work." Jack was sweating now. He hoped they would keep talking so his heavy breathing and pounding heart wouldn't be heard. Looking through the crack in the doors he could see Harry put his arms on Sheila's shoulders. He could almost reach out and touch them.

"Oh Daddy, don't worry, I'm almost a woman now."

"I know, graduating and everything but can't a father worry about his little girl a while longer?" Sheila put her arms around her dad's waist.

"Of course you can Daddy," she assured. "Now, I better get back to bed," she said, covering her body with the sheet and blanket.

"Goodnight sweetheart I'll see you later." Harry closed the door. The bedroom light had never been turned on. Without saying anything, Jack threw his clothes out the window. He kissed Sheila on the forehead and exiting the same way he came in, lowered his naked body to the ground. From the other side of the house he could hear Harry's truck drive away. He quickly dressed. Sheila was leaning out the window. She had a small transistor radio in her hand.

"Here baby take this so you can listen to our song if they play it," she said, handing it to Jack. He jumped the hedge and jogged down the street to the company truck.

He climbed in the cab and started the engine. He was still sweating and not just from the run. Putting the truck in gear he headed down the street toward the highway. That was close. Was he crazy or just in love? Someday, he thought, everything would be known. Well, maybe not everything. A red light appeared in his mirrors. He had gone but just a few blocks. Jack pulled the company truck to the side of the road and waited. He could see it was a City Police car. The officer approached carefully.

"Where you going young man?" he ask.

"To work, officer. Did I do something wrong?" Jack answered

nervously.

"We had a report of a possible burglar in the area. Lemme see your driver's license."

Jack leaned forward and reached back to his hip pocket for his wallet. It was gone.

"I musta left it at home officer." Jack knew exactly where it was.

"Well, most burglars don't carry wallets. Now where have you been?" the cop demanded.

Jack saw his excuse lying on the seat beside him. "It was probably me officer. I stopped by my girlfriend's house so I could pick up this transistor radio." Jack held up the radio and showed the officer. "It gets pretty lonely waiting at those fields while their loading."

The policeman looked down at the flying red wings of the company logo painted on the door.

"Work for Cal-Ag, do you?"

"Sure do. My father owns it."

"You're Alan's kid? Well, it's been a long time since I've seen you."

"Yes, sir. All grown and even flying too."

The officer smiled. "Yep, me and your dad both are Elks."

"Oh yea, great club," said Jack, looking to get out of this predicament and somehow get to a phone and call Sheila.

"Gave your mom a ride home the other night. Boy had she had a few too many."

"My step-mother," Jack corrected.

"Yea, yea, now I could take you back home but your dad is probably already at work."

"That's right officer he left before I did." It was a lie but couldn't be checked.

"Well, I've already called this in so I'm gonna have to write you up for driving without a license. All you have to do is show up in court with your license and the judge will probably let you go...this time."

"Thanks officer," Jack said, reaching for the ticket. "I'll be sure and show up. I'm sure I left it at home."

"Better turn around and go get it," the policeman advised.

"Yes sir, right now," Jack said, starting the engine. He slowly drove around the corner. Going one block he turned another corner and waited. He had to talk to Sheila. If her mother found his wallet first all hell would break loose. He waited until he thought the officer had moved on and then drove to the highway and out to the field.

He had arrived earlier than everyone except Brownie, who was in the office sipping fresh made coffee and going over the day's assignments.

"Morning Brownie," said Jack. Entering the office he shakily poured himself a cup of the steaming brew.

"Thought you didn't drink coffee?" Brownie asked.

"I need something this morning," Jack answered.

Brownie was inquisitive now. "Rough night?"

"No, rough morning. Would you believe I got pulled over in the company truck?"

"With you, I would believe anything." Brownie smiled.

"They thought I was a burglar."

"Well, not surprising. Look at yourself."

Jack looked down at his still unzipped pants, his shirt was half buttoned from the top and his shoes were untied. "I was kinda running late this morning."

"Well, you're here plenty early for me," assured Brownie. "Now bring your coffee and let's get these gals warmed up."

Jack and Brownie warmed up the three planes that were going to be used today and made sure the wheels were chocked and wings tied down while idling. The pilots, Alan, Pat and Gary, were at the field now and checking over their flying assignments in the office. The other loaders and flaggers were headed out to their respective landing strips and fields. Brownie climbed in the truck Jack had driven to the airfield. Jack jumped in the passenger seat and they soon were headed away from the field on Airport Drive. At the junction of the highway there was Lee's Motel and a pay phone.

"Stop Brownie," Jack said suddenly, "I need to make a call."

"Now? Right now?" Brownie asked, slamming on the brakes and steering the truck toward the phone booth. "Why didn't you use the office phone?"

"Just thought about it. Just now," lied Jack, digging in his pockets for a dime.

He jumped out of the truck, leaving the door open. Brownie left the engine on and settled back to watch Jack in the booth. He put the dime in the slot. Dialed and waited. Three rings, four rings. "Hello," came a sleepy voice at the other end. It was Sheila's mother. Jack was silent.

"Who is this?" asked the waking woman at the other end.

Jack pondered rather to ask the voice if he could talk to her daughter. But, just for a moment. He quietly replaced the receiver on the hook and went back to the truck.

"No answer," he told Brownie before he was asked. "I'll try later."

"Oh yea, where we're headed there are lots of phones," laughed Brownie.

Jack was silent all the way to where Brownie dropped him off at the edge of the cotton field to be sprayed. He grabbed his pole and flag out of the back of the truck, said bye to Brownie, and walked to the corner of the field. Brownie drove off wondering why the kid had been so quiet this morning. Jack counted off the rows of cotton for the first pass, made a mark in the dirt and sat down to wait for the loaded plane to arrive.

It wasn't long before Jack heard the sound of the big Pratt and Whitney engine in the distance. The dark spot in the morning sky was quickly getting larger. Jack waved his flag and the man in the cockpit turned the plane toward him. The pilot of the duster lined up for his first pass. Jack watched the red nose cone turn slightly and head straight for him. He looked downward and started to count the rows for the next pass. The biplane roared behind him. Passing him on its first run down the field spewing the yellow sulfur out of the spreader mounted between the wheels. The dust, with the aid of the prop wash, curled gracefully under the leaves and then upward, until gravity caused the particles to fall delicately onto the top of the cotton plants. Jack was standing ready as the plane lined up again after a hundred and eighty-degree turn. The pilot, adjusting the stick and rudder, made the Stearman fly slightly sideways so he could peer over the edge of the cockpit toward the flagger. Once lined up he straightened her out. Crossing the road he pushed the dump lever forward and the poison spewed once again from the spreader. Jack waited and waved. Keeping the plane lined up as it approached from the far end, Jack watched the wheels. They were three to four feet above the plants. Following the rows toward him, it was not his father flying. Alan would be lower, sometimes actually putting the landing gear between the rows of plants and returning after a run with leaves and stems decorating the undercarriage. The farmers liked that. Thought they were getting their money's worth. They had no concern of the dangers to the pilot. Just wanted a good job. Jack waited until the plane was fifty yards away and roaring towards him. There were power lines at this end of the field. The good, experienced pilots would go under the wires when possible but Jack knew this pilot. Pat waited until he could go no farther down the rows and pushing the throttle forward to full he pulled the stick back. The plane's response was quick. She lifted her nose toward the sky. As they cleared the wires over the top, Pat shut off the dust and it was blown back onto the end of the rows by the prop generated wind. Later he would make a border pass around the field to make sure all the plants were dusted. On and on it went through the morning. His cousin Pat leaving when empty and returning loaded with 1800 pounds of bug killer. When empty, the plane would disappear back to the landing strip and Brownie. Waiting in the dirt, Jack would aimlessly throw clods of hard soil at the power poles and think of his girl and that morning.

    The day was done. Pat dipped his wings on the final pass and waved to his cousin Jack, now standing at the opposite end of the field from where he started. Jack waved and sat down to wait for Brownie to pick him up. It seemed like forever before the truck arrived to pick him up and head back to the field and a phone.

    Back at the office of Western Dusters, Sheila was alone at her desk, busy writing monthly statements to the farmers that owed her father. Her purse, with Jack's wallet tucked inside, was in the leg space below her desk. The day's flying was done and Harry had left the field to talk to customers in the hopes of landing a few new accounts. Sheila was having a hard time concentrating on her work. The door to the office opened and Carter appeared. His silhouette against the late morning sun made a striking figure in the doorway. He said good morning to the girl at the desk.

    "Good morning Carter," Sheila responded, not lifting her head up from her work.

    Carter had used the employee's small shower in the hanger to get cleaned up and put on a new set of clothes. He leaned against the door opening and crossed one boot over the other. Lighting a cigarette with his Zippo, he wanted Sheila to look at him.

"Man, what a day we had out there," he said.

Sheila remembering her father's accident responded, "No rougher than yesterday I guess."

"Oh yea, guess not," Carter answered. "But he flew great today. Your dad's quite the daredevil I would say." Trying to make up for his error.

Sheila finally looked up from her work to see Carter still posing in the doorway. She noticed his cleanliness and clothes. Not like most loaders who wait to get home to shower and shave. "Did you need something?" she asked the striking young college student at the door.

"No, not really, thought I would just stop by and say hi," Carter said as he approached the desk.

"Thanks, I am pretty busy right now." Sheila again turned her eyes toward her work and away from Carter.

Carter approached the desk and the back of Sheila. "Something I can help you with? I am pretty good with figures."

"No thanks, Dad doesn't like anyone to see what is owed him." She knew he was standing behind her.

"Are you sure? We could get through a lot faster and maybe go get some lunch."

"No, I really can't Carter." Sheila was losing concentration again.

Carter stood close behind her. He took his hand and placed it on the back of the girl's head. He spread his fingers. Letting his hand travel downward. The strands of silken soft blond hair separated between his fingers until he reached the middle of her back. He repeated the performance again and finished just as Sheila stood up and walked away from the desk.

She looked at him. Slightly afraid but knowing if she told her father Carter would be fired. "What are you doing? Do you know who you work for?" she threatened.

Carter smoothly responded, "I work for a guy that has the most beautiful daughter in the world. And, I would like to take her to lunch."

"I can't Carter I have too much work to do," she said in a pleading tone.

"I said I'd help you. Why don't you let me and we can get out of here?"

"You know I can't, now please leave me alone so I can finish." She took a step toward her desk.

"Why don't I just sit here and wait until you're finished," Carter stated, plopping himself down in the chair at the desk. "Come on," he said, patting his lap with his hand, "we can work together."

Sheila backed away again and looked at the phone on top of her workplace. "I can call my dad you know." Her voice was meek and halting.

Carter picked up the receiver and laid it beside the phone. "Looks like the line is busy to me," he said pushing the chair away from the desk. His foot hit Sheila's purse in the opening. He looked down at the black bag with the wallet lying on top.

"Your dad must pay you quite a bit for you to carry a wallet."

"Leave it alone, Carter," Sheila demanded.

He opened the wallet. "Not too much money in here. Guess I had better buy you lunch, eh, beautiful." The girl standing against the wall made no response. Carter unsnapped the little flap that held the photo file and lifted the cover.

"Whoa, what have we here?" he smiled at the senior picture of Sheila and flipped it over to an official state document, Jack's driver's license. "Wow, I knew you guys were close but this is real good stuff." Sheila approached where Carter was sitting and darted out her hand in a futile attempt at reclaiming her property and Jack's. Carter whipped the purse and wallet above his head and stood up.

"Give it back to me or I'll tell my father," an angry Sheila demanded.

"You tell him what? That you're so much in love with his competition's son that you carry his wallet around for him."

"I'll tell him you tried to rape me." The trembling girl warned.

"That's a laugh. Right here in the office I suppose? He's not stupid you know. Now how 'bout that lunch?" Carter asked again handing the purse and wallet back to Sheila.

Sheila relieved, but knowing that Carter could tell everyone, had no choice. "Okay, Carter, but just this once."

"We will see about that, beautiful. You know I am not always like this. It's just that you are so lovely and when I saw you sitting at this desk it was like something just happened and I knew we could be good together." He opened the screen door of the office for Sheila. "I think you will find out that I can be, and will be, a very mature gentleman."

Sheila walked out the door and towards Carter's vehicle without a word. He opened the door for her and she slid into the passenger seat. As they drove off she glanced at the other side of the field and saw Brownie and Jack just getting out of the truck. She slid down in the seat a little farther as Carter whizzed through the airport entrance toward the highway, town and lunch.

CHAPTER FIVE

Jack ran to the office to use the phone. He dialed Sheila's number. No answer. Darting back outside he looked south to the Western Dusters' office and saw Sheila's car parked outside. Racing back inside he dialed the business number. No answer. Now he was in a near panic. He ran out the office door and smack into Brownie. Bouncing off the brawny mechanic he didn't apologize.

"Brownie, you gotta do me a favor."

"Slow down kid," advised Brownie, grabbing Jack by the shoulders. "Why the rush?"

"Gotta find Sheila, you gotta help me."

"Okay, okay, but slow down."

"You used to work over there," he said, pointing to the southern end of the airfield. "I need you to go over there and see if you can just see Sheila. Her car is parked out front but there is no answer when I called the office."

"Man, if you think she is hurt or something get your ass over there," said Brownie, releasing Jack from his grip.

"She's alright, I just need to know where she's at."

"All the time?" Brownie asks. "Isn't that a little possessive?"

"Brownie, just go," Jack pleaded. "I'll check the lounge."

Brownie meandered toward the planes and office of Western Dusters wondering how he would explain his presence if confronted by his old boss. Jack dashed to the Airport Managers Office and lounge. Inside he found emptiness. There was a beer can on one of the tables and a half played-out game of solitaire. As he left out the back door he heard the flush of the men's toilet. Standing on the grass of the old parade ground he looked past the airport tower and its rotating beacon of green and white. He gazed down the rear of the few hangers. Looking for movement or person he saw nothing. Jack returned to the Cal-Ag hanger and waited for Brownie. He tried the phone again. Still no answer.

Brownie returned from his foray and reported the office door unlocked but no one inside. Jack was mute.

"Now, you wanna tell me why I made that trip?" Brownie mused.

"Brownie, I need the rest of the day off. Gotta get my wallet and everything."

"Just a minute, let me check the schedule." Brownie went into the office and sorted through some papers and returned to the hanger area. "Okay, but don't make a habit of it this time of year. You know we're gonna get boo-koo busy."

"I know and I won't. Don't worry and thanks."

"You know, your ol' man plans on getting you over the fields this summer," admitted Brownie. "I wasn't supposed to tell ya, but hell, you'd find out soon enough."

Jack's eyes opened wider in amazement. He felt he was ready now but didn't think his father would let him fly this year. "Thanks, I won't say anything," said Jack rushing past Brownie to his car. He sped off in a spray of loose gravel. Leaving Brownie smiling and shaking his head.

In town, Carter and Sheila were sitting down at Emelio's Italian Restaurant. The fanciest place to eat in a town of ten thousand. A place that Sheila had only gone with her parents. They were seated at a window table. The waiter brought water and took their order.

"Would you like some wine with your meal?" Carter asked, knowing she was under age.

"No, I don't drink," responded Sheila, thinking of her and Jack's escapades on weekends.

Carter tried his best to make conversation but Sheila's answers were short and quick.

"So, you're graduating soon," he asked.

"Next Friday."

"Bet you can hardly wait."

"When it gets here, it gets here."

"Going on to college I hope."

"Yes, of course."

"Any particular school or course of study?" Carter said still trying to expand the dialogue.

"Not yet," Sheila said. "What's taking our food so long?"

"What's your hurry? When it gets here, it gets here." Carter smiled and uttered a meek laugh.

"Don't mimic me Carter," Sheila scolded.

"Sorry, just trying to liven' up the talk a little." He knew he shouldn't have said that.

Sheila was silent. The waiter brought the food and she slowly began to eat her lunch.

Minutes passed without a word being spoken between them. Carter looked outside and saw a familiar truck pull up and his boss exit the cab and head inside.

"Well, look who's here," he told Sheila.

The girl looked up just in time to see her father meet one of his farmer clients at the door. The waiter seated them and Harry looked around. There was no use hiding. Sheila and her father looked at each other. Harry excused himself and walked over to his daughter and Carter. "Well, who is buying who lunch?"

"I hope you don't mind me asking your daughter to lunch sir?" asked Carter.

"Certainly not, young man. Honey, how are you doing?" Harry asked, looking down at his pretty daughter.

"Oh fine, Daddy," was her short reply.

"I'll have her back at the office real soon sir," Carter interrupted.

"Oh, don't hurry. You two enjoy your meal. And I'll take care of the check."

"Sir, you don't have to do that."

"I know and any way," Harry placed his hand on Sheila's shoulder, "if this, soon to be young lady, doesn't enjoy it, I'll take it out of your paycheck." Harry smiled at both of them and returned to his own lunch and client.

Sheila sensed a chance and spat out, "I guess your check is going to be a little short this week."

Carter responded, "Come on girl, I've been trying real hard."

"Oh yea, you tried real hard back at the office too." Sheila, angry again, found herself not making much sense to the college student across the table or to herself.

Carter leaned forward. "Don't forget, what I know can hurt you."

Sheila turned her head and looked out the window. She saw a familiar convertible, with her Jack at the wheel, slowly drive past. He was peering in the windows of the few businesses that lined the street. Sheila turned her head back towards Carter, hoping Jack had not seen her.

But he had. At the end of the block he made a U-turn and drove by again to confirm his sighting. Sheila didn't see the second pass. Jack wanted to stop and have a confrontation in the restaurant, or outside, but he saw Harry's fancy company truck parked outside and knew Sheila's dad was also inside. Jack parked down the street and waited. Carter and Sheila finished their lunch. Sheila had hardly eaten any of her meal. Carter pulled Sheila's chair away as she stood up and escorted her past her father's table.

"Thanks for lunch, sir."

"You're welcome Carter, see you two back at the field." Harry smiled. He smiled again, as he watched Carter through the window, open the door for his daughter, start the engine, and drive cautiously out of the parking area. They drove down the street past a glaring Jack. Seated in his car, he turned his head toward the couple and frowned as they passed. Afraid to see the expression on her lover's face, Sheila stared straight ahead. But Carter smiled as he drove by and extending his arm outward gave Jack a thumbs up. Jack was mad, upset and still without his wallet. He waited a few minutes then headed home. Pulling in the driveway, he stopped behind his stepmother's Thunderbird. He slammed his car door and walked slowly to the house slamming the front door behind him. There, Gail, his stepmom, hearing the slamming doors, asked if everything was all right.

"Not really," answered Jack.

Gail walked over to her stepson. "I can help if it's girl problems."

Jack had never learned to really love this second mother. No one could take the place of his "real mom" who had died of tuberculosis when he was in second grade. He called this later one "mom" only because his dad wanted him to.

"Thanks Mom, but I'll be okay."

"Are you sure there's nothing I can do."

Jack, thinking of his wallet and the ticket he had gotten early that morning, suddenly realized something. "Actually Mom, you can do me a favor." He explained what happened with the police and looked Gail in the eye. "When that notice to appear in court comes in the mail, will you make sure Dad doesn't see it?"

"Well, I don't know. Don't you think he'll find out anyway?" Gail asked.

"Yea, but the later the better. You know he's going to let me fly this summer?"

"He had mentioned it to me, but how did you find out?" she wondered aloud.

Jack, not wanting to betray Brownie's confidence, answered, "With the workload and business increasing all the time I just figured he would have to let me rather than hire another pilot. That's why you gotta help me, Mom."

"Okay Hon, I'll make sure I check the mail." Gail looked up at Jack and placed her hands on Jack's shoulders. "Don't worry, mum's the word from Mom."

Jack turned away. Gail's hands dropped to her side and she went back to the kitchen. He was soon dialing the phone. Calling an office number.

"Good afternoon, Western Dusters," answered Sheila's voice.

"Well, hello. How was lunch?" Jack said sarcastically.

"Jack, oh Jack we have to talk."

"I guess we do and I hope you have something of mine I need."

"Yes, yes and that's what we have to talk about," said an excited Sheila.

"I hope your mom didn't see it," Jack paused, "actually I guess it doesn't really matter now."

In the Western Dusters office Harry, returning from his luncheon, had just entered.

Sheila, looking up at her father entering, changed her conversation. "We'll call you back on that sir? I am sure we can get it sprayed by early week."

Jack sensed something had happened. Still angry he told Sheila, "Just leave it in my car. It's in front of the lounge." He slammed the receiver down on the phone.

Sheila made up a conversation. "Thank you very much for calling and we will be getting in touch with you." She returned her receiver gently to its holder.

"Who was that?" her father asked.

Sheila was worried, but answered fast. "One of our accounts. He wanted to know when we could get to his vineyard and I told him we already have it scheduled."

"Good job, Honey." Harry left the office and headed toward his hanger to check on the work being done on his wrecked plane.

Sheila waited and when her father had entered the building she left the office through the back door. She walked behind the row of hangers. Across the entrance road and to the far side of the Manager's Office and Lounge. She saw Jack's open convertible out front. She walked alongside the far wall to the car. Reaching over the driver's door she tossed the troublesome wallet under the seat.

"Sheila.....Sheila," came a whispered tone from the doorway of the lounge. She looked up and saw Jack standing in the doorway. Just far enough inside as to not be seen from the outside except by direct view. Sheila raced up to the doorway and inside. Jack backed away from the entrance as Sheila rapidly approached. She stopped for a moment, looked around, saw no one else and again started speedily toward Jack.

"Oh Jack, let me explain," she pleaded as she tried to wrap her arms around him.

Jack backed away and grabbing her arms from around him tossed them downward.

"Nothing to explain. I saw it all at the restaurant."

"Jack, please let me tell you what happened."

"Where's my wallet?" asked Jack.

"In your car. Under the seat," the tearing girl answered.

Jack turned away and started to walk toward the rear door.

"Wait, Jack, don't leave. I love you." Sheila started after him. But he was out the back door and headed around the building. Still inside, she followed his path through the side windows until he reached his waiting car in front. Sheila dared not go outside and continue the futile conversation. Someone would see them from the south end of the field. She stood in the doorway and continued her pleading.

"Wait Jack. Come back inside. Let me explain. Carter means nothing to me."

Jack heard her words but did not hesitate. Sitting down in the car, he reached under the seat, pulled his wallet from underneath and finally returned it to his hip pocket. He turned the ignition key, looked up at Sheila, tears now visible on her cheeks, shook his head and drove off. She turned to a table, sat down, folded her arms on the table, lowered her head onto them and sobbed. Soon, she felt a strong but gentle hand on her shoulder. Raising her head and wiping the tears away she was surprised to see the man standing, with a comforting look on his face. It was Brownie. Working outside, under the wing of a Cal-Ag' aircraft, he had seen it all.

CHAPTER SIX

The following days Jack kept busy working long hours. Late in the morning, after loading and flagging, he would wash each duster and spray rig until nearly spotless of chemical residue, oil, grease and exhaust stains. From the wash rack he could look across the field to the office where Sheila was working. He would see Carter go in and out of the office several times during the day. Sometimes staying for long periods of time. Every time Carter would leave the office Jack would want to run to Sheila and tell her how he really felt. Now, he wanted to tell everyone exactly how he felt towards her. Sighing, he returned to his work. Scrubbing the fuselage until the black and gold paint and the red emblem of twin flying wings glistened in the summer sun. Later in the day he would help Brownie with the daily routine maintenance of each plane. Late afternoons would find him in a Stearman flying low over the grass between the parallel runways of the airfield. Practicing short turns at each end of a pass. He was getting good at low level flying. But even while flying, he found himself quickly glancing to the office at the south end of the field. He wanted to "buzz" that building so badly. And then, when Sheila came running out to wave, dip his wings to her...for her.

Wednesday came and went. Only two days until Sheila graduated from high school. They had made plans after the ceremony to go to Fresno and the dance at the Rainbow Ballroom then spend the night and early morning at the nearby lake watching the sunrise. Alan had already told his son he could take the next morning off. Dad was cool. But now Jack figured he might as well be working. What else was there? He was working as the thought of his girl, being with Carter, raked his mind. Of them together, dragging the strip, eating, talking. Worse, laughing, necking, kissing. He was torn between the pain and the anger. Angry with himself for being, as Brownie told him later, an asshole. Angry, because he just couldn't quite get enough courage to tell Sheila's parents how he felt. How they felt about each other. Or, did she still love him? To expose these feelings, would it change anything? He decided on Thursday he would make an effort to reconcile these thoughts. Getting both the hurt in his heart and Carter out of his mind and Sheila's head forever.

That morning it was business as usual. By noon, after six hours of flying, the pilots were finished with their assigned fields. Shortly after 1:00, Jack was finished at the wash rack. He looked across the field and saw that Sheila's car was not parked at the office. She must be getting ready for graduation. That would mean she would probably be at the school, maybe helping with the final decorations for the dance. He checked with Brownie to make sure everything was finished. Not everything, but the mechanic let him leave. Jack went home and cleaned up. The shower washed the fine yellow dust and spray residue down the drain. Afterward, he changed to a clean pair of jeans and a black pullover short sleeve shirt. He shaved, combed his dark brown hair, and splashed a little after-shave, what Sheila called "foofoo," on his face. He felt confident. Jack closed the front door. He glanced through the kitchen window to a beautiful, red haired woman busy at the sink. "See ya later, Mom!" Gail looked up and waved with a soapy hand. As Jack climbed over the door of the convertible into the seat he thought, Dad has a real winner with this one.

He got to the high school and drove slowly by the gymnasium. There were a couple of hotrods out front and a Chevy and Studebaker that the auto shop class used for practice. Sheila's car was nowhere in the parking lot nor parked on the street. He looked at his watch: two o'clock. Were they finished already? He drove around the two-block square that made up the high school grounds. Because of tomorrow's graduation, most teachers and students had left the campus. Sheila's car would be easy to spot. He made the round one more time. Nothing. He hoped she hadn't gone home. Maybe, if she had, this was the time to knock on the door and explain all. Could he face her father and mother? What would be their reaction? He would make that decision when he got there. Five minutes later he arrived at Sheila's house. The driveway was empty. He went around the block. The neighbor was trimming his hedge. The same hedge that Jack had hurdled a few nights earlier to get to his girl. Now he couldn't even find her.

He drove back to Main Street. At the west end was the drive-in. In the parking lot was Sheila's car. Was she working the day before graduation? He parked in the spot next to Sheila's vehicle. Before entering the dining area he looked in the window. Carter was sitting by himself. A half drank mug of beer in front of him. Sheila was nowhere in sight. He pushed the door open and walked past Carter without a word. He sat down in a booth at the opposite end of the dining area. He was facing Carter across the room and could also see the entrance. Only another teenage couple, sharing a milkshake, was in the room. Jack ordered a coke. The jukebox had just finished blasting out "Summertime Blues." Eddie Cochran's guitar licks were still ringing in Jack's ears when he saw Sheila drive up in Carter's car and get out. She entered the dining room but suddenly stopped when she saw Jack at the far end. She hesitated for an instant and then turned to Carter and sat down in the booth on the opposite side of the table from him. They talked quietly. Jack strained to hear the conversation but he was too far away. His eyes darted back and forth between their table and the menu in front of him. A few more minutes past. Carter finished his beer. He and Sheila got up and started outside. As he held the door open for her she went through the entrance, returning the car keys to his open hand. The waitress arrived with Jack's Coke but Jack was headed toward the door.

"Jack, your Coke," she told him. He walked briskly by her without saying a word. Leaving her standing at the table, holding the cold beverage in her hand.

He walked outside. Carter and Sheila were standing between Sheila's car and Jack's. He had to talk to her. She had her back toward him as he approached the pair. Carter saw him coming and grabbed Sheila's hand. Holding it firmly, but not too tight.

"Well, if it isn't the junior fly boy," Carter said, turning the surprised Sheila around to face Jack. "Daddy let you out from under his wing?"

"Cool it Carter, I need to talk to my girl."

"Not today, she's with me and I wouldn't call her your girl, anymore. Right honey?"

Sheila was silent. She just looked at Jack.

Ignoring Carter, Jack said, "Baby, we need to talk...now." He was looking into her eyes.

Sheila felt the hand holding hers tighten even more. "Come on honey, let's get outta here. This guy's a jerk and you know it." Carter turned toward the back of the two cars parked side by side. He pulled

Sheila with him. Jack followed closely. Sheila looked back while being tugged along by Carter. She could see the fire; the determination as Jack looked beyond her, to the man he wanted to banish from her life. He imagined that he saw her trying to get away from the grasp of Carter.

"Wait a minute asshole. I think she'd rather go with me."

Carter stopped just as he rounded the back end of Jack's car. He let go of Sheila's hand and pushed her toward her car. Jack stepped in between them and faced Carter. The girl stood nervously behind Jack. She wanted to say something but remained silent.

But not Carter. "Awful persistent for a jerk off," he said, leaning against the back end of Jack's convertible. His clenched fists at his side.

"You know, for a college student, your vocabulary really sucks," Jack said. Getting even closer to Carter.

"Those aren't my words. Those are what your ex-girl friend told me about you."

Jack turned around toward Sheila and started to approach her. Carter took a couple of steps, grabbed Jack's shoulder hard and with a whip of his arm, turned Jack around. Again they were face to face.

"Listen, you son of a bitch. Why don't you let her tell me a lot more about you by leaving us alone," yelled an angry, but confident, Carter.

Jack was hot. He responded. Pushing Carter with both hands, onto the trunk of his car. "Listen fucker, she's going with me."

With that, Carter sprang from his back and at the same time hit Jack in the middle of his chest. Jack staggered backward. Out of breath for a moment, he was bent over gasping for air. Sheila screamed. Carter approached the hunched over man, but Jack saw him coming and landed a blow with his right hand just above Carter's belt buckle. It didn't seem to bother the slightly larger man. Jack swung again but missed. Carter countered with a short jab that landed squarely against the side of Jack's jaw. He tasted blood in his mouth. With the blow, his teeth had cut the inside of his cheek. Jack rushed forward. Tackling Carter at the waist, both men went to the ground. Sheila was jumping up and down yelling, "Stop it, please stop!" From inside, the teenage couple, waitresses, and cooks were all watching. The owner was on the phone with the police. Jack and

Carter rolled on the gravel of the parking lot trying to get an advantage. Both landed short punches. But, at such close distance, neither combatant could accomplish much damage. Sheila was now in tears. She was still yelling at both of them to stop when the police arrived. Just as Carter finally managed to roll on top of Jack and pin him to the ground the black and white patrol car, with two officers inside, screeched to a stop beside the fighters. Jumping out, one cop yelled, "Hold it right now you two. Break it up." Carter unclenched his fist and started to stand up. The other cop, now out of the car, pulled him away from his foe. Jack quickly jumped up from his prone position. He stood, with the officer holding back his arms and fists, a menacing look directed at his foe. Both young men were squirming in the officer's hold. Trying to get free.

"Alright you guys, that's enough or we'll handcuff you both. And Jack, haven't you had enough trouble for one week?" Jack looked back over his shoulder at the uniformed man holding him. It was the same officer who had pulled him over in the early morning a few days before.

"I guess so," he responded.

"You young man," the cop said, looking at Carter, "what started all this?"

"He did," said Carter, nodding at Jack.

"I didn't say who," said the officer, looking at Sheila, "I said what." Carter said nothing. "Now, if we let go of you two and you go at it, we're hauling you both in and leaving this pretty girl for neither of you. You got it."

"Yes sir," was the reply from Jack.

"Sure officer," said Carter, "she's going with me anyway." He winked at Sheila.

Jack again started toward Carter, but the cop quickly grabbed his arms again. "I said take it easy." Jack relaxed and took a step back.

"That's better," said the senior policeman. "Now I think I can sort this out. Jack, that's your car right?"

Jack, dusting himself off, answered, "Yes, sir."

"Do you have a car miss?" the officer asked Sheila. She pointed to the vehicle next to Jack's.

"Good, I suggest you get in it and go home." Looking at Carter he asked, "And your car?"

"Right over there officer," answered Carter pointing to the car Sheila had arrived in earlier.

"Alright, now let's all of you get in your cars and get out of here." Looking at the two men, he added, "And if I hear anymore about this, you'll both be in a lot of trouble."

Sheila got in her car and started the engine. The two former fighters turned away from each other and the policemen. Jack got in his car parked next to Sheila's.

Glancing at her with a slight smile, he winked. Carter passed behind Sheila's car trunk. He tapped on it with his fist. Sheila looked away from Jack and into the rear view mirror. She did not turn around. The police waited until all three vehicles had left in different directions from the parking lot. The black and white, with its flashing red lights now turned off, headed back down Main Street.

Jack drove slowly away from the drive-in. After a few blocks he pulled over and stopped. Minutes passed by and so did cars. A few honked, but Jack stared straight ahead. Hunched forward, his forearms resting on top of the steering wheel. A half-hour passed. Finally, he started the motor. Flipped a U-turn in the middle of the street and headed straight for Sheila's place.

He parked across the street from the house. Walking up to the front door he noticed only Sheila's car in the driveway at the side of the house. Before knocking he heard music playing from inside. He pounded hard on the wooden door. Nervously he waited. Who would open the door to answer his knock? Again his clenched fist beat on the portal. The music stopped and the doorway opened. It was Sheila. Jack could see she had been crying.

"Is your mom or dad home, I have something to tell them," he said to Sheila from outside.

"No Jack, they won't be home until tonight. What are you going to tell them?"

Jack was ready. He had thought about it long enough. "Everything. How I feel about you. Our secret meeting places, our dates. They need to know that I love you more than anything I have ever loved before or will in the future." Sheila stood transfixed in front of Jack as he continued. "But before I tell them I need to tell you, baby, how sorry I am for the way I acted. These days have been hell. I can't live the rest of my life without you." He grabbed both her hands and pulled them up to his chest. "I think about you all the time baby. Even in the air. I can't get you out of my mind."

Sheila, her hands inside of Jack's against his chest, finally spoke. "But Jack, you're so jealous."

"Of course I am," Jack admitted. "You are the only one I love and I'm not going to lose you...to anybody."

"But we can't keep doing this," said Sheila.

"That's why I wanna tell your parents."

"I didn't mean that. I meant arguing, fighting," clarified Sheila.

"We won't have anything to fight about after I talk to them."

Sheila wasn't so sure. "I don't think that'll change their minds. Maybe Mom's, but Daddy's, never."

"Then he'll just have to live with it, right?"

Sheila was silent. Jack looked in her eyes and asked again. "Right?"

His girl was silent. Her head bowed.

Putting his hand under her chin he lifted her head and looked into her eyes. He asked a different question and important one. "You still love me?"

Sheila was returning the look. Jack could see the liquid glaze over her eyes. A tear building in each corner. Waiting to trickle down her soft cheeks as gravity took hold.

The young girl couldn't answer with words but couldn't wait. The tears rolled as she put her arms around her lover and placed her head on his chest. Jack held her tightly. He was relieved, thankful, and now worried.

Her head was still lying on her boyfriend's chest, as she pleaded, "Jack, please don't tell my parents just yet. I can do it after graduation."

But Jack was adamant. "I think it would be better if I just waited until they come home and we both let them know."

She was just as firm, but still in a quiet pleading tone. "We can wait one more day, honey. We'll tell them at the stadium. On the field after the ceremony they will be in a good mood.

Jack wasn't so sure. "I can't wait, what if Carter shows up between now and then?"

"He doesn't matter," Sheila reassured, placing her hands on Jack's cheeks. "Nothing matters now that we are back together." She leaned forward and kissed Jack firmly on the lips. Before parting, she slid her tongue in his mouth and caressed the inside of his still sore cheek.

That did it for Jack. "Okay, I'll get a pass and meet you on the field after graduation."

"Sit up high Jack," she said, "so I can see you," referring to the stadium where the ceremony would take place. She was tugging at Jack. They headed for the couch in the middle of the living room.

Sheila stopped to put a record on the hi-fi. Soon they were dancing to a slow song, just moving their feet back and forth. More concerned with embracing, Jack lowered his hands to Sheila's buttocks. He grabbed them and pulled. He felt the firmness of her vulva pressing against his already hard organ. When they were near the couch they parted and sat down. He pushed her back against the arm and slipped his hand under her dress. "Jack, I've missed you so much."

"Honey, if I could only tell you how much I love you." Jack searched for the right words but decided on action instead. His hand had reached her panties and he began the search.

"Ouch," Sheila squealed.

"Wha'd I do baby? Asked Jack, pulling his hand slightly away.

"You pulled a hair, silly," answered the girl. "Out of practice," she joked.

"You want me to stay in practice on someone else?" Jack said smiling.

"Better not." Sheila raised up and pulled Jacks hair and head down to her bosom. His hand came out from underneath her dress and slipped inside her blouse. "I am out of practice in this area too," he said. His hand began to gently massage the pinkish circle surrounding one of her nipples. She pushed him back and grabbed for the zipper of his pants. He grabbed her hand and soon they were rolling off the couch and onto the floor. Laughing, wrestling and kissing. Sheila squirmed as Jack tried to pin her hands and arms on the floor. Achieving this, he sat straddled on her stomach. He looked down at her. "Oh baby, have I missed you." He leaned forward and as his lips touched hers he let go of her arms. They wrapped around his shoulders. They continued the long kiss. Tongues exploring, lips gently squeezing, pushing, changing positions. The last song on the record was over. The needle repeated its track over and over. No music, just the steady rhythm of the little point at the end of the arm returning to the same groove in the record at a speed of thirty three and a third RPM. On the floor, again and again, the two lovers were renewing feelings of hope and smashing the pain of separation.

CHAPTER SEVEN

The high school's Memorial Stadium was decorated in the school colors of blue and white. Relatives and guests of the graduates were filing in through the gates and finding seats on the wooden benches of the north side bleachers. On the green grass of the playing field stood row upon row of folding chairs. The graduates would soon be sitting on these hard steel seats while listening to the tedious speeches from their former teachers. They would face the speaker's podium on a makeshift stage with ramps on either side. Beyond that platform, a track separated the field from the bleachers where three thousand people would be staring back at them.

Jack was walking toward the entrance. He had not been able to locate a spare ticket. Being a graduate two years earlier he was hoping he could talk his way into the ceremony. As he approached the open wrought iron gate and turnstiles he saw his former baseball coach.

"Hey coach," he said as he arrived at the gate. "They got you working overtime tonight."

"Jack," the coach exclaimed, surprised at seeing him. "How have you been? Still learning to fly?"

"Doing great. Almost ready to start dusting, just waiting for Dad's okay. How was the team this year?"

"We did okay. But I could have used your arm in the outfield." The coach remembered Jack's all league performance his senior year and the championship the team had won.

"Well, there's always next year." Jack stepped back to let some guests with tickets pass through the turnstiles.

"Yea, I think we'll do pretty well with the pitching we have," said the coach, taking the tickets and ripping them in half. "You going in Jack?"

"Well, I'd like to coach. I have a real close friend getting her diploma tonight. But you see, I've got a little problem. I forgot my ticket and I don't have time to go back home and get it. Besides, by the time I got back here, I'd have to park blocks away."

"Forgot your ticket?" asked the coach as he stepped away from the turnstile. "Tell you what. When you get really good at flying you give me a ride sometime, okay?"

"You got it coach and thanks a lot." Jack shook hands with his old mentor and, pushing the bar of the turnstile, entered the stadium.

The bleachers were filling up fast. Jack looked toward the top rows. There were a few empty places up high. Just where Sheila had wanted him to sit. He started up the steps from the track, nodding at a few acquaintances as he went. At the top row he took a position a couple of seats from the aisle. He gazed out onto the still empty field. Jack looked at his watch: seven-fifteen. Only fifteen minutes until the ceremonies began. He looked around the bleachers. Sitting this high and to the rear of everyone it was hard to identify friends or former classmates. But, to his left, about half way down from where he sat, was a familiar figure. It was Carter. There was no mistaking that blond hair. Next to him sat Mrs. Gebhardt and on the aisle seat was Harry Gebhardt. What was Carter doing here? Was he a guest of the Gebhardts? How did he get a ticket when Jack couldn't?

A blast from the horn section of the school band signaled the start of the graduation ceremony. School district officials, the high school principal and administrators took their seats on the stage. The U. S. Flag was raised on the pole near the scoreboard and the entire school band played the Star Spangle Banner rather awkwardly. Cheers followed and then silence. Jack looked across the field to the bleachers on the opposite side. He knew the routine. The graduates' grand entrance never changed. The male graduates in their blue caps and gowns and the girls in their white. Soon the sound of Elgar's "Pomp and Circumstance" came from the uniformed players on the field. The band playing it loud and bungling just a few notes from the classic march. On the opposite side of the stadium, on the walkway above the top row of seats, appeared the procession of graduates. Alternating boy and girl they formed a blue and white procession that walked to each end of the south bleachers and proceeded down to the track and onto the field. Again facing each other, they began walking toward one another. At the center section they joined again, boy with girl, to walk in pairs to their seats. At the end of the line, girls walked side by side, the school not having enough boys graduating this year to make it even. Jack looked for that long blond beautiful hair of Sheila's. But with the caps and the distance he couldn't make out one blond from another. As the graduates approached the spectators they filled the rows of chairs on the field. Jack began checking each row as the seats were occupied. Finally, four rows from the front, halfway in, he spotted Sheila. He stood up and began to wave. She was waving, but not towards him. He looked down and to the left. Also standing and waving to their daughter were the Gebhardts. So was Carter. Jack wanted to yell and jump so his girl would turn and see him. But, he didn't want to make a scene for fear the people also there for Sheila would see him. He sat down.

The procession was finished and the first speaker took the podium. He rambled on about the future of the young graduates and the world of today. Typical rhetoric, same scenario. Jack just looked at Sheila down there in that sea of blue and white. He waited and waited for her face to glance his way. She was looking in the stands for him. When her gaze finally appeared to be looking at him Jack raised his hand high above him and stood up. Sheila, her hands resting on her lap, raised her left hand up to shoulder level. Waving slowly and for just a few seconds she lowered it again to her lap. Jack sat down quickly. She had seen him. She knew he had made it. The speeches went on. After what seemed hours, the school board members stood. The full name of each graduate was announced over the public address system. They walked up one side of the ramp to receive their diplomas from a board member and down the opposite side of the ramp. Returning to their seat, each graduate garnered applause from the audience in the stands. Some students more than others, depending on their popularity. When Sheila Gebhardt's name was announced her cheerleader friends, parents and relatives all stood and cheered. Carter stood and whistled and waved. Jack sat quietly but applauded. As the procession receiving diplomas continued, Jack began thinking of what lay ahead that night. After the ceremonies were finished parents and guests would hurriedly leave the bleachers. Spilling onto the track and football field to find their waiting son or daughter. Congratulatory hugs and handshakes would be exchanged. Mothers would be crying. Fathers would be smiling. Most likely out of relief that they had shoved another offspring out of the nest and into the world. Pictures would be taken for posterity. Jack wondered how he would approach that scene of happiness and pride. When would Sheila tell her parents? The last graduate was receiving her diploma. There was loud applause from the stands as she left the stage. The graduates and crowd all rose together as the school band played the alma mater. At the end of the tune the graduates tossed their caps in the air. The crowd in the stands filled the aisles and hurried as fast as they could down the steps onto the field. Jack, being on the top row, was slowly inching downward with the multitude. Behind the parents, aunts, uncles and grandparents he waited for them to slowly descend the steps. After every few feet he would glimpse down on the field. Making sure not to lose sight of Sheila in the mass of humanity that was now covering most of the football field. Finally at the bottom and on the track, Jack discovered that from this view it was impossible to pick out anyone except by chance. But he knew the general area that he had last seen Sheila so he headed in that direction. Searching, looking, people were everywhere. As he maneuvered through the horde, he heard laughter and giggles from siblings of the graduates. He saw smiles on fathers' faces and tears in the eyes of mothers. Relatives were snapping pictures. Flash bulbs punctuated the glare from the stadium lights. Suddenly, he spied Sheila. Standing with her parents, classmates and friends were hugging her. Mr. Gebhardt, Dad, camera in hand, was taking pictures. Carter stood at her side.

Jack approached from behind Sheila's parents. She saw him coming and so did Carter. Carter reached for Sheila's hand. A girl friend, also in a white graduation gown, came bounding up to Sheila. They threw their arms around each other, giggling and laughing. The hugging stopped just as Jack came up beside Mrs. Gebhardt.

"Good evening Sheila," said Jack. "Good evening Mr. and Mrs. Gebhardt." He extended his hand to Mr. Gebhardt. It was not taken.

Sheila chimed in. "Good evening Jack." Harry Gebhardt looked at his daughter and then returned a cold stare to Jack.

"What are you doing here, Jack?" he asked.

"I am here to congratulate your daughter, sir," answered the young man, looking at Sheila.

"You're not welcome at this occasion," Harry said with a stern voice. "Not welcome at all."

Carter saw his chance. "Would you like me to escort this guy out of the stadium, Mr. Gebhardt," leaving Sheila's side and advancing toward Jack.

"No Carter, I think he has enough sense to leave on his own accord," answered Harry, still with the intimidating look toward Jack. Mrs. Gebhardt stood silently at her husband's side.

Sheila's friend, who had been so exuberant just seconds before, nervously excused herself.

Jack looked at Sheila. "I think your daughter has something to say to you sir."

Harry looked at his daughter. Sheila moved away from Carter and with a couple of steps stood next to Jack. "Jack is taking me to the dance tonight, Daddy."

"The hell he is young lady! You may have graduated but you're still my daughter." Harry was angry now.

"Daddy, you can't stop me," said Sheila. "I love Jack and he loves me."

"That's bullshit young lady. Now come over here and stand with your mother."

"Harry, watch your tone, all these people can hear you," pleaded Mrs. Gebhardt.

The parents and students nearest the confrontation had suddenly stopped talking and were watching what was occurring.

"Young man, I am not going to ask you to leave again. Now for the last time get out of here," Harry demanded.

Jack stood firm and looked at Sheila. "When I leave sir, it will be with your daughter. I believe that is what she wants and I know that is what I want."

Sheila's father started forward. Jack and Sheila, still holding hands, took an equal amount of steps backward. Mrs. Gebhardt, seeing the anger in her husband's face, interjected, "Harry, not here, he's just a boy."

"Boy, my ass!" Harry spat back, "This 'boy' as you say, knows all about a good time and how to get it. Look at his cousin Pat, it runs in the family, all that carousing around down in Fresno every night. Do you want your only daughter associating with a family like that?" He looked at his wife but she was looking at her little girl. She started to answer but her daughter said it for her.

"Daddy, I'm going out with Jack. I will see you when I get home tonight." She grabbed Jack's left hand and held it tight.

Harry Gebhardt had seen and heard enough. "Carter," he said, like an order at work, "maybe you better take this bastard and escort him to the gate. And make sure he leaves."

It was the words Carter had been waiting for. "Yes sir," he said, announcing his full intentions. He stepped in front of Harry and started toward Jack. But Jack was ready. Still holding his girl's palm in his left hand, he took one step forward for leverage with his left foot and just as it landed, swung his right fist. Thrown with all his might, it landed squarely on the side of Carter's mouth. His adversary, white dinner jacket and all, crumpled to the ground. A nearby lady gasped, "Oh my goodness." The nearby throng came closer to see what all the fuss was about.

Sheila was stunned but happy. Harry Gebhardt looked at Carter, lying on the grass of the field, groaning and trying to raise himself to his hands and knees.

He started toward his daughter to pull her away from Jack. "Sheila, come here right now," he demanded.

"No, Daddy. We're leaving."

Harry kept coming toward them and now Carter was rising to his feet, ready for revenge.

"Come on babe, let's get outta here," Jack said hurriedly turning Sheila around, away from the angry men.

"Stop right there, you bastard," Harry demanded. Grabbing for his daughter's arm, he managed to just touch the sleeve of his daughter's graduation gown before she pulled away. He kept coming for another try. But Jack wasn't waiting any longer. He started to walk faster. Sheila followed, but her father kept coming towards them. The young lovers began to run. Sheila lost a high heel shoe, but quickly recovered it. Taking off her other one, she held them both in her free hand. Barefoot, except for her nylon stockings, she could now keep up with her boyfriend. With Jack leading the way they darted between the people. When they wouldn't move, they brushed them aside. Harry was trying to follow but couldn't keep up with the youthful speed of the two lovers running hand in hand toward the east gate. He finally stopped. Watching with scorn as Jack and his daughter raced out the exit and down the road toward Jack's waiting car. He thought he could hear them laughing as they ran. A still groggy Carter caught up with his boss just as he turned around to go back to his wife.

"You want me to go after them sir?" he asked. "I'll find 'em and bring her home. After I beat the crap outta that son-of-bitch."

"Just forget it," Harry answered. "I'll see my daughter later tonight and she won't like what I have to say. As for Jack Lawrence, I'll fix him later."

Jack and Sheila ran all the way to Jack's car. The top was down. Jack opened the passenger door for his girl. Sheila threw her shoes on the floorboard and scooted in. Jack jumped into the back seat and then into the drivers seat. He started the car. Leaving the black mark of screeching tires behind, they headed toward Fresno. Once on the highway Jack pulled over and put the top up. Latching the hooks above the windshield to secure the front bow of the convertible roof. When he reached over to latch the right side, in front of and above Sheila, she grabbed and hugged him. Completing his task with one hand while in her arms Jack turned and kissed her passionately on the lips. As cars sped past on the highway, Sheila opened her door and got out of the car. She unzipped her graduation gown and stepped out of the cumbersome outfit. She threw it in the back seat with her cap and stood looking at Jack. Jack was eyeing her beauty. She was dressed in a deep blue, tight fitting, low cut evening dress that ended just above the knees.

"Well what do you think?" said Sheila, running her hands down either side of her hips.

"You are," he paused, "you are the most beautiful thing I have ever seen in my life," stuttered Jack, taken aback at this girl of his, now suddenly a young lady.

"Good enough to spend the night with?" Sheila asked. Then thinking of how that sounded added, "Well dinner and dancing anyway."

"At least that baby," replied Jack, slapping the space on the seat next to him. "Now let's get to the Rainbow so I can show you off."

Sheila slid in next to Jack. She put one arm around his shoulder and the other on his thigh. "Please Jack, let's don't get home 'till the sun comes up," she pleaded.

"I'll see to that baby. You don't have to go home at all you know." He put his hand on top of Sheila's hand that was still on his thigh.

She laid her head on Jack's shoulder as he pulled on to the

pavement and headed toward Fresno. "I have to go home. For my mother anyway," she sighed. Jack turned up the radio and Sheila, her head still resting on Jack's shoulder, closed her eyes. Her hand moved from his thigh to around his waist. In this state of contentment she was no longer thinking of the anger of her father or the heartbreak of her mother. She was with the man she loved and with whom she wanted to spend the rest of her life.

At the Rainbow Ballroom Graduation Dance, Sheila met friends and classmates that had seen what happened at the stadium. Together, Jack and Sheila tried to stay on the dance floor to avoid the many questions. But at every break by the band people would approach and ask, "What was that all about, back there? Man, you really laid it on that guy, Jack. Sheila, are you going home after this? I wouldn't want to face your father after what you did." Finally, Sheila had answered enough. "Let's get out of here honey. I'm hungry," she said to Jack.

Jack was ready also. "Okay beautiful, anything you want."

"Let's go to Bob's and get a cheeseburger, fries, anything and just drive around."

This sounded good to Jack. "Okay, let's go."

Out the big double doors of the dance hall they went. Leaving the sound of the band, the food and beverages, their friends and the questions behind. Let the rumors and innuendoes fly and spread. They didn't care. They had each other.

Jack stopped to fill up with gas. They stopped at Bob's Big Boy, ordered double cheeseburgers, large fries and cokes to go and roared off into the night toward the lake.

Jack was driving carefully and slower than usual. The road to the lake was winding and the pavement narrowed the closer they got to the reservoir. Cresting a hill, there was a turnout into an old gravel quarry by the river. Jack pulled onto the dirt road and drove the short distance to the river. Parking under a huge elm he turned off the engine. The motor's silence brought the sound of water, released from the dam's spillway, splashing over the boulder-strewn riverbed. Though just past midnight, the June evening was still warm. They finished eating and for awhile just sat together quietly. Listening to the soothing sounds of the river and looking at the stars through the branches of the elm.

Jack broke the silence. "What are you going to do when you get home?"

"I don't want to think about it, Jack. I just want to stay here. It's so beautiful," replied Sheila.

"But you're gonna face them sooner or later baby," continued Jack.

"I know. I think Mom will be understanding," Sheila said, hoping for the best.

"And what about your father?" asked Jack. Knowing that would be the real challenge.

"If I can get Mom on my side, I mean our side, that will help a lot. Especially when Daddy gets mad."

"Do you want me stay when I take you home?" Jack was ready to defend his girl and love once again.

"No Jack, I think that would just make Daddy angry all over again. It may take a little while but I think Daddy will just have to realize that we love each other and he either accepts it or something bad will happen." Sheila wasn't quite sure of her words or how to back it up but she knew who and what she wanted and it was right next to her.

Jack didn't quite understand either. "What do you mean, bad?"

"Well, you know, I'll move out or maybe not go on to college. Something...but I couldn't stay there and live in that house when he's mad."

Jack was thinking. "If I start flying soon for my dad, I'll make a lot more money. We could get a place of our own."

"We'd have to get married, honey," said Sheila.

"Well, eventually, but maybe not right away."

Sheila, now concerned on what the town and friends would think of this "unlawful" relationship, squeezed her man and said, "Jack, honey, I don't know. What would people say?"

"The heck with people. If they can't understand they aren't really friends," Jack replied, stroking the girl's hair.

"I know, but Mom's reputation and Dad's business might suffer," worried Sheila.

Jack was thinking of the two of them living together. "I thought you weren't worried about your dear old dad."

"I'm not, when it comes to us. But, he does have to make money for Mom."

"Oh, he's got a good business. He makes a lot of money. Especially this time of year," Jack said.

Sheila, remembering the phone calls at home, "He's losing business to your dad almost every week. And it really makes him mad."

"Well, Cal-Ag has been around longer, with more experienced pilots. Besides, there are plenty of fields out there for everyone. And if we don't keep increasing our acreage I might not ever get to dust or spray. Dad's not going to fire Pat or Gary just to let me fly a Stearman." Jack wanted to change the conversation. This was supposed to be a special night, a romantic night. He started the car's motor.

"Where we going?" Sheila asked.

"Oh, I don't know. I know I have to take a leak," replied Jack. "How 'bout you?"

Sheila, looking down at her almost full Coke said, "I'm fine."

Jack drove to where the dirt road joined the pavement. Just before the junction he stopped and leaving the car running, jumped out and relieved himself near the trunk of the vehicle.

"Ah, that's better. Now honey, anywhere special you want to go?" he asked.

"Let's just drive around and listen to the music for a while, okay?" asked Sheila.

Jack turned up the radio and turned onto the paved road. He drove down in front of the dam. Over the bridge, crossing the river, running with what little water the Corps of Engineers decided to release down stream. Back on the north side of the lake he headed into the foothills. On these back roads this late, there was no traffic behind or coming towards him. He drove slowly. Sheila, sitting by his side, slid her hand across his lap and buried it between his legs. Jack felt his penis swell. He put his hand inside his pants and straightened the stiff joint from its bent position inside his shorts.

"Jack, do you have a condom?" Sheila whispered in his ear.

"Of course baby, why?"

"Jack," Sheila continued in his ear, "love me Jack, love me like you never have before."

"Out here?" Jack asked, somewhat perplexed.

"Yes, here Jack, anywhere, just tonight."

Jack stopped next to a small pasture, wooded with small oaks and elm trees. "Is this all right baby?" he asked turning off the motor.

"Yes, it's fine," answered Sheila opening her door and getting out.

"Where you going?" Jack wondered.

"It's a beautiful evening. Just look at the stars and the moon." The young girl was twirling about while looking up at the stars.

Jack got out on his side. He reached in the back seat and got his flight jacket in case his girl got cold. Sheila was looking across the open and empty pasture. "Let's go for a walk."

"I thought we were going to...."

Sheila stopped him. "We will and we are," she said. Taking Jack by the hand she began to walk out onto the pasture. The green grass was still dry and barely ankle high.

"Over there," she nodded toward one of the oaks in the middle of the field.

Once there she started to sit down near the trunk of the tree.

"Wait a minute," said Jack. He took his jacket and laid it on the grass. "There, wouldn't want to mess that pretty dress."

"We won't," said his girl turning her back on him. "Unzip me."

"Sheila," said a shocked Jack, "Out here. Let's go back to the car."

"Right here, please baby. The back seat of a car is for everyone else. Not for us."

Jack shrugged and unzipped the back of Sheila's dress. She let it fall to the ground on his jacket. "Keep going, baby," she said to him. Reaching around and pointing to the two hooks of her brassiere.

Her lover fumbled with the tiny clasps but with just a little trouble had them unhooked. "Out of practice," said Jack.

"Who have you been practicing with?" chuckled Sheila turning around and showing her breasts to the man undressing her.

"Okay, I'll confess," Jack said smiling. "There's a first for everything."

Sheila put her hands on Jack's chest. "Good answer."

She began to unbutton his shirt. He helped and tossed it to the side. She stepped toward him, placing the soft skin of her upper torso against the hair of his chest. "Love me Jack. Love me like you will love me always."

Jack laid her down on his coat. Her legs extended beyond the warmth of his jacket to the grass. He took his shirt and tucked it under her thighs and calves. His hands worked their way, slowly, inch by inch, up her legs. He pulled her panties gently down her legs and off of her trembling toes. Back at her waist he turned Sheila over and began the journey back down her legs. That trip finished, he lowered his lips and planted a gentle bite on each soft buttock. He rolled her back over. She moaned. He whispered his love in her ear and with his lips gently bit the nape of her neck. He grasp her breasts in each hand and kissed her lips, dashing his tongue in and out of her open mouth. She whispered in his ear. The words were a return of the love chant he had just made known to her. He spread her legs and lowering his head between them began to caress her open love area. She groaned a satisfied moan as she felt him grab her swollen clit with his lips. He rose and wiped his mouth on the sleeve of his shirt underneath Sheila. The girl, roused and excited grabbed his member and attempted to push it between her legs to probe the orifice Jack's lips and tongue had just explored. Jack, raised on one elbow, found the succulent opening and slowly pushed his member inside. She jerked, but allowed his penetration to continue. Now they were joined. They sprawled and tangled, limb on limb. Hugging, kissing, squeezing, raising, pushing until he had given her the last full measure of devotion.

They lay there together for a while. Jack on top, but resting his weight on his elbows. Slowly, his member diminished in size. He pulled out and sat up beside her. "Honey, we better get going. It's getting late," he whispered, caressing her still naked breasts.

She rose and stood up. Jack followed. She looked in his eyes. She cocked her head. Then kissed him one more time before they both started dressing. He helped with her dress and put the jacket, now warm from body heat, around her shoulders. They walked slowly through the grass to the car. Jack looked to the east. He saw the faint orange glow over the Sierras of the coming dawn. In an hour, by the time they got home, the sun would be cresting the mountain peaks.

CHAPTER EIGHT

Jack turned onto the street where Sheila lived. The Gebhardts lived on the next corner. A block later he pulled his car into the driveway of her house. Parking alongside Debbie Gebhardt's Cadillac he left his car running. With the dawn, Sheila's father had already left for work.

"Oh honey, thanks for a wonderful night," said Sheila, leaning over and kissing Jack on the cheek.

"Are you sure you're gonna be all right?" he asked.

"Don't worry darling, Daddy's gone and Mom, I think, is okay with us. By the time Daddy gets home he will have cooled off and Mom will talk to him."

"Okay babe," agreed Jack. "We better get some sleep. How about a goodnight kiss?"

He leaned over, putting his right arm around Sheila. They kissed a long time. Then Sheila opened the car door and scooted out. Straightening her dress, she leaned into the back seat and picked up her graduation cap and gown. She blew Jack another kiss. "Call you tonight, Okay?" and began to walk towards the house.

"Call me if you need me, honey. Otherwise I'll see you later on." Jack put the car in reverse, and backed out of the driveway. Waving to Sheila standing at the doorway, he headed home to bed.

Sheila entered the house and found her mother doing the ironing. "Good morning, Mom."

"Morning honey," her mother answered not looking up from her task.

Sheila worried, asked, "What did you and Daddy do after the ceremony?"

"We were going to dinner but we ended up coming straight home," her mother said, finally looking up from her chore and placing the iron on its end. "You know your father is very upset with what happened last night."

"I know Mother, but he was going to find out sooner or later. And so were you."

"But did you have to tell us on what would have been the

proudest night of our lives?"

"I didn't mean it to happen the way it did. It's just that Jack and me had the evening all planned for weeks and didn't want anything to spoil it."

Debbie Gebhardt's voice grew stern. "Well you two certainly spoiled it for me and your dad."

Sheila approached her mother. "Oh Mom, I wouldn't do anything to hurt you or Daddy, but I do love Jack, very much."

"And does he love you?"

"Yes, and he would do anything to make me happy," said Sheila, trying to convince her mother. Mom will be a much-needed ally when she faced her father.

"I don't know, Sheila," her mother stated. "Our two families could never get along or be friends."

"Never?" asked Sheila.

"Never," confirmed Mrs. Gebhardt. "How long has this been going on?" she asked.

Sheila thought she might as well not lie any longer. "Since I started my senior year."

"He's so much older than you are, honey," said her mother. A fact she knew really didn't matter if her daughter was truly in love.

"Just a couple of years, Mom. Besides isn't Daddy older than you?" asked Sheila. "Why is it any different?"

"Your father had a good job and a steady income when we first met. You are barely eighteen and Jack Lawrence is still working for his own father."

Sheila, trying to bolster Jack's image in her mother's mind said, "But he already has a pilot's license and will soon have his Ag permit to start dusting. You know there is good money in that, Mother. Look what we have here and where Daddy takes you. We will be alright."

Her mother was sensing more than just a fleeting romance now. "I suppose you want to marry this boy?" she asked.

"Eventually," Sheila confirmed. "Don't most people in love get married?"

"Don't be smart," admonished her mother firmly.

"We haven't talked about marriage," Sheila said, head down, "or even much thought about it." Then Sheila remembered Jack's plan about living together. "But I was thinking, if I get another job during the summer I could move out on my own."

This caught her mother by surprise. "You already work at the drive-in and for your dad in the office. You won't have the time to do any more work."

"I'm going to quit the drive-in. I can't work there now that I've graduated. And I don't think Daddy will want me working at the field anymore after last night."

"So now you are just going to go out on your own with nothing and with little income. What about college?"

"I can go to Fresno and get a degree. I have a couple of scholarships and Mother, you said you would help out as long as I continued in school."

"Honey, it's your dad that makes all the money in this family and after last night I don't think he's going to be much help. Especially if you move out of this house."

"Do you think he would let me stay here and go with Jack? Do you think I could stay here when he gets mad at us? It would be impossible, Mother. Don't you think it would be better if I just move out?"

Mrs. Gebhardt now was worried that she was about to lose her daughter. She put her arm around Sheila and looked into her eyes with a mother's gentle expression. "Oh honey, let's talk about this later. You're tired and maybe, if the three of us can sit down to dinner tonight, we can straighten this whole mess out. Your father will have had time to think about it and I am sure we can work it out together," she repeated. "Now, why don't you get some sleep. I'll wake you this afternoon in plenty of time."

Not seeing any reason to go on with this, Sheila agreed. "Okay Mother but please, wake me before Daddy comes home." She turned and walked to her room, quietly closing the bedroom door. She undressed and crawled naked into the security of her bed, falling quickly asleep. In the other room her mother unplugged the iron. Going into the kitchen, she poured herself a cup of coffee and sat down at the table. Staring out the window, her eyes glazed over. She wiped them with her apron.

Jack was awake in the early afternoon. He drove to the airfield and stopped alongside the Cal-Ag hanger. His dad was in the office going over the next day's flight assignments. He went inside and sat down opposite his father's desk. Alan Lawrence looked up from his work. "Hi, son, how'd it go last night?"

"Just fine, Dad. Got in probably just after you left this morning."

"Had a good time with Sheila, huh?" his father asked smiling.

"Yep, quite a gal and now she's graduated," answered Jack proudly. "Well, better get to work." Jack rose from the chair and was going to leave when his dad interrupted. "Just a minute, son. I've got something to say to you." He walked to the office door and yelled at Brownie working on a plane in the hanger. "Brownie, get Bobby in here will you?" He returned to behind the desk with the field plans laid out in front of him. Brownie turned and walked outside the hanger and yelled to a teenager washing a plane. The washer looked up and Brownie motioned him to come to the hanger. The boy dropped the hose, turned off the water and trotted toward the mechanic.

"Bobby, the ol' man wants to see you in the office," ordered Brownie, pointing to the door. The boy went inside.

"You wanted to see me, sir?" the young worker asked, standing in the doorway.

"Come on in," said Alan, "I want you to meet my son. Jack, this is Bobby. He just started today."

Jack didn't rise from his seat, but nodded and acknowledged the new guy, "Nice to meet you, Bobby."

Bobby, recognizing the younger Lawrence, answered, "Hello Jack, pleased to meet you." And then added, "Hey, didn't I see you last night at the graduation?"

Jack looked across the desk at his father before answering. "Yea, I was there. What were you doing at the stadium? You don't look old enough to be a graduate."

"No, next year," the boy answered. "My sister was graduating this time. Man, that was quite a scene on the field wasn't it? What happened anyway? I didn't see it all."

"Oh, it was nothing. Just a little misunderstanding." Jack answered; hoping the boy wouldn't press it any further.

But he continued. "All I remember is you decking that guy and you and that girl taking off running toward the gate."

Alan Lawrence wanted to hear more about this from his son, but with just the two of them. "That'll be all Bobby. Tomorrow morning, be here by 4:30. Report to Brownie. You and him will be working with Jack out on the west side."

"Yes sir," the boy said, turning and leaving the office.

"Thanks and close the door behind you," commanded Alan. The boy quietly closed the door. Jack and Alan Lawrence sat across from each other, the big oak desk separating father and son. His dad looked down again at the field layouts spread on the desktop. After a minute, he looked up to see his son gazing out the window. Watching the boy returning at a walk to the wash rack.

"You going to tell me about what happened last night or do I have to wait to hear it from someone else. Probably at a club meeting or social night?" Alan asked his son.

"Like I said Dad, it was just a misunderstanding. This guy Carter was really rude and tried to take my girl. He came at me and I just beat him to the punch."

"You hit him with everyone around?"

"Dad, I didn't have much choice. I tried to be polite towards the Gebhardts, but things got out of hand."

"Harry Gebhardt was right there?" His father wanted all the answers now.

"Well actually, he kinda started it. I was polite and told him I was there with his daughter and that Sheila and me were going out together."

"Oh boy, I bet that went over well." Jack could see a faint smile come over his father's face.

"You wouldn't believe it, Dad. Mr. Gebhardt just blew his cool. I thought he was going to take a swing at me. Poor Sheila, I just had to get her out of there."

"So, who's this Carter fella?" queried his dad.

"Some college jerk who works for Western. He's been after Sheila since he got here. But she doesn't want anything to do with him."

His dad continued, "How'd he get into the ceremony? I thought it was just family and close friends."

"Harry Gebhardt thinks he's God's gift to the family and the company. College educated and all."

Dad smiled again. "You would think with a college education he would choose another occupation."

Jack kept going in defense of his actions. "With just one more year 'till he graduates you'd think he would act a little more civilized, too. I really don't think he plans on working in the ag business, Dad. I don't know what his major is but it certainly isn't manners or charm. Except to Sheila of course."

"Well son, that's what girls and love will do to guys."

Jack leaned forward and put his hands on the desk. "With Carter it's girls. With me it's love."

His dad smiled and again looked down at the charts.

"Can I go now, Dad? I gotta lot a work to do." Jack felt he had made his point.

"Just a minute son. I think you'll want to hear this." The ol' man took his pencil and outlined a rectangular field on the map in front of him. He handed it across the desk to his young and only son. Jack took it and laid it on his lap. "What's this?" he asked.

"It's sixty acres of cotton on the McMillan ranch. You'll be working it tomorrow."

Jack was puzzled. He figured he'd be showing the youngster loading and fueling techniques. These charts were for the pilots only. "So what am I looking for? I know how to get to the landing strip."

His dad chuckled. He had waited a long time for this. "I know you can drive there. Can you land there?"

Jack looked up from the map. "What?" he exclaimed.

"Gary has to attend an airport managers meeting tomorrow so we're short a pilot. Besides I have been watching you and so has Brownie. We both agree you're ready to go."

Jack couldn't believe what he had heard. He jumped up and leaned over the desk. "Dad, I don't know what to say. I have been working so hard on my turns and low level flying. But I thought you would never let me actually fly ag this year."

His father leaned back in his chair and looked at his son. "It's just a small field. But, it'll be a start. Look on the chart. No wires, no standpipes. Just nice, smooth, straight, runs are all I want. Okay son? And locate the flagger as soon as you come out of the turn."

"You got it, Dad. Man, thanks. Thanks a lot."

"Just do it right. I have all the confidence that you are ready," said his reassuring father. He got up from behind the desk. Walking around to Jack he extended his hand to his son. When Jack took it, Alan grabbed his shoulder. Pulling Jack close to him, he gave his only son a hug. "Now take the rest of the day off. Go home. Study the landing strip. Getting to and from the field. You'll be in 'three-seven.' That's the best flying duster we got. If you see Mr. McMillan watching from his truck, don't get nervous. Just do what you've been doing in practice and you'll be fine. Now get out of here. And no partying tonight!" concluded his dad, smiling one more time.

"No sir and thanks again, Dad." Jack swung the door open and bounced out into the hanger area. Brownie was on a ladder checking the spark plugs on a big Pratt and Whitney engine. He turned and saw Jack running towards him.

"Brownie, Brownie, I'm flying tomorrow. My first field."

"I know kid. You think you're ready?"

"Oh, I'm ready. I've been ready for a long time," answered Jack, pumping his fist in the air.

"Don't get cocky on me already kid," cautioned the mechanic. "Just do it right and make the ol' man proud."

Jack was walking briskly to his car. He yelled back at Brownie still on the ladder. "Don't worry, I won't let him down...or you! See you in the morning, bright and early."

Brownie waved with a wrench in his hand and went back to his work. Jack sped off the field. As he left, he saw Harry Gebhardt's truck parked at the office. He could hardly wait to tell Sheila.

Jack drove right to her house. He parked in the front, next to the curb. He walked up the sidewalk to the front door. Standing in front of the screen, he took a deep breath and rang the doorbell. A minute passed. He rang the doorbell again. He could hear someone approaching from inside. The door opened. Mrs. Gebhardt stood looking at Jack through the screen.

"Hello Mrs. Gebhardt, can I please speak to Sheila?" Jack was trying to be as polite as possible.

"She is still asleep Jack. Besides, I don't think this is a good day to see her."

"I'm sorry about what happened last night Mrs. Gebhardt, but I have something real important to tell her," pleaded Jack.

"I think you have done quite enough to this family for the time being Jack. Why don't you just leave now and let us work this out," said Sheila's mother. A resolute tone in her voice.

Jack, still trying to be polite, asked, "May I call her later this afternoon or this evening?"

"I don't think so Jack," answered Mrs. Gebhardt beginning to close the door.

"Wait, Mrs. Gebhardt, let me explain. I want you to know how I feel about your daughter," said Jack, leaning forward and placing his hands on either side of the locked screen.

"Goodbye Jack." Mrs. Gebhardt finished closing the door. Jack could hear the deadbolt slide into the slot in the jam. He turned and leaned against a post supporting the roof of the porch. Head down, he pondered what to do next. Maybe Sheila's mother was right. Maybe the previous night had been too much of a shock. Though he was still excited about his job the next morning he decided to either call Sheila after he was finished flying or see her tomorrow evening. Jack walked slowly to his car. Pulling away from the curb, he drove around the corner. From her bedroom window Sheila watched the convertible, with Jack at the wheel, drive away.

CHAPTER NINE

At the airfield, Harry Gebhardt was smiling. He had just taken his newly repaired Stearman for a test flight. Everything had gone well. Tomorrow, he would be in full operation again. Harry congratulated his mechanic and left the hanger. His crash helmet and goggles tucked under his arm, walking into the office he removed his flight overalls and placed them in a tall locker. Putting the bright red helmet and shaded goggles on the top shelf he closed the locker door. On the outside, in red letters, was printed "Chief."

Carter was sitting at the desk normally occupied by Sheila while working for her father.

"Everything go all right on the test flight sir?" he asked.

"Just like she was never hurt," Harry answered, referring to his favorite aircraft.

"Good, now we can get back to normal around here," said Carter.

"I'm glad you mentioned that Carter," said Harry. He sat down at his own desk in the back of the office. "You know just because of what happened last night doesn't mean you have to stop seeing my daughter."

"Oh, I wasn't planning on it sir. Sheila is a wonderful girl. After I graduate next year I would like to think her and I, with your permission of course, could begin planning..." Carter paused.

"A future?" offered Harry.

"Yes sir...a future," answered a hesitant Carter.

"You are a fine young man Carter. A hard worker and, from what I hear, a college student with good grades. But you realize that for you and my daughter to have a future you have to get her to stop seeing...and even thinking about Jack Lawrence."

"I know, and that's going to be hard." Carter rose from his chair and began to pace around the room.

"I don't think it's going to be as hard as you think, young man." Harry leaned back and put his boots up on his desk. He folded his arms across his chest and continued. "Tonight the family is going to sit down to dinner. I'm sure my daughter has had a chance to work her spell on her mother. By the time I get home Mrs. Gebhardt will be ready to sit me down in my easy chair, hand me the evening paper and have my favorite meal prepared."

Carter stopped pacing. "Sounds like you're outnumbered."

"Not in my own house," said Harry. "Besides, that's where you come in. We normally finish dinner by 6:30. You need to show up about 7:00."

Carter was wondering. "What'll I say? What do you want me to do?"

"Sheila will answer the door," Harry answered. "She'll be thinking it's Jack."

"And when it isn't, won't she be disappointed?" interjected Carter.

"Don't worry. Just be nice. Like you always are to her. I'll see to the rest." Harry took out his wallet and handed Carter a twenty-dollar bill. "Take her to a movie or something, maybe the drive-in theater. Get her to forget about Jack. Forget about him forever."

"What if she doesn't want to go out with me?" Carter was making sure of everything.

"Carter, listen to me. I told you, don't worry. Be there at 7:00. By then she'll want to go out with you."

"Okay, seven o'clock it is," affirmed Carter. "Not a minute later."

"That a boy," said Harry, rising from behind the desk. Grabbing his keys from the center drawer he passed Carter on the way to the door. Slapping Carter on the back he told the smiling man, "Between the two of us we'll get my daughter to straighten up and fly right."

"Yes sir, we sure will," Carter was already thinking of that night's plan, both Harry's and his own.

At the Gebhardt's home Sheila was showering and Debbie Gebhardt was preparing a pot roast with mash potatoes, gravy and fresh cut asparagus. Her husband's favorite dinner treats. For a finishing touch she had baked a pumpkin pie. Finishing her shower, Sheila pulled on a pair of tight pedal pushers. Putting on a white, button down blouse, she left the top two buttons unfastened. The hint of cleavage between her breasts just visible in the opening. She put on a pair of short white socks and stepped into her black and white oxfords. Sheila looked in the mirror. She debated whether to roll her hair and sit under the dryer or just brush it dry. Jack liked the long straight look. The natural feel of the velvet soft strands. Grabbing a brush Sheila walked out of her bedroom.

"Smells good, Mom," she said, passing through the kitchen and out the back door.

"Thanks honey, I hope your dad likes it," replied Debbie Gebhardt.

Sheila sat down at the outdoor patio table. Positioning her chair so that the summer sun would be to her back. She began slowly brushing the strands of her hair. Extending each stroke the full length. First one side then the other. The long blond strands of her hair, separated by the bristles, fell gently onto her back at the end of each caressing movement. The brush strokes were automatic. Her thoughts were of Jack and the night before. The pasture, the thrill and sense of adventure. Her nakedness in the moonlight under the oak tree. The lusty feel of her lover's body against her skin. The gentleness of his manhood as he ever so slowly penetrated her young and tender opening. The ecstasy of their joining as one. She remembered the sweet gentle breath of the northwest breeze cooling her hot body afterwards. As she continued brushing, a stirring began to be felt between her legs. From the kitchen window, Debbie Gebhardt could see her daughter smiling as she dried her hair in the sun.

"Whatever is for dinner it sure smells good," hollered Harry as he entered the door. "If the neighbors get a whiff we're sure to have company."

"My, aren't we in a good mood," said Debbie. "Have a good day at work?"

"Yep, plane's fixed. Jobs are waiting and we are rolling into our summer season."

"That's good honey. Why don't you sit down and read the paper. Dinner will be ready in a little while."

"Where's my girl?" asked Harry.

"She's out in the yard. Do you want me to call her?"

"Naah, that's alright. I'll talk to her at dinner." Harry grabbed the evening news and sat down in his easy chair.

He had not finished the front page when Sheila walked through the room to return the brush to her bedroom. She had passed by him without speaking. On the return trip, it was different. "Hi Daddy," were the only words she spoke.

"Hi Sheila," was her father's only reply.

She helped her mother set the table. Soon dinner was ready. Debbie called to her husband, "Come on dear, before it gets cold."

Harry put the paper down. He walked to the dining room and sat down at his customary place at the head of the table. On his right was his wife. On the left his daughter. Nothing was said. Dishes were passed. Servings spooned out until plates were full. Initial samplings were eaten. The only sound was the tapping of silverware against the china. Finally Sheila couldn't stand it any longer.

"How'd it go at work today, Daddy? Did you miss me?" she asked.

"It went fine and no I didn't," her father answered bluntly.

Sheila looked across at her mom. Hoping for some help in this already awkward situation. Debbie, head down, continued slowly eating.

Sheila tried again. "I bet you were busy with fixing the plane, huh Daddy?"

"She'll be back in the air tomorrow. Just in time too. With the busy season."

His daughter kept up the effort. "I know I am little behind with the office work Daddy, but I'll be out there first thing in the morning."

"Actually, Carter finished the day's paperwork. That young man is quite a whiz with figures and math," Harry beamed, touting his favorite worker.

"I guess you'll need me out there tomorrow to call in the chemical orders, pay bills and do the invoicing?" asked Sheila, hoping that was the case.

Harry looked at his silent but attentive wife. "Why don't you stay home and help your mother with the housework. If you want to come out after lunch, you and Carter can finish off the billing in no time."

Sheila remembered the last time her and Carter were alone in the office. "I'm sure I can do it myself, Daddy. Doesn't Carter have other work to do?"

"He's a good, fast employee. Always looking to help out. Do you have a problem with him working in the office?" Harry asked his daughter.

"No, I guess not," answered a condescending Sheila. "It's just that it has always been kinda of my job to do."

Harry looked at his wife. "Do you mind Carter and Sheila working together?"

"No honey, not if you feel it is for the good of the company," answered Debbie sheepishly.

"Good, now let's enjoy this delicious meal your mother has fixed," Harry said, looking at his watch.

Sheila was quiet again. She wanted to say something about the night before but could see her mother had retreated from reinforcing any statement that she was going to make about the previous evening or her night with Jack. Her father still ruled the roost. Finishing her meal, Sheila began to clear her side of the table.

Harry again looked at his watch. "That's alright baby, your mother can finish the dishes. Why don't you go in the living room and turn on the TV."

Sheila was confused. She always helped Mom with the dishes when they all sat down together for dinner. She began again to put some dishes in the sink. Harry looked at his wife and with anger in his tone said, "Debbie, get up and let you daughter relax a little this evening."

Leaving her unfinished meal and without saying anything, the obedient wife went over to the sink and began running the water for dishwashing. Nodding to her daughter she whispered to Sheila, "Go on honey, I can finish in here."

Sheila sighed, left the kitchen and went to her bedroom. She closed the door, turned on the radio and raised the volume. The Gebhardt's phone rang. Debbie sensed who the caller was, but her hands were already deep in the soapy dishwater. Harry answered after the third ring. The caller asked if he could speak to Sheila. Harry, recognizing the voice from the night before, replied that his daughter was out for the evening and hung up. Minutes later the phone rang again. Harry picked the receiver up and repeated, "Hello." On the other end of the line, the caller, without speaking, gently placed the receiver back on the hook. In her bedroom, radio blaring, Sheila danced to the music. Oblivious to the ringing phone.

"Sheila, get out here and watch TV with us," Harry yelled. He went to her room and knocked on the door. The rock and roll music coming from inside was silenced with his pounding. Sheila opened the door.

"Yes Daddy, what do you want?"

"Why don't you come out and join us? Your mom is almost finished and we can watch TV together."

Sheila didn't want to say no and upset her father. "Okay, I'll be right there."

Harry returned to the living room. He sat down in his easy chair and picked up the paper to start reading again. His wife came in with a large piece of pumpkin pie. Placing it on the end table next to her husband she let him know about dessert. "I think you'll like this honey."

Harry lowered the paper. "Pumpkin pie too. This is turning into a very special evening." Seeing his daughter coming down the hall he added, "certainly better than last night." Then continued, "Oh, hi honey. Turn on TV. See what's on the news."

Sheila had heard the remark but didn't have a response. Didn't want to respond.

Harry had just taken a bite of the pie when the doorbell rang.

"Would you get that Sheila? My mouth is full."

Sheila opened the door. Carter was standing there holding a bouquet of flowers.

Swallowing his bite of pumpkin pie, Harry said, "Let the young man in honey."

Sheila unlocked the screen and Carter pulled it open. "These are for you, Sheila," he said holding the bouquet of spring flowers out to the girl.

"Well, aren't you going to thank him, Sheila?" asked Harry, rising from his chair.

"Thank you, Carter," answered Sheila. Obeying her father's order.

"My these are so pretty," chimed in Debbie. "I'll put them in some water for you honey." Sheila's mom took the flowers and headed for the kitchen to look for a vase.

Harry was now at the doorway. He shook Carter's hand. "Come on in and make yourself at home."

Carter was now at the point he had been practicing. "Actually sir, I came to see if Sheila would like to go to the movies with me tonight. There is a new Kirk Douglas flick that just started at the drive-in."

"Kirk Douglas, one of my favorites, and Mother's too. Isn't that right, Debbie?"

Debbie hadn't heard anything. She was filling the vase with tap water for the flowers.

"Yep, he's her favorite alright," laughed Harry, "sometimes I even get a little jealous."

Carter, doing what he knew best, responded, "With your happy marriage sir, I don't think you have anything to worry about. A beautiful house, successful business, a pretty wife," he turned to Sheila, "and a lovely daughter."

"No, son, probably not. Sheila grab your sweater, this man can't wait all night."

Sheila was startled. It was the first time her father had used the term "son" when referring to any boy. She was also surprised at Carter's charm. Of course her parents *were* present. She knew Jack was going to call or come by. Before she obeyed her father and left with Carter she had to try one time to reach him. "Just a minute, I'll be right back." She excused herself and went to the kitchen. As her mother watched she dialed Jack's number. While waiting for someone to pick up on the other end she looked at her mother sitting silently at the kitchen table. The flowers, now in a glass vase, adorned the center of the tabletop. There was no answer at the Lawrence house. Sheila hung up and redialed the number. There was still no answer. She left the kitchen. Not speaking as she passed her mother. She returned to the living room. The two men were still standing and talking. "All ready to go honey?" asked her father. "Where's your sweater?"

"I don't think I'll need it Daddy," answered Sheila going out the front door. Leaving Carter in the front room.

"Well, if you get cold this young man can always keep you warm," yelled Harry, winking at Carter.

Carter returned the wink and shook Harry's hand. "Thank you sir."

Harry held the front door open for Carter as he left the house. Sheila was already in the car. Carter jumped in the driver's seat, started the car and moved the vehicle slowly away from Sheila's house. Harry returned to the front room. Debbie had made herself a cup of coffee and was seated on the living room sofa. Harry sat down next to his wife, placed his arm around her and stated what seemed so obvious to him, "That Carter is quite a fellow isn't he honey?"

Debbie, between sips from her cup, answered, "If you think so."

"Oh, I know it. Wouldn't it be nice if your daughter married someone like him?"

His wife placed her cup on the coffee table in front of her. She turned to her husband. "I think Sheila will marry who she wants to, Harry."

Her husband was not amused with his wife's sudden change of tone. "Only with my blessing, she will. She's still my daughter and still living under this roof."

Debbie slipped out from under Harry's arm on her shoulder. She picked up her cup and headed for the relative safety of the kitchen. Turning to look back she told her husband, "Don't drive her out of this house Harry. If we lose her you might lose me too."

Harry didn't respond to his wife's idle threat. He again picked up the paper and began perusing the pages of the evening news. His wife quietly closed the sliding door that separated the kitchen from the living room. It would be a long night again.

At the drive-in theater, Carter parked in the center for a good view of the screen. Before placing the speaker on the edge of the door he politely asked Sheila if she would like anything from the snack bar. "No thank you, Carter," she responded.

Soon the show started. Previews of upcoming features were shown on the screen. Exciting clips that were the best parts of the movies. During the movie, Carter sat behind the wheel. Sheila was up against the inside of the passenger door. During the first feature both were engaged in polite conversation. At intermission Carter again asked if Sheila would like something to eat or drink.

"A Coke and popcorn would be nice," she answered.

He opened the car door. Careful not to catch the speaker cord. "Be right back," he said.

While he was away Sheila thought of how nice he had been. His attitude was completely different than before. Had her father talked to him? No, her father didn't even know of the episode in the office. She was perplexed. Halfway through the evening and he hadn't made an advance toward her. Just polite and engrossing conversation of college courses, life in general and the scenes being played out by the actors on the screen.

"Here you go, Sheila," Carter said, passing the Coke and box of popcorn through the window opening on the passenger side. He walked around to the driver's side and sat down behind the wheel.

"Mind sharing that popcorn?" he asked. Sheila put the large box on the seat between them. Carter grabbed a handful, putting his Coke between his legs he used both hands to eat the kernels one and two at a time. They talked a little during the second feature. When it was over it was nearly midnight. Carter headed out of the theater lot and drove slowly down the main street. The car radio was playing softly.

"Would you like to stop at the drive-in and get a shake or something?" He asked.

"No thanks, I'm ready to go home," answered Sheila. "Besides we both have to work tomorrow."

"Yea, I guess so," said a disappointed Carter. "I worked in the office today. Boy, you do quite a bit of work in there, don't you?"

Sheila saw her chance to end this right now. "Yea, I get quite a bit done when I'm left alone and not bothered."

Carter became apologetic. "I'm sorry about the other day. I really am. I don't know what happened." He was pulling up to the curb at the Gebhardt's house. "I really made a fool of myself."

"You sure did. You scared the hell outta me," agreed Sheila, turning and looking at Carter. He turned the car off, ran around to the other side and opened the door for Sheila. She got out and together they strolled slowly up the walk to the front porch. The house was dark. Only the corner street light provided illumination. Sheila started to open the door but Carter interjected. "Wait Sheila. I just want you to know that I am truly sorry about the other day. I had a wonderful evening tonight and hope you did too."

Sheila hesitated then responded, "I had a nice time too. Thanks for the movie and stuff Carter. Now I better go inside."

Carter gently grabbed her hand. Intertwining his fingers with hers. She opened the door with her free hand. Carter held the screen open for her. "Thank you, Sheila. I guess I will see you in the morning."

"I guess so," Sheila said, closing the screen and locking it. "Good night Carter."

CHAPTER TEN

Jack opened his eyes. He looked at the alarm clock on the table next to his bed; only three in the morning. He couldn't sleep. He debated whether to just lie in bed or get up and go for some early morning coffee at the truck stop. His father would be getting up in a half-hour. Should he wait for Alan? Together they could have coffee before heading to the airfield. Father and son, two pilots talking experiences. Nah, wouldn't work, Jack decided. He had heard all of his father's tales and he certainly was too young to have any of his own. He rose from his bed. After a quick shower and dressing he was headed toward the coffee shop near the airfield.

"Black coffee please and one of those bear claws," Jack said as he sat down at the counter. The nervous young pilot, the waitress, and the cook in the kitchen were the only people in the restaurant. She brought him his coffee and pastry and returned to reading the early morning paper. Jack sat quietly. Thinking of the field he was going to fly, he went over in his mind the approach and turns. He tried to visualize the flagger at the far end. Lining up with the waving white rag tied on the end of a pole. The door opened. A burly trucker walked through the entrance. Straddling a stool at the other end of the counter he sat down with a thud. "Hey sugar," he thundered in a deep voice, "howza 'bout some coffee?"

"Hold your throttle Sam, I'm comin," answered the waitress.

"Bring the sports section over here with the coffee would ya?" The trucker asked.

Sugar the waitress, brought the coffee and paper. "Your Dodgers lost again, Sam."

"Damn it! Those Braves are good," said Sam. "That negro kid Aaron can sure hit the ball."

"Maybe, but you guys can't hit Spahn or Burdette," added the waitress.

"Listen Sugar, what makes you the baseball expert?"

"Well maybe, if you and your trucker buddies would stop more often, maybe I wouldn't have so much time to go over the box scores." The waitress smiled and leaning over the counter, pinched the cheek of the husky truck driver.

Returning to Jack, she asked, "Want anything else honey?"

"No this will do for now." Jack threw a dollar on the counter. "Maybe I'll see you at lunch."

"I get off before then sweetie, but come back tomorrow morning," said the waitress, winking at Jack.

The truck driver looked up from his paper to see Jack wave to the waitress as he walked out the door. The young pilot started his car and headed toward the airfield, leaving the lonely waitress and solitary trucker still talking baseball inside the coffee shop.

Jack parked along side the Cal-Ag hanger. The lights inside signaled that Brownie and some of the loaders had already arrived. The hanger door was wide open when Jack walked around to the front. On the tarmac, lined up wing to wing, sat his father's planes. It was still dark. The silhouettes of the biplanes looked like a squadron left over from an old war movie. Jack laughed to himself. He would like to see Errol Flynn fly as low and good as he knew his father could.

"Good morning, kid," said a familiar voice. "We'll have your plane ready to go in no time. Better get your gear on."

"Be right behind you Brownie," Jack said, passing the mechanic and the new worker Bobby, heading toward the planes.

Jack went to his locker where his flight jacket, helmet and goggles were kept. Outside he could hear the familiar voices and commands as the crew readied the planes. "Contact" the turn of the prop. Jack listened. Nothing. Then the usual, "Shit" from the propman. "Off," said Brownie turning the switch. "Contact," was repeated. The switch was again turned on. This time, as Jack closed his locker door, he heard the engine roar to life. He looked outside. The big radial engine of his duster was belching orange flames out the exhaust. Brilliant in the early morning, as the engine warmed the exhaust would soon turn a glowing blue. Jack walked into the office. He laid out the chart of the fields. He had studied his assignment so long it seemed he should know every plant in every row.

"Mornin' Son," said Alan, startling Jack a little. "Are you ready to go?"

"Ready as I'll ever be, Dad," answered Jack, rolling the chart up and returning it to the file cabinet.

"Nervous?" asked Alan.

"A little."

"Good," his father assured. "It'll make you more careful."

"Any pointers, Pop?" Jack smiled.

"Just fly right. In dusting, it's low and slow. From the time you get in the plane, Son, become part of it. Feel what she feels. You know the 'airspeed' and 'altimeter' don't work. But, I had Brownie put in a new 'tach.' Keep a check on the oil and manifold pressure. When you come down on the field learn to sense the cushion of air. You'll feel it. Especially in row crops like the cotton you'll be dusting today."

Alan's son was sitting on the desk. This was a refresher course but he found himself trying to remember everything his father was saying. "You mean it's different with a vineyard?" asked Jack.

"Oh yea, a lot different." Alan answered. "But don't worry about that now. Just concentrate on what has to be done today. One job at a time, one field at a time, one pass at a time. How's the helmet feel?"

Jack pulled his helmet down over his ears and adjusted his goggles. "Feels okay."

Alan had another tip that Jack had already learned the hard way. "Make sure you tighten that chin strap. That thing will sail on you if air gets inside." His dad tapped the top of his son's helmet with his fist. "You'll wind up with a sore and stiff neck. And stay low in the cockpit. No use getting the hell beat out of you by the wind."

"Okay Dad," said Jack. "I better get out there. See you when I get back."

"Knock 'em dead, Son," said Alan pouring himself a cup of coffee. "When you get outside, send Brownie in here will you?"

"Sure," answered Jack. He walked out of the hanger toward his plane warming up at its place in the line.

"What's your hurry, kid?" asked Brownie stepping off the wing after getting out of the cockpit.

"No rush, just a little excited is all. Guess I'll be waiting for you at the strip."

"Bobby and Junior have already left. I'll be right behind them. But, don't wait for me. Have them start loading as soon as you get there. It's going to get hot real quick today and we have to get a lot

March 15, 2002done." Brownie patted the young Lawrence on the shoulder and began walking toward his truck. Jack suddenly remembered his dad's last words.

"Hey Brownie," he yelled over the roar of the Stearman's engine. "Dad wants to see you."

Brownie nodded and gave Jack a thumbs up. He walked into the office. "You wanted to see me, Pappy?"

"Yea Brownie. Keep an eye on the kid today. I want a full report on his flying technique. Even though we both know he'll do fine I'd like to know what you feel and if you get a chance, talk to McMillan. I'm sure he'll be out there watching. The field is not too far from the strip. After the last load, jump in your truck and watch his passes will ya? Hopefully he won't forget to border the field."

"Sure Pappy, I think you worry too much. Jack's a good pilot. And besides, you taught him." Brownie smiled at Alan.

Jack's father returned the smile. "Yea, I guess that's why I want him to be the best."

"Pappy, he's got a long way to go to catch you. See you later and don't worry, I'll watch him." Brownie walked out and jumped in his truck. He passed the duster. Jack was in the cockpit. Shoulder harness buckled, he began to taxi the plane out to the runway. At the far end, before take off, he ran up the engine and checked the few gauges that were working. Brownie was soon on the road headed toward the landing strip. Jack turned the biplane into the wind. Everything was ready. More throttle and the Stearman raced down the asphalt. The tail raised and when the attitude of the nose was right, Jack eased the control stick back. The plane rose from the field into the cool morning air. Jack banked the plane westward. He felt the wind from the prop and the airspeed. It buffeted his helmet. His head was too high in the cockpit. When he got to the strip he would have to remove one of the seat cushions. His face felt cold. He gained altitude. Trying to find the warmer inversion layer in the early morning, Jack passed over Brownie's truck headed for the landing strip. He would arrive there before the mechanic.

Jack saw the landing strip. It was short, but wide and paved. He passed over on the downwind and turned to line up for his final approach. With this short strip he would have to three point the landing. All three wheels, the two front and the tail, touching down at the same time. The landing would have to be slow. Touch down would have to come as close to the beginning of the strip as possible. Long and fast meant disaster. He was on his final approach now. Jack "set" the nose at the attitude. At this correct attitude he couldn't see over the front end. Pushing and holding the right rudder pedal and moving the stick a little to the left the biplane cocked its nose to the right but continued to fly in a straight line with the landing strip. With the plane cocked to the right, Jack, looking out the left side, could easily see the runway ahead. He adjusted the rate of descent with the throttle. Keeping the nose up, at the last moment he kicked the plane back to its straight flying position with the wheels just a few feet above the ground. All three tires hit the pavement together. Careful not to push the brakes at the top of each rudder pedal at the same time, Jack alternated the pressure on the pedals, slowly bringing the duster to a halt. He held one brake and increasing throttle turned the plane around. Taxiing back to the stacks of sulfur and the loaders he leaned out over the cockpit, watching the edge of the landing strip until he again swung the plane's lower wing over the sulfur bags. Bobby set the chocks in front of the wheels. Jack unbuckled his lap and shoulder harness and climbed out.

"Nice landing," said Bobby as Jack jumped from the left wing to the ground.

"Thanks," beamed Jack. "Let's get her loaded. Brownie's not here yet, I guess?"

"On his way," Bobby answered, climbing into the cockpit with his grape knife. Soon the other loader was tossing the bags of yellow dust up to the space between the cockpit and hopper. Bobby sliced the bag open, flipped it over and dumped it into the empty abyss. Jack walked over to the loader's truck and sat in the driver's seat, his feet resting on the edge of the door opening. He left his helmet on. Next time, he thought, he would bring a thermos. Soon the plane was loaded. Jack returned to the cockpit. Now it would get serious. He sat down on the seat. Again feeling the prop blast he remembered the seat padding. He pulled a cushion from underneath him and tossed it out of the cockpit. Bobby ran over and picked it up. Placing it on the floorboard of the truck, he gave a thumbs up to Jack. The pilot wasn't looking. Already preparing for a takeoff with full weight, he headed toward the very end of the strip. There, holding the brakes, he looked down the runway to make sure it was clear. He pushed the throttle forward as far as it would go. The engine roared. Loose asphalt and gravel were sprayed by the propwash under the plane, past the tailwheel, into the neighboring field. Jack released the brakes and the biplane gained speed quickly. Fifty feet from the end of the asphalt the Stearman took flight. Jack banked slightly to the left and headed toward his first field.

Soon he was there. He saw the flagger. He took a deep breath. This was it. Coming in high, as if he had wires or poles to cross, Jack lined the plane up with the man at the far end of the field waving the white banner. He eased the throttle back. Just before the plane settled on the field Jack pushed the hopper release. The "money handle" opened the hopper gate and the sulfur poured out the bottom. The prop created a swirling effect to the dust. Curling the bug killer under the leaves, then upward, to finally settle on the plants. Flying across the field at about 80 miles per hour, Jack could feel the cushion of air between the field and the underside of his lower wing. This was what his father meant. Approaching the end of the pass he eased in the power. Pulling up straight, Jack shut off the dust and put in more throttle. He needed turnaround power. Keeping the nose up he began his turn. Banking the plane to the right, it gracefully angled in the morning air. The early rays of sunlight reflecting off the gold paint of the wings. Halfway into the turn Jack started coming back on the throttle. He had overshot the flagger a little. But this was on purpose. It was easy to correct and allowed him to spot the flagger to line up for his next pass. He set the power and the plane eased down on the crop. Each pass was lower and slower. Jack gained confidence after each run. As the weight of the sulfur decreased, less power was needed and his turns became shorter.

He was empty now and returned to the strip for another load. Brownie had arrived.

"How'd it go kid?" he asked as Jack stepped to the ground.

"Great Brownie, just great."

"Having fun are we?"

"It's fun, but that's because this is different," said an enthusiastic Jack. "It's sure different than practice. But, I think I'm doing a good job."

"Good," said Brownie calmly. "The farmer that owns that field and a lot more acres will be out there soon. Don't pay any attention. Just concentrate." Brownie looked at the loaders gathering up the empty bags. "You're loaded. Let's get the show on the road."

"Alright, I'm off." Jack hurriedly returned to the cockpit.

The plane was soon over the field again. Jack could see farmer McMillan's truck parked on a dirt road. A little more nervous with a spectator, he put his mind to the task. Each pass was lower. He had already learned to use the cushion of air his father had talked about. He didn't notice when two other farmers drove up along side McMillan's pickup. Jack could feel his tires hitting the tops of the cotton plants as he crossed the field. The three ranchers were standing, sipping coffee from McMillan's thermos, watching the young pilot at work. One of them asked, "Who is that? That helmet doesn't look like Alan Lawrence's."

"It's not," replied McMillan. "It's his kid."

"Well, he's pretty good for a kid."

"He had a good teacher," McMillan said, "best damn pilot around. Been doing my fields for years."

"Look how low he gets," the other grower said. "His wheels are practically between the rows."

McMillan was starting to gloat. "He can fly my fields anytime...or his old man."

The farmers stood mesmerized. Drinking from their metal cups, they watched Jack make each low pass then turn smoothly and with ease to start another run across the field. While he was off loading they would talk shop. But the conversation would always change to the technique of the young flyer when he returned to traverse the rows of McMillan's cotton field. On his last load, Brownie had also watched the skill of the youngster. Jack had finished the field. He turned, and using what sulfur he had left, applied the yellow dust to the edges of the assigned acreage. His border passes complete, he returned his focus to the three farmers on the nearby dirt road. Brownie watched as Jack flew over the top of them, waved and dipped his wing tips. They raised their cups in unison and waved back. Jack banked his Stearman toward the airfield and home. He was smiling. He was now an ag pilot. This was something. Something he could hardly wait to tell Sheila.

Jack, back at the field, wanted to keep going. He was excited. He taxied to his aircraft's parking spot and shut off the engine. He jumped down from the wing. Removing his goggles and helmet he walked briskly to the office. No one was inside. He sat down in his father's chair at the desk. On a notepad was scribbled the pilot's assignments and acreage. His dad was still flying. Jack wanted more assignments and looked down the list of names on the paper: Alan, Alan, Alan, Gary, Pat, Gary again, Alan again and finally the name Jack, read the list. Brownie's truck pulled onto the airfield and the mechanic went to the office.

"Nice going kid. That was a real fine job you did out there. Nice personal touch with the farmers too."

"I want to go some more. I can get some of this done," demanded Jack, pointing to the notepad.

"Easy kid, those can wait," Brownie said, "besides it's gettin' too hot to dust. You know heat means danger with sulfur."

"Yea, I know, just excited I guess." Jack returned to his father's chair. "When's Dad gonna be finished?"

"Should be back real soon," answered Brownie. "Well, gotta check your plane. How'd she fly today?

"Just fine, Brownie. You're the best mechanic around."

"Yea, best mechanic, best pilot and now maybe another."

"I'll never be as good as the 'ol man," Jack said.

"Hey, you never know kid. Just keep practicing and who knows," Brownie was trying to be reassuring but didn't want the young pilot to develop that attitude that had led to the demise of so many other flyers. The feeling that nothing could go wrong. That they were invincible. He had seen too many pilots mangled in the crash of a Stearman or burned in a dusting accident that should have been stopped because of the rising temperature.

"Well, I better go," said Jack rising from the chair. "I'll be home if you need me."

"Arn't you gonna wait for your dad?" asked Brownie.

"No, gotta get cleaned up and tell Sheila about today," Jack answered. "You can give Dad the details." The young ag pilot placed his gear in his locker. He told Brownie goodbye and was soon driving down the road on the way home. He was going to see Sheila one way or another today. With, or without her parents' permission.

Brownie watched him drive down the road to the highway and

then turned to the work at hand. When the 'ol man returned from his first assignment, the chief pilot would have to switch to a spray rig for the rest of the day.

Motioning to Bobby, leaning against Jack's duster, he hollered, "Hey Bobby, come on we gotta get three-seven warmed up."

Bobby walked over to the sprayer and began turning the prop to get oil up into the cylinders. Brownie climbed in the cockpit and the starting process began. The engine was not yet running when the mechanic heard Alan's plane over the field. Just as Alan parked his duster the two crewmen successfully brought the sprayer's Pratt and Whitney radial engine to life. Brownie climbed out, checked the wood blocks in front of the wheels, and went over to talk to Alan. Together they walked toward the hanger. Jack's dad took his helmet off so he could better hear his mechanic.

"Well Brownie, how'd he do?"

"Just fine, Pappy. You would have been proud," he answered.

"Was McMillan out there to watch?" the chief asked.

"Of course. He and a couple of other ranchers."

"Did you know them?"

"No, they weren't our customers. But they watched Jack until he was finished with the field." Brownie new what the businessman and pilot had in mind.

"Maybe I should call McMillan and find out what he thought of my son's job on his field. I could ask him who his buddies were."

"That would be good, but I have an idea he liked it. Jack gave him a little buzz at the end and the three of them got a thrill out of it."

Alan was suddenly concerned. "He didn't make them duck or hit the ground did he?"

"Oh no, not at all. I think they got a kick out of it," Brownie assured.

"Did you see his technique? How were his turns?" Alan wondered.

"Everything was fine. He put his wheels right down on the field and his turns were smooth and short. Pappy, he was real good. You better get three-seven loaded. It's gonna get hot soon." Brownie was right. Alan grabbed his helmet and headed toward his spray rig. The senior pilot was soon airborne and on the way to his next job.

About the same time Alan Lawrence was leaving the airfield Jack was pulling into the empty driveway of his house. He ran inside. There was nobody home. He picked up the phone and called Sheila's number. After a couple of rings the voice of her mother said, "Hello."

"Is Sheila home, Mrs. Gebhardt?" asked a hesitant Jack.

A surprise came from the other voice. "Yes Jack, just a minute, I'll get her."

Seconds later an excited Sheila said, "Hello honey, I've been waiting for your call. Are you all right? How'd it go? Was your dad happy with your flying? Are you through for the day?"

"Whoa, slowdown babe," interrupted Jack. "I'm fine. Let me get cleaned up and we can meet somewhere."

"Hurry up Jack," said a bubbly Sheila. "I can hardly wait to hear about it." Then came an unexpected question from his girl. "Can you pick me up?"

"At your house?" asked a confused Jack.

Looking at her mom nodding approval, Sheila answered, "Sure it'll be fine."

"Alright!" Jack exclaimed. "I'll be there in an hour."

"I'll be waiting honey...I love you Jack."

Jack answered in kind and hung up the phone. He couldn't believe what had just happened. Had Sheila's parents suddenly changed their minds about him? Certainly not her father, he thought. He decided when Sheila was through with all her questions, about his flying, he would have a few questions of his own about this change of heart.

CHAPTER ELEVEN

Jack walked up to Sheila's house and knocked on the front screen door. Debbie Gebhardt opened the large, carved oak main door. "Hello Jack, just a minute, I think Sheila is ready."

"Thank you, Mrs. Gebhardt." Jack waited outside. He heard Sheila's mother call for her.

"Hi Jack," his girl said as she opened the screen and bounded out of the house to give him a kiss on the cheek. "I'm going, Mother. Be back after lunch."

"Okay, honey," responded the voice from inside.

They settled in Jack's car and they were off. "What's with your mom?" Jack wanted to know.

"She just decided that if I'm going to stay in that house she better accept the guy that I love," answered Sheila.

"You threatened to move out?" Continued Jack.

"Sure did. Mom couldn't handle that. Me, her only daughter, out on her own at eighteen."

"Sheila, that's blackmail," laughed Jack.

"Call it anything you want, but isn't it nice that you can call or walk right up to the front door now?"

"Yea, I guess so. And your father, what does he think about this?" Jack knew Harry was the key to the whole situation.

"Oh Daddy, he doesn't know. I suppose Mom will tell him sooner or later."

"So if your dad is home I better keep clear, is that it?" Jack inquired.

"Oh, I'm sure me and Mom can smooth it all out tonight," answered Sheila, scooting over and putting her arm around Jack. "Now, about you. You flew good today, huh?"

"Yea, it was great, all those hours my dad made me practice really paid off. Man, what a ride. You shoulda seen me baby. Plane right down on the crops. Farmers watching. Even Brownie said I looked good."

"Oh honey, I'm so proud of you," Sheila told Jack, planting another kiss on his cheek. "Are you flying tomorrow too?"

"I guess I'll be flying almost everyday now. All the way through defoliation in the fall."

"Does Cal-Ag have enough business to keep four pilots busy?" asked Sheila knowing her dad's business could barely keep three working.

"Well, we might be getting a few more accounts with me flying now," answered Jack proudly.

"Well, aren't we the ace pilot now, a regular barnstormer," said Sheila with a laugh.

Jack pulled into the Town House Restaurant and turned off the car. "Hey, I can make a living at this you know and I'll be able to get a place of my own."

"A regular bachelor pad?" asked Sheila smiling.

Jack put his arm around his girl. "No, a pad for Sheila, for us."

"What do you mean for us?" The girl was hoping Jack was talking something permanent.

"You know, just an apartment. That way we won't have to meet at places like this or just draggin' main in this jalopy in order to see each other."

"Oh," said a disappointed Sheila. They got out of the car and went into the restaurant to have lunch.

Back at the airfield, Harry Gebhardt was through flying for the day. He and Carter sat in the office going over the day's results.

"Nice job today, Mr. Gebhardt, everything went well," said Carter.

"Yea, but we have to do better. This has to be our best season ever. I want to buy another rig this winter and get Sheila started in college after summer. By the way, how did your date go last night?"

"Real good, we went to the drive-in and watched that movie I was telling you about," answered Carter, not wanting to go into details.

"Is that all? You just sat and watched the movie?" asked Sheila's dad.

"Well, I bought her a Coke and popcorn."

Harry laughed. "Listen son, you pick her up tonight and take her to Fresno for dinner. Understand?"

"Yes sir, how late can we stay out?" Carter was hoping the second date would lead to something more than the first one the night before.

"Oh hell, I don't care. Just give her a good time."

"Oh, I will sir," said Carter, a sardonic smile now on his face. "I certainly will."

"Good, that's more like it," Harry said, rising from his desk chair. "Now help me with these planes."

"I can do it sir," said Carter rising also. "You better take it easy. You've been putting in a lot of hours these last few weeks. Fixing up your plane and everything else."

"Hey, it's make or break time, son. Besides, I'm in good shape. Hand me my cigarettes and let's get going."

Carter grabbed the pack of cigarettes off the desk and tossed it to Harry. They fell clumsily from his hand to the floor. "Damn it," exclaimed Harry, reaching down to pick up the cigarette package. They walked out the office to the hanger. Soon, Carter, Harry and the Western Dusters' mechanic were working on the two Stearmans that needed repairs, changes or upgrading. Harry Gebhardt was a hard man to work around. He was very demanding and seemed to be always in a hurry to get even the smallest job completed. Later that afternoon, the three of them were almost finished when the phone rang. Carter ran to the office and picked it up. It was a farmer that wanted to speak to Harry.

"It's for you Mr. Gebhardt," yelled Carter, leaning out the office door. Harry, standing on a ladder, working on an engine, stepped down to the floor, missing the last rung and stumbling slightly.

"For chrissakes, Carter. Don't yell so loud near the phone. And damn it, you can call me Harry." He rushed by Carter and picked up the receiver. "Hello, this is Harry Gebhardt." Carter stood in the doorway listening to the one way conversation. He could see the expression on Harry's face become stern.

"But Tom, I've been doing your fields for the last couple of years. Haven't you been happy?" Harry sat down on his desk, listening to the farmer on the other end. "He's just a kid, he can't be that good." Harry responded then paused again. "I'm sorry you feel that way, goodbye." Harry Gebhardt slammed the receiver down on the hook. "God damn it Carter. That Lawrence kid is flying for his old man now. I guess he put on quite a fucking show over McMillan's land today. Tom Magarian wants Cal-Ag to do all his dusting and spraying now." Harry picked up his crash helmet and flung it across the room. The helmet hit the corner of a file cabinet and spun crazily to a stop on the floor.

Carter had never seen his boss like this. "You win some, you lose some, sir."

"Shit, we can't afford to lose any more. I'll never get that other rig this winter."

"Or get Sheila through school," Carter added.

"Carter, just get outta here," Harry yelled, motioning with his hand to the door.

"Okay, guess I'll see you tonight?"

"Yea, see you tonight," answered Harry, sitting down at his desk. Carter walked out of the office. Leaving Harry Gebhardt staring out his office window, across the airfield, to where the black and gold Stearman's of Cal-Ag were lined up, all of them cleaned and ready to go in the morning. He slammed his fist down on his desk. From the right lower drawer he pulled a bottle of Jack Daniel's whiskey.

At the Town House restaurant, his daughter and her boyfriend were just finishing lunch. Jack called for the check and left a rather large tip.

"Jack, don't you think that's a little too much?" asked Sheila.

"Naw, she was good and besides, I can afford it."

"You never left me a tip like that. I'm guess I'm not that good."

"I didn't always have it then," Jack said. "But, you were always that good," then he added, "better."

Sheila smiled as they got up from the table. "You better get me home. I have some work to do in Daddy's office this afternoon."

"Okay Baby. I've got to go to the field to check tomorrow's flight assignments anyway." They were soon headed home, Sheila as close to Jack as she could get on the bench seat of his car.

At the Gebhardt house, Jack walked Sheila to the front door. They kissed on the porch and Sheila opened the screen. "See you tonight, honey," she said.

"Sure, I'll pick you up. Maybe we can go to the drive-in movie or something."

"Uh, how 'bout Fresno or the lake?" a hesitant Sheila asked.

"Man, I get a job and now I can't get off cheap," laughed Jack.

A relieved Sheila said, "That's right, from now on you're treating me like a lady, not your girlfriend." She stepped out from the screen and kissed her lover again. "Call me before you come over," she cautioned.

"I will, honey, I love you," said Jack blowing her another kiss.

"Love you too, darling," Sheila said closing the screen again. Jack jumped in his car and headed to the airfield.

"Mother, I'm home," hollered Sheila through the house.

"How was lunch honey?" her mother asked from the kitchen.

"Fine, I'm going to change and go to the office."

"That'll be good, your dad is still at the field. I'm sure they're busy today."

"Mom, if he's the owner, how come he has to spend so much time running the business? He does most of the flying and is always watching his crew and mechanics work on the planes. If he doesn't do it himself, which is most of the time, Daddy should spend more time with you."

"Oh he does. Especially in the winter," answered Debbie Gebhardt. "It's been like this every summer since you were born. Now you better get changed and get to the field." Sheila sighed and went to her room to change. Her mother returned to her work in the kitchen. Soon her daughter was out the door and headed to the airfield.

Entering the office of Western Dusters, Sheila found her father sitting at his desk, his head resting on his arms. An empty whiskey bottle next to him. Just inside the doorway, she began tiptoeing to her desk but the screen door slammed shut behind her. Her father began to stir. He raised his head and wiped the saliva from his chin. "Oh, hi honey. You startled me. Just catching a quick nap." Sheila looked at the bottle. Harry grabbed it by the neck and dropped it in the waste basket next to his desk. "Through for the day, just celebrating a little." He was slurring his words.

Sheila wondered. "Celebrating what, Daddy?"

"Your gradu...graduation...what else? Didn't get to do much of that the other...the other night."

Sheila sat down at her desk and began to go through the day's paperwork. Harry started to get up but couldn't get his feet under him. He leaned against the back of his chair. "So, whaddya think of Carter? How was your date?"

"Fine Daddy," answered Sheila, not looking up from her work.

Harry was trying to talk straight but the words were a little jumbled. "Did you go to dinner or Fresno?"

"Daddy, you know we went to the drive-in."

"That's right. I remember now. Carter's a nice guy isn't he?"

"I guess so." Sheila couldn't look up at her drunk father at the other desk.

"He's gonna pick you up tonight," Harry slurred.

Sheila finally looked at her father. "I can't go out with him tonight."

"Whaaat, why not?" demanded Harry, leaning forward on his desk.

"I've got other plans, Daddy," said Sheila returning her eyes to her work.

"Well, change them. He's picking you up and that's all there is to it." Her father again slammed his fist down on the desk.

"Can't I do what I want, Daddy? It's my life you know."

"Oh yea?" stammered her father. "Who gives you everything you have? A room, food, nice clothes, everything." Harry was sobering rather quickly. "You are still just a teenager and still at home."

"But, maybe not for long, Daddy," Sheila again glared at her father.

"And what is that supposed to mean?" demanded Harry.

"It means, when I get a job or find someone else who will take care of me I'm movin' out."

Harry reached down in the wastebasket for the whiskey bottle. He raised it to his mouth and swallowed the few drops that were left. Dropping it with a crash back in the basket he stood up. "If you mean that Lawrence kid you can forget it. I want you to never set eyes on him again. Do you understand?"

"You can't stop me, Daddy." Sheila was also standing now.

Harry, bracing his hand on his desk, walked around to his daughter. "He's nothing but trouble. Trouble for this family, trouble for this business. You are not to see him, do I make myself clear?"

Sheila was trembling now. "Daddy, I'm going out tonight," she paused. "I'm going out with Jack."

Harry was in a rage now. "God Damn it girl, what did I just say? You will not see Jack Lawrence ever again. If I see you with him anywhere I'll throw you out of the house." He was standing, a little wobbly, over his daughter now. She could smell the whiskey on his breath. She was still standing looking up at his red face.

"Maybe that will be better," Sheila said loudly, "I can make it on my own."

"You are going to college young lady and nothing is going to stop it." Harry swayed a little forward and backward trying to maintain his balance.

"I'll do what I want now Daddy...maybe I'll just marry Jack," said Sheila.

Her father raised his hand. Sheila stepped back. Harry pushed her down. She landed hard in her chair. "You stay here and get that work done. I will talk to you tonight."

A tearful Sheila, watched her father walk out the door, hitting his shoulder against the jam. He yelled to his mechanic, "Call me at home as soon as this bitch leaves the office."

He got in his pickup and headed out the airport road, straddling the dotted white line, to the highway.

CHAPTER TWELVE

Sheila had watched her father's truck weave its way down the road. Now out of sight, she watched the mechanic in the hanger working. She looked across the field. Jack's car was parked in front of the Cal-Ag hanger. He was in the office. No doubt going over the flying assignments for tomorrow. She waited patiently until the mechanic stepped behind the plane in the hanger. Closing the office door quietly behind her Sheila walked to the back of the row of hangers. She was soon inside the hanger of Cal-Ag and saw Jack with Brownie in the office. She entered through the open door.

"Sheila! What are you doing here?" exclaimed Jack.

"Hello, Sheila how are you?" said Brownie.

"I'm okay, Brownie. Jack can I see you for a minute." Brownie saw the tears beginning to form in the young girl's eyes and the redness of her cheeks.

"Well, I'll leave you two alone," he said and headed for the planes. "I've got plenty to do out there." He closed the door behind him leaving Jack and Sheila alone.

"Whatsa matter baby?" asked Jack. Sheila ran to him and put her arms around him. The tears flowed down her cheeks.

Jack held her tight and asked again. "What's wrong Sheila? What happened?"

"Oh Jack, me and Daddy just had a big fight. He was drunk and I thought he was going to hit me."

"Did he hurt you? Are you all right?" Jack said, gently pushing Sheila back and looking at her face.

"I'm okay. Just scared. He's never acted like that."

"Let's go talk to him. I'll straighten him up," Jack said.

"No we can't. Anyway he's gone. Just hold me for a minute, Jack."

He pulled her toward him and stroked her hair. "Anyhow, what started all this?" he asked.

"I told him we were going out tonight and he said I could never see you again."

"Well, here you are." Jack was trying to make his girl feel better.

"So much for that order."

Sheila wiped her eyes and uttered a faint laugh. "Yea, I guess I am." Then she remembered the mechanic. "Oh crap, Daddy told the mechanic to call him if I left the office. I can't go back over there. He'll call Daddy for sure if he catches me gone.

"It'll be okay." Jack assured her. "Your mom's home and she can help calm your dad down. Maybe he'll sober up a little by then."

"Oh Jack, I don't want to go home. Let's go right now," pleaded the girl.

"Go where?"

"Anywhere, right now, I just wanna be with you."

"Okay honey," Jack said, holding her tight. "Let me put these things away and we can go on our date starting right away. Nobody says we can't start early. Aren't we old enough to make our own decisions?" He folded up the charts and put them in the corner. "Come on, we'll leave your car here. Do you have your keys?"

"Oh no, they're in my purse in the office."

"That's okay. We'll drive by and you jump out and get 'em."

"What if Daddy's help sees me and calls?" asked a worried Sheila.

"So what? Not much anybody can do about it now," answered Jack. "Come on, get in the car and let's get going." He opened the door for her and she slid in.

Stopping at the side of the Sheila's office, Jack let the motor run. Sheila jumped out and ran inside to her desk. Jack watched the mechanic. He was busy hanging a spray boom from a wing. When Sheila ran out of the office the door slammed behind her. The mechanic looked up just in time to see her in Jack's car speeding down the road. In his mirror, Jack could see the mechanic running to the office. Undoubtedly, to make a phone call. Driving with his left hand, he put his other arm around Sheila and pulled the girl to him. She rested her head on his shoulder. They were quiet when they hit the highway headed south.

"Where do you want to go baby? Are you hungry? Wanna get some lunch or something?" asked Jack.

"Anywhere Jack, just somewhere we can sit and talk."

"Well, I don't have to be back till the morning. Let's get something in Fresno. Is that okay?"

"That's alright. Just...just drive." She snuggled closer to Jack. He reached over and turned up the radio. They listened to Rock and Roll all the way. Listening to their music, their songs, neither said a word.

At the Western Dusters office the mechanic was calling the Gebhardts' house. Debbie Gebhardt answered but said that Harry had not arrived home yet. The mechanic hung up without leaving a message. He finished hanging the spray boom and locked up the office and hanger. Soon he was headed out of the airfield, finished for the day.

In Fresno, Jack pulled off the highway into the large park where the municipal zoo was located. "Let's see if we can find anybody we know in there."

Sheila laughed. "Maybe a close relative."

"That's better. That's my girl," said Jack, giving her a kiss. Sheila was feeling better. The drive and the music had calmed her fears. There was something about being in Jack's arms. He always had been able to make her feel good, make her laugh and forget all the problems at home they had created with their love for each other. It was no different now. Together they walked through the zoo, laughing at the monkeys swinging from their tree branches and the seals playing in their pool. They shared a Coke together and sat on the large lawn beside the elephant pit. Sheila leaned back on the grass and gazed at the azure sky above. Jack rested on his elbow looking at her face. People walked by but the young couple paid no attention. For a long time neither said a word. Both were thinking the same thing. About the future, their future.

It was late afternoon now. At home Debbie Gebhardt was fixing dinner and beginning to worry a little about her husband. There was a knock on the door. She turned off the stove and went to answer the caller.

"Hello, Mrs. Gebhardt," said Carter. "Is Harry home?"

"No Carter, he's not here. Isn't he still at the field?"

"Not this late," answered Carter. "I'm here to pick up Sheila and take her to dinner. Is she ready yet?"

"Ready! She's not here either. Come on in. I'll call the office." Debbie picked up the phone and dialed the office number. There was no answer. "That's strange. It's not like Harry not to call if he's going to be late. Carter would you mind going downtown to see if

Harry's there?"

"Sure Mrs. Gebhardt. And if Sheila gets home, tell her I'll be back to pick her up." Carter left, as a worried Debbie Gebhardt nodded and sat down on the couch.

Driving down main street, Carter was perplexed. Where was Harry? Where was Sheila? He thought his boss and him had everything set for the evening. Passing Irene's Tavern, he spotted the familiar pickup of Harry's. He parked and walked in through the swinging front door. The smoke filled, dimly lit cocktail lounge was not very crowded. At the bar sat Harry, a half-empty beer mug and an empty shot glass in front of him. Carter sat down on the stool next to his boss.

"Hi Harry, howya doin'?" he asked.

"Hey Carter, when'd you get here?" slurred Harry.

"Just now." Went to the house. Just your wife is home. Do you know where Sheila is? Remember? We had a date tonight."

Harry raised his beer and emptied the contents. "I don't care where she is. Bartender! Give me another round, whiskey and a beer. And get this young man a drink too."

The bartender came over with Harry's drinks. "Nothing for me," said Carter. "Don't you think you oughta be callin' it a night sir?"

"Don't lecture me, God damn it. I'll go home when I'm ready." Harry's voice was getting louder. The few bar patrons were beginning to stare.

Carter put his hand on Harry's shoulder. "Come on Harry, let me drive you home."

Harry threw Carter's hand off with a jerk of his upper torso. "I can drive home. Shit, I can fly home. I can fly better than any Lawrence, that punk kid or his washed up old man. Just go home Carter. I'll see you in the morning." Harry returned his stare downward into his beer. He took the jigger of whiskey, tilted his head back and emptied it in his mouth. He followed the shot by gulping down another half a mug of beer.

Carter saw it was no use. "I'll see you in the morning sir, take it easy, okay?

"Yea, yea, don't worry about me," said Harry. "You better worry about getting Sheila away from that asshole, Jack. That's your main job. Or don't you remember?"

"Yes sir, don't worry I'm workin' on it." Carter stood up. Leaving Harry at the bar, he headed home, still wondering where Sheila had disappeared to. At his apartment, he grabbed a beer and put a TV Dinner in the oven. He had forgotten to call Mrs. Gebhardt.

Debbie Gebhardt was at home trying to keep the family dinner warm. By 8:00 o'clock that evening she had given up. She covered the evening's meal and placed it in the refrigerator. Going into the living room she sat down at her favorite end of the sofa. Leaving the television off, she picked up a magazine. She sat reading and listening for a car or truck.

A few minutes later the phone rang. "Finally," Debbie muttered to herself. As she walked to the table to pick up the phone she wondered if it would be Harry or Sheila.

"Hello," she didn't wait for a response. "It's about time you called."

"This is Memorial Hospital," said the voice from the other end. "Is this Mrs. Harry Gebhardt?"

Suddenly Debbie couldn't talk. Everything raced through her mind, all the possibilities. "Mrs. Gebhardt?" the voice asked again.

"Uh....yes, this is she."

"Your husband has been in an automobile accident and is here at the hospital. The doctors think you should be down here."

Now Debbie was in a panic. "What happened?" she screamed into the receiver. "Is Harry all right?"

"He's in surgery right now Mrs. Gebhardt. I'm really not at liberty to say," said the nurse on the phone. "We'll know more when you get here."

"I'll be right there." Debbie hung up the phone. She undid her apron and tossed it toward the kitchen. It fell to the floor in a heap. Before leaving, she scribbled a note to her daughter and squeezed it between the screen door and the jam.

Debbie arrived at the hospital and ran to the emergency room entrance. At the desk, a nurse was at work filling out forms. "Excuse me, I'm Mrs. Gebhardt."

"Oh yes, just a minute," replied the nurse. "I'll get the doctor." She went through a door to the emergency room treatment area. Soon she returned. "The doctor will be out shortly. Would you care to have a seat?" She motioned Debbie to the waiting area. But, instead she moved aside and paced back and forth around the room. After what seemed an eternity a man with a white jacket and stethoscope hanging from his neck opened the door. He motioned Debbie to follow him. He introduced himself and held the door open for the wife of his patient. Debbie didn't have to ask how her husband was before he began to explain.

"First of all your husband will be okay. He's still in recovery, but soon you'll be able to see him," the doctor explained.

Debbie sighed. "What happened doctor? He was supposed to be home for dinner."

The doctor went on. "It seems your husband was involved in an auto accident." Then he added, "Does he have a history of drinking?"

"No, not at all," answered a shocked Debbie. "He's a licensed pilot and a business owner. He has an occasional social drink at community functions but he's never been drunk." Debbie tried to change the subject. "How serious is he doctor? When can we go home?"

"He'll recover fully Mrs. Gebhardt," answered the doctor. "He should be home in four or five days. You'll be able to see him in a little while. In the mean time, I think that officer wants to see you." The doctor pointed down the hallway to a uniformed city cop standing near the small cafeteria. Debbie thanked the doctor and walked to the policeman.

"I'm Mrs. Gebhardt. You wanted to see me."

The cop tipped his hat. "Hello Mrs. Gebhardt. Let's sit over here. Would you like a cup of coffee?"

"No thank you," she answered sitting down at a table in the cafeteria. "Is there a problem officer?"

"I hope not. I Just have a couple of questions. Did your husband come home tonight?"

"No, he was at the airfield most of the day and didn't call me. He is usually home by dinner time. Is he in some sort of trouble?" Debbie was worried now.

"Well, we found his truck in a ditch. He had rolled it over a couple of times and was lying beside it unconscious," the cop explained. "No other vehicle was involved as far as we could tell. He didn't have any enemies did he?"

"Harry? Of course not!" Debbie answered. "He's well known and liked in town. Our daughter just graduated from high school."

The officer continued. "You know he had been drinking heavily tonight? We found a bottle in the truck."

"Harry's never been drunk before officer. I don't understand. Are you going to arrest him right here in the hospital?"

"I don't think that will be necessary," the cop assured. "No one else was involved and there was no damage. Except to his own pickup. You're going to have enough problems when he gets home Mrs. Gebhardt." The cop again tipped his cap and thanked Debbie. She watched him walk out the emergency room entrance then returned to the nurse at the desk.

"Can I see my husband now?" she asked.

"I think so. Let me check." The nurse soon returned to show Debbie to her husband's room. Entering, she saw her husband lying in a bed. Bandages around his upper head, his right arm in a cast. His bandaged left leg dangled from a suspension device at the foot of the bed. She leaned over and whispered, "Harry, Harry, it's me. Harry, I love you." Harry opened his eyes and mumbled something indiscernible. Just then the doctor entered the room. He checked on Harry's condition and asked Debbie to step out to the hall for a minute.

"Didn't you say he was a pilot Mrs. Gebhardt?"

"Yes, a successful ag pilot in this county," she answered. "Why do you ask?"

"Well, I'm afraid he won't be able to fly for quite a long while."

Debbie paled at the thought of the future. "This is our busiest time of the year, doctor. We only have one or maybe two other pilots and all our farmers can't wait."

"They are going to have to if they want your husband to do the job. His injuries are too severe." The doctor went on, "Until they are healed and I sign a required release he is to stay home and recuperate. His arm is broken and he has a badly sprained ankle. Maybe even torn ligaments, not to mention a slight concussion."

"How long are we talking, doctor? I mean before he can fly?" Debbie asked.

"Four to six weeks at least. Maybe more. I'll be by to check on him after he leaves the hospital. If you need anything you can call my office. The nurse has the number." He put his hand on Debbie's shoulder. "Why don't you go back in and see him."

"Thank you, doctor." She turned and walked back to her husband's room. He was sleeping. She sat down in the chair next to his bed. She stared at his bandaged body and began to cry.

CHAPTER THIRTEEN

After their visit to the zoo Jack had taken Sheila to a nice dinner. In the car on the way home, the tired girl had fallen asleep on Jack's lap. As he pulled up to the curb at her home she woke. Raising, she wiped her eyes and brushed her hair.

"It doesn't look like anyone is home," said Jack. Sheila looked past the walkway to the front room windows. The house was strangely dark.

"They must have gone out to dinner. Come on and walk me to the door." Sheila got out and with Jack holding her hand walked to the front porch. She fiddled in the dark looking for her keys. When she opened the screen door she didn't notice the slip of paper that fell from the jam landing on the welcome mat. She unlocked the front door and turned on the front lights.

"Thank you, Jack. You turned a miserable day into a day to remember." She stepped out of the open doorway and kissed her lover hard and passionately. Jack returned the passion.

"Would you like to come in?" asked Sheila.

"I guess, but just for a minute. I don't feel like facing your father right now."

"Wipe your feet," said Sheila.

Jack scraped his shoes on the welcome mat. Accidently turning up the corner of the mat so the screen door could not shut he looked down to straighten it.

"What's this?" he asked, reaching down to pick up the slip of paper. He turned it over and read the brief message Sheila's mother had scribbled.

He looked up at Sheila. "Come on, we gotta go." He grabbed her by the arm and pulled her out of the doorway.

"What's the matter with you, Jack?" He gave her the note. She read it quickly.

"Oh no...come on!" Jack was already pulling her to the car. He slammed her door shut and leaping over his side landed squarely behind the wheel. He squealed the tires of the car away from the curb. This late there was very little traffic as they headed toward the hospital. The radio was quiet. So was Jack.

He pulled up to the front entrance and let Sheila out. As he pulled away to find a parking spot he could see Sheila asking questions of the person at the front desk. She was gone by the time he got to the desk but the volunteer told him what room Harry Gebhardt occupied. He walked down the hallway. As he passed the nurse's station he could see Sheila and her mom talking outside the room. He approached the pair.

"Hello Mrs. Gebhardt. Is Mr. Gebhardt okay?" he asked.

Debbie looked at Jack and back at Sheila. "Yes Jack. He's hurt badly but he'll be fine. It will just take time, the doctor says." Jack could tell Mrs. Gebhardt had been crying. He waited outside the room while Sheila and her mom went in to see her father. There were no chairs except at the end of the hall. He walked over to the nurse's station and asked about the condition of Harry. They offered him the details and he returned to lean against the wall outside the room. Finally, Sheila came out. She looked pale. Her mascara was smeared from her crying.

"How's he doin' honey? Is it bad?" asked Jack. Sheila described what Jack had already learned from the nurses.

"Are you going to stay here with your mom? Do you want me to stay with you?" Jack was trying to handle the situation as best he could.

"Mother wants me to go home," answered Sheila. "She's gonna spend the night here with Daddy. I'm supposed to go to the field at sunrise and tell everything to the crew and our other pilots. The assignments are all ready for tomorrow but I don't know what to do after that."

"One of the other pilots can take charge. Wasn't Ben his right-hand man anyway?" asked Jack.

"Yea, I guess. But we'll never keep up without Daddy. If those farmers can't get their fields done they'll just go elsewhere." She reached out for Jack's hand. Jack knew what the farmers only option was.

"It'll work out baby. Let's just play it day to day. How's your mother?"

"She's scared we'll lose the business and everything else. And if that happens we'll probably lose Daddy too."

Jack pondered the thought of the two girls living alone. "When your dad gets better the farmers will come back. He has a good business going. There's plenty of fields out there for both companies. Come on baby, I'll take you home." Jack waited outside while Sheila went in the room one more time. Then he drove her home. It was almost midnight. He had to work in five hours. He walked his girl to the door and waited inside while she turned the lights on in each room. They kissed on the porch and before leaving made sure she had locked the door. Even very tired, neither would sleep much tonight.

The next morning at Cal-Ag it was business as usual. When Jack pulled onto the airfield he looked at the planes of Western Dusters. Only a duster was warming up. Inside the office he could see his girl, Carter standing beside her, trying to explain to the personnel the circumstances of the night before. As he taxied his plane down the runway the Western crew was just headed out to the planes. Another one was started. At least they had two pilots, Jack thought. As he checked his instruments Sheila left the office. Turning out the lights, she got in her car and headed to the hospital. Jack pushed the throttle forward and took off to do his day's work.

For the next couple of days Jack didn't see Sheila. She spent most of the time at the hospital during the day. Allowing her mom to get some rest. Sheila would go home in the evening and she and Jack would talk on the phone for short periods. She didn't want to tie up the line in case the hospital or her mother called. During the day he could see Carter in the office going through the required paperwork, answering the phone. Explaining to customers why their crops had to wait. Harry's number two pilot Ben did his best to keep up, but even with the help of their part-time flyer it was impossible this time of year. Every late morning and into the afternoon, Cal-Ag's phone would ring several times. Another cotton or grape farmer needing his field done.

Then the weather turned. A rare cold front brought high winds and cumulus clouds to the valley. Crop work was suspended until the front blew through. Jack knew it would be overtime and a lot of hours in a couple of days. But for now it was a break that allowed him to see his girl. He missed her and wanted her to know that he would be there for her. Just after lunch, with Brownie at the truck stop, he headed for the hospital. Walking down the hall toward the room he saw Carter standing outside. Jack ducked into the cafeteria and waited. If Carter was outside, Sheila must be in the room. He decided to wait outside also. Walking confidently down the hall the two of them made eye contact.

"Hello Carter, how you doin'?"

"Hello Jack, what are you doing here? Come to see how much longer you can rub it in?" said Carter, folding his arms and leaning against the wall.

"I don't know what you're talking about. I just came to see how Sheila was doing."

"Don't play dumb with me," Carter said, raising his voice. "We've already lost a third of our accounts." The nurses at the station looked up from their work.

"Look, I can't help that. It's not my fault Harry had that accident. From what I hear, you should have drove him home that night," said Jack, leaning against the opposite wall. "It's as much your fault as anyone else, I'd say."

Carter started toward Jack but a nurse came over and ordered both of them to be quiet or leave. Just then Sheila came out the door from seeing her father.

"Jack," Sheila exclaimed. "It's nice of you to come. Carter, I guess you can go in now."

"We'll settle this later," said Carter to Jack. He started to open the door of the room but Sheila stopped him.

"You won't tell Daddy Jack is here, will you?" Sheila pleaded.

"And give him a relapse. He's going home tomorrow. I am not going to upset that timetable." Carter entered the room. The door closed behind him.

"Come on, I'll buy you a Coke in the cafeteria. It looks like your dad is doing better." Jack took Sheila by the hand. It felt good after these few days of not seeing her. They took a seat at a table. A couple of nurses on break and an elderly couple were the only people in the cafeteria.

"Man, am I glad to see you baby," said Jack, reaching his hands across the table.

Sheila clutched both of them. "Oh Jack, I missed you so much too."

"With your dad going home tomorrow we should be able to see more of each other," he said hopefully.

"I'll still have to be there sometimes and when I'm not I'll probably be working at the office. Jack, I have to tell you something." She squeezed his hands.

"I don't think the business is going to survive the year. Mother says we've lost too many accounts because of the accident. And word has gotten out that Daddy was drinking."

"Hey all pilots have an occasional fling," said Jack. "Look at those end of season company parties we both have. My dad gets plastered once in a while. It's part of that image left over from the war or something."

"Anyway," Sheila continued, "Mother is worried about losing the house and the cars. One of the planes is not paid for yet either. If the hanger rent gets too far behind the city will evict us. I don't know what to do. I wanted to start college in the fall. Now, I may have to work just to keep us in a house."

"We can work it out. I'll get a place of my own and you can stay with me," suggested Jack.

"I can't leave my family now, Jack. Especially Mother. She'd never make it. I've got to help her at home and get a job."

"Well, I can help too." Jack had a plan. "With all this increased business, I am flying my tail off right now and probably through 'till winter." Sheila looked up. "I can give you money to help pay the bills. If I live at home for a little while longer I won't have many bills."

"Oh Jack, I couldn't ask you to give my family any money."

"Okay, don't ask," said Jack. "I'll just give it to you and you can do what you want with it."

Sheila leaned forward. "Jack, you don't know how much I love you. I could never tell you."

Jack smiled, "Fine you can show me someday. It's settled then. I'll give you half of what I earn."

"Half," said Sheila, "that's too much."

"No it isn't and besides I might as well start now and get used to it." Jack laughed and leaned back. Sheila smiled and lowered her eyes. As the elderly man and woman watched, he stood up, kissed her on the cheek and left the hospital. Sheila sat at the table finishing her Coke.

In Harry Gebhardt's room, Carter and his boss were talking about the lost accounts. Carter was explaining. "We can keep up without you sir. Not that we don't need your expert flying, but every day we get phone calls from farmers switching to Cal-Ag. Word of mouth has it that Jack Lawrence is the best pilot around next to his dad. And you of course."

Harry was feeling better now. The concussion gone, he was fully aware of what had been happening. "When I get outta here, I'll bring those farmers back."

"Sir, it'll be at least another five weeks before you can even think about flying. By then the season will be two-thirds finished," said Carter. "You'll get back for the tail end of defoliation and maybe a little grain spray. We've got to do something about the competition real soon."

"Like what?" asked Harry.

"You know, make it harder for them to keep up with their assignments too. Maybe hire one of their pilots at a higher pay scale."

"Hell," said Harry, "I can't hardly afford to pay the one's I have now. Besides, I guess if they earn the business they can have it."

Carter leaned over the bed. "That's not like you sir. They're stealing your business. Spreading rumors that you're a drunk. Washed up...finished. It all started when Jack Lawrence got his license. Did you know he was outside your room when I came in?"

"What, Jack here in the hospital?" Harry painfully raised his body to a sitting position. "What was he doing here?'

"What else, he came to see your daughter." Carter continued. "The last time I saw them they were necking outside the hospital, waiting for me to come out."

"Damn it Carter." Harry was ready to leave now. "I thought you were going to keep an eye on her for me."

"I can't be at the field trying to keep the business going and keep them apart too. Besides, when your wife is here and Sheila is home at night by herself I've seen Jack's car parked out front. No telling what they're doing inside."

An angry Harry blurted, "Jack inside my house?"

"And with your daughter sir. I bet they have some fun times. All alone and everything."

"Shut up Carter," said Harry angrily. "Nothing you haven't done."

"But I would never do anything to your daughter until we are married sir. She's a great girl and I wouldn't do anything to change that. Now what are we going to do about Jack?"

Just then Sheila entered the room. "Hi Daddy, I'm back, nice to see you feeling better. All ready to go home tomorrow?"

"Yes honey, I sure am. Would you mind leaving me and Carter alone for a few more minutes?"

Sheila was confused but answered, "Sure Daddy, I guess so."

"Thanks honey. We just have a little business to discuss. I'll send him out when we are done and you can come in and watch TV with me, okay?"

"I'll be right outside, Daddy." Sheila left the room. Carter made sure the door was completely closed. They talked quietly and intently for a long time.

CHAPTER FOURTEEN

Harry Gebhardt was home from the hospital, but he wasn't happy. The weeks were passing too fast as his injuries healed. Too fast, as he marked each day on the calendar, he watched helplessly as the most profitable months of business were being lost. His wife, Debbie, did the best she could. Fixing his meals, making sure he was comfortable, foregoing her household chores to watch television with him and constantly attending to his needs. She knew only one thing could really make him happy and that was to be flying again. He would spend hours in his little office at home. Behind the closed door, Harry would sit at his desk going over the paperwork of the business. He would try to write with his broken right arm and in frustration throw the pen against the wall. Using his chair he would roll back and forth from file cabinet to desk. Every afternoon, Carter would bring him the results of the day's activities at the field. From the work sheets and invoices Harry could see his business faltering. His dream of another airplane was gone, along with the customers who he thought were loyal and the employees he now couldn't afford to keep.

At the field, Sheila worked everyday until the crews were finished. She answered the phone, handled customers and kept up on the work orders and supplies of tools, equipment and chemicals. She assured the bill collectors that everything was okay and they would eventually get paid. After the pilots had returned from their morning assignments Carter would saunter into the office and sit down at Harry's desk.

"Everything went ok this morning," he told Sheila.

"That's good," the girl said, not raising her eyes from the work in front of her.

Though Carter had not mentioned their date that never happened the night of the accident, the beautiful young high school graduate was still on his mind.

"Your father looks like he's doing better everyday," he said. "When does he go back to the doctor to get the cast off?"

"I really don't know," answered Sheila. "Why don't you ask him?

You see him every afternoon, don't you?"

"Yes, but we just talk business. Every time I bring up the subject of when he'll be able to fly again he gets angry and throws me out."

"Why don't you use some of that tact and cunning you think you're so good at?" said Sheila, defiantly.

"Well, it doesn't work on everybody you know," Carter answered.

Sheila laughed and looked toward Carter sitting at her father's desk. "You don't have to tell me. Maybe it just doesn't work on us Gebhardts. Or is it that we can see right through you, Carter? Have you ever done anything for anyone other than yourself?"

Carter rose from the desk. Walking over to Sheila, he put his hand on her shoulder. "I'm doing something right now, don't you think? Your dad doesn't pay me any more or any less. Even with all the extra stuff I do, I'm making the same dough."

Putting her hand on his, still resting on her shoulder, Sheila said, "I know Carter, Mother and I appreciate it." She stood up and removed his hand. Picking up her pile of papers she added, "Don't you think you better get this home to Daddy?" She handed the pages to him. Taking them, Carter stepped closer to Sheila. The girl sat back down at her desk. "Better get going. Daddy's waiting."

"Yea, right," a disappointed Carter responded. "I'll run into town and drop these off. Do you want me to pick up something for lunch and bring it back? We could eat right here in the office while we get tomorrow's assignments ready."

"No thank you," Sheila answered. "I'm not hungry. I'll have tomorrow's jobs already for the pilots by the time you get back."

Carter tried again. "Are you sure I can't bring you something? It's on me."

"No thanks, not hungry," Sheila again answered.

"Okay, your loss Sweetheart." Carter headed out the office door. "See ya in a little while."

Sheila watched him get in a company truck and drive out the road that led to town. She looked across the field toward the Cal-Ag hanger. Locking the office door behind her, she began to walk across the tarmac. She saw Jack through the office window standing over a desk. She bounded into the room without knocking. "Hi Jack, ready for lunch?" she beamed. At the other desk was Alan Lawrence. "Oh, excuse me Mr. Lawrence, I didn't know you were here. I can come back later."

"That's alright Sheila," smiled Alan. "We were just talking about airplanes and field assignments."

Stepping back toward the door Sheila was apologetic, "Really, I can come back Mr. Lawrence."

"Nonsense," replied Alan. "You and Jack go to lunch. We can get this finalized when you two get back. By the way, how's your father doing? Is he going to be back in the air soon?"

"A couple of more weeks at least," answered Sheila. "I hope sooner. Our business really needs him."

Alan was now a little embarrassed. "Sorry about all the lost customers. You know how it is with these farmers and ranchers. They just can't wait."

Standing next to Sheila with his arm around her, Alan's son added, "I bet you'll get'em back as soon as your dad gets better."

"I hope so, Mother is really getting worried."

Standing up, Alan advised, "You two better get to lunch. We got a lot to do this afternoon to get ready for tomorrow. Go on now and enjoy."

Jack and Sheila turned to leave the office but Alan had forgotten one more item. "Jack, would you go by Ortho Chemical and make sure they deliver that Malathion out to Road 17? Have them put it just south of Avenue 14? We are flying off of it tomorrow."

"Sure Dad," answered Jack. "We'll do that first and then go on to lunch."

"Thanks," said Alan sitting back down at his desk. "Have a nice time. See you this afternoon."

Sheila and Jack were soon in Jack's car. They turned the radio up loud while speeding to town.

Stopping at the chemical company, Jack set the parking break and left the car running. "Be right back," he told Sheila. The girl nodded approval and began singing the words to the song on the radio. Jack ran inside to check the order and verify the delivery spot. The cashier at the counter checked the amount of chemical and the place to be delivered. "Tell your dad everything will be there." Looking up he noticed the girl in the car. "Jack, isn't that Sheila Gebhardt in your car?"

"Sure is, we're going to lunch," he answered. "That is if you'd hurry up with the receipt and order."

"How's her old man doing? I hear he got in a really bad accident. Been drinkin' down at Irene's. Really messed himself up, huh?"

"Wouldn't know about that. Is there anything else you need me to sign?" asked Jack.

"I'm not trying to be nosy or anything," the clerk responded. "That guy who works for Western was just in here. He placed an order for Parathion but I had to tell him I needed a company check or cash."

"Bet that made his day," chuckled Jack.

"I didn't have much choice. Their account is past due and with Harry not flying my boss says that's the way it's gonna have to be."

"Past due?" Jack was surprised. "How much?"

"I can't tell you. But enough to be on a cash basis until it's cleared up," answered the clerk.

Jack grabbed the receipt off the counter. "Thanks, I'll see what I can find out and let you know." He left and joined Sheila, still singing in the car.

"Honey, do you know it's 'cash only' for your dad here?"

"I thought so," answered Sheila. "This won't be the only place either."

"You gotta tell me these things baby. I said I would help out." Jack reached in his wallet and produced a bundle of twenty-dollar bills. He counted out five of them and handed them to Sheila.

"Jack, what's this?" the girl asked.

"I told you I'm gonna help," he smiled. Putting the cash in her purse, he told her, "Here take it. There's more where that came from."

"Oh Jack, I can't let you do this." Sheila reached down to return the money but Jack leaned forward and put his hand on hers.

"Don't be silly. I want you to have it. Give it to your mom if you want. Or put it in the company account. Spend it on yourself. Wherever you think it should go is fine with me."

Sheila left the money in her purse. Leaning over she gave Jack a hug. "Thank you honey, thank you so much. I'll give it to Mom to buy groceries. That should get us through the month."

"I get paid at the end of the week. You get some bills together okay, and I'll help you pay them," Jack advised.

"You can't pay the company bills with money you made flying for your dad," Sheila answered.

"Why not? It's my money," Jack replied. "Dad doesn't care how I spend it. I still pay my own way. Besides, you know I'm making a ton right now with all this flying."

"But it won't last." Sheila knew that winter meant very little business. "By November we'll both be broke."

Jack would not be detoured. He put his arm around her and started the car. "Silly, we'll be together by then and you'll have a job. Dad will still pay me for maintenance and the little flying we do. Besides, he said I could do a little charter work this winter too."

"Charter work?" Sheila asked.

"Yea, you know honey," Jack answered. "Flying people all over the country. At a price of course. Fuel and time. We do pretty well during the off season." Pulling into the parking lot of the restaurant, he continued, "Now can we enjoy lunch? Just the two of us?"

Sheila kissed him on the cheek before they entered the restaurant.

At the Gebhardts' house, Carter had just delivered the day's activity sheets. Harry was going through them. Slowly turning the pages with his good hand, he saw the bad news his daughter had printed out on the paper. "We lost the Agajanian account I see," he told Carter. Further down he noticed something else. "Damn it, we just did the last job for Pico Hills Ranch. Now they're going over to Cal-Ag." Slamming the cast on his right arm down on the desk he looked at the nervous young man standing over him. "Carter, that was our biggest account. You should have made sure we got those fields done."

"Sir, I just take them as we get 'em," explained Carter. "If we can't hire another pilot until you get going again, I can only do the best I can. I can't fly you know."

"Oh, how I wish you could," said Harry. "Oh, how I wish you could."

Carter had more bad news. "Ortho says, 'no cash, no chemical.' We maxed out our account I guess."

"I'll have Debbie or Sheila transfer some funds tomorrow," countered Harry. "We have enough until then. At least according to you."

"Yes sir, we have enough." Then Carter remembered the earlier conversation. "Sir, that stuff we talked about in the hospital. Were you serious? I mean, I think I can do it."

Harry looked up at Carter. "I was serious, but it's never to be talked about except between us. Do you understand?"

"Of course, do you think I'm stupid?" Carter smiled down at Harry. He didn't answer the question. "Well then, which plane and when?"

"Not yet, I'm still thinking about it," answered Harry. "Let me see what the doctor says."

Carter, disappointed at the lost opportunity, was ready to leave. "I better get back to the field. I left your daughter doing the assignments for tomorrow. I'll double check 'em when I get back."

"Good idea son, and keep an eye on her, will ya?" asked Harry. "She hasn't been seeing that Lawrence kid, has she?"

"Of course not sir, and I won't let her either," Carter assured his hobbled boss. "I watch her all the time."

"I bet you do," chuckled Harry.

"You know what I mean sir."

"I really don't," said Harry. "And I don't want to know. Now get outta here."

Carter told Harry, "Take it easy," and left the room. He passed Mrs. Gebhardt in the front room without saying a word and was soon headed back to the field.

At the restaurant, Jack and Sheila had just finished their lunch. While Sheila used the restroom Jack paid the bill with a check. He balanced the amount and mentally added what he was going to get paid in a couple of days. Sheila returned and they left the café.

"I gotta stop at Ortho again on the way back," he told Sheila.

"I thought you got all that taken care of on the way in?" his girl asked.

"Forgot somethin," he answered. "It'll just take a minute okay?"

"Sure Honey, work can wait. The more time I spend at the field the less I have to spend home with Daddy. He's such a grouch and so mean to Mom."

"Hey, I probably would be too if I were in his condition. And what about the time you spend with me? Doesn't that count?"

Sheila laughed. "Of course, that's the most important time of all."

She scooted close to him. "Will there be more of that in our future?" she asked meekly.

"There will if I have anything to do with it," Jack answered. He put his hand on her thigh and squeezed it gently. "You'll probably be seeing more of me than you want."

"I've seen all of you already and I like what I see," laughed Sheila.

Jack squeezed a little harder on her thigh. "That's not what I meant."

Sheila squealed and laughed again. "How 'bout all of you...all the time."

Jack pulled up to the front of the chemical company. "Be right back, baby."

He jumped out and entered the sales area. The same clerk was at the counter. "Forget something, Jack?"

"Yea, I did," he answered, removing his checkbook from his hip pocket. "I forgot to pay a bill. Will you take a postdated check? It'll be good on Friday."

"Sure Jack, your check is always good around here," answered the clerk.

"Okay, how much is the bill for Western Dusters?"

"Jack," said the clerk, "I can't tell you that."

"What if I want to pay it off and bring it current, will you tell me then?"

The clerk was dumbfounded. "You want to pay off Harry Gebhardt's account. Does your dad know about this?"

"It doesn't matter, it's my money. Now hurry up. I've got my girl in the car and it's getting hot outside."

"Just a minute, Jack. I've got to check with the boss. I'll be right back." The clerk left and entered the back office. Through a window Jack could see the manager and clerk talking. The manager looked at Jack and then went to a file cabinet.

Outside, Sheila waited. Looking in through the large front window she could hardly see Jack at the back counter. Behind her, passing by on his return to the airfield, Carter saw the familiar blond figure waiting in Jack Lawrence's car. He noted the time and gunned the engine of the company truck. Speeding down the street to the field, he would be waiting for Sheila at the office.

The clerk soon returned with the delinquent account. He handed it to Jack. Circled in red was the amount that was in arrears. Jack wrote a check for the exact figure and dated it for Friday. Handing it to the clerk he told him, "Tell your boss, this'll be good after noon, Friday."

"You got it Jack. I'll tell him," said the clerk sticking the check under the cash in a drawer. "Why are you doing this anyway?"

"None of your business," answered Jack. Leaning over the counter and grabbing the young man's collar, he pulled the clerk toward him, "And if my dad comes in here don't say anything to him about this, got it?"

"Okay Jack, mum's the word," acknowledged the clerk.

Jack left the chemical company and soon, with Sheila still sitting next to him, was returning to work. He pulled along side the Cal-Ag hanger.

Sheila kissed him flush on the mouth. "Thanks for the wonderful lunch, honey. I'll call you tonight."

"Okay baby, I'll be home after 6:00." Jack watched his girl walk across the tarmac. Her hips swayed back and forth in her jeans. He knew he had done the right thing at the chemical company.

Sheila entered her office. "Couldn't have lunch with me, but you could have it with Jack," was Carter's first words. He was sitting at his customary place, Harry's desk, his boots planted firmly on the left corner. "Wait 'till your dad hears about this little fling in the summer sun."

Sheila said nothing, but sat down at her desk. She put a piece of paper in the typewriter and began to pound on the keys.

"I thought we had something going, but I guess it'll take a little more persuasion by your dad and me," said Carter, getting up from the desk.

Sheila was nervous but kept typing the letter.

"You could at least say something," Carter continued. "If you don't want me to tell your dad, fine, I won't."

"That would be good of you, Carter," Sheila said, stopping her typing. "He has enough to worry about."

"Alright, promise me one thing. If I don't say anything at least go out on another date with me. Give me one more chance," pleaded Carter.

Sheila pondered the situation. She couldn't win. "Okay, how 'bout tonight, around seven?"

Carter smiled. He reached down and gave Sheila a little peck on the cheek. "Okay girl, I'll pick you up at seven. We'll have a good time," Carter promised.

Sheila wiped the kiss from her cheek and returned to her typing. Carter went out to the hanger to tell the mechanics of his good fortune and how Harry was doing.

CHAPTER FIFTEEN

Late that afternoon at the Cal-Ag hanger Jack, his cousin Pat, and Alan Lawrence were in the office. The chief pilot was at his desk. Sitting opposite was his son and nephew.

"Pat, there's been a change in plans for tomorrow," said Alan. "I need you and Jack to drive out to the Brown strip and get your plane back here."

"I thought it was going to stay out there overnight," replied Pat. "Wasn't I supposed to meet the loaders there in the morning?"

"That was the original plan. But with this new Pico Hills account, we need to get them satisfied first."

"Hey, you're the boss," Pat said to his Uncle. "Let's go kid, it's already late."

"Okay, I'll drive and drop you off. I've got to get right back," Jack said rising from his chair.

Pat smiled. "Hot date with blondie tonight, heh kid?"

Jack knew all too well about his cousin's playboy attitude. "At least I know I'm not going to catch something from her. Not like the chicks you date."

Pat laughed and looked at Alan. He was smiling. "You know what blond babes like, don't you kid?" he asked Jack.

"No, but I have a feeling your gonna tell me, Mr. Sex Machine."

"When you chase a blond around the house and they get all nice and sweaty, that's when they are really hot to trot. They start takin' off their clothes to cool off and that's when you have 'em right where you want 'em."

Jack had heard enough. "Come on Pat, let's go. See ya later, Dad."

They climbed in the truck and started the 30 minute drive to the landing strip on the Brown ranch. All the way, Pat told stories of his weekend adventures. He was a good looking young pilot and he knew it. He never had a problem with getting girls. Pat was a strong, athletic looking man with curly black hair and a face that would have looked good on a movie screen. He was a carefree individual, often putting concern aside to play a joke on someone or get a laugh from one of his many girlfriends. He had set up Jack with a girl at the local motel near the airfield. There he had lost his virginity. A secret Jack and his cousin never shared with anyone else.

Now Jack was interested in only one girl. He looked at his watch. He was going to be late. Finally at the Brown strip, he pulled alongside the Stearman. Leaving the truck running, they both walked to the plane. Pat climbed in the cockpit while Jack turned the prop. Soon the engine was coughing and sputtering to life. Jack returned to the truck. He looked at Pat in the cockpit. His cousin was checking the few instruments that actually worked. Jack looked at his watch and back to the pilot. Finally, Pat gave a thumbs up, signaling everything was okay. Jack stepped on the gas and the truck headed down the county road back to the airfield. Pat taxied to the far end and turned his plane into the wind. A few minutes later he would lift off the paved strip.

Flying above the same road Jack was traveling, Pat could see the company truck ahead. There were no power lines or poles on either side of the road so Pat devised a little prank to play on his cousin. Jack was driving as fast as the road would allow. He heard the noise of the Stearman's engine behind him. Pat had slowed his plane to almost the same speed as the truck. Approaching from behind the truck the biplane descended. Jack could see the prop and wings of the Stearman in his mirror. "What the hell's he doin' now?" he mumbled to himself. A moment later, the plane disappeared from his mirror. Jack leaned forward over the steering wheel and looked upward through the windshield. Where did Pat go? Suddenly there was a tremendously loud thump on the top of the truck. The center of the roof caved inward, revealing the outline of a tire. The truck, with the extra weight applied for an instant, swerved to the edge of the road. Jack, struggling for control and cursing his cousin at the same time, managed to bring the truck to a stop on the dirt shoulder. Ahead of him, Pat made a turn and headed back toward Jack. His cousin had opened the door of the truck. Standing on the lower edge of the cab opening, Jack looked over the roof at the large dent in the center. Black tire marks scarred the gold paint on the top. Pat wiggled his wings as he passed over Jack. Another turn and he came over the top again. Jack could see his cousin's head leaning back. His pearly white teeth showing a big smile. Jack raised his hand and extended his middle finger toward his cousin. He climbed in the truck and continued his return journey to the airfield. Pat was going to be in trouble, he thought. But, he wasn't going to tell his father. Alan would find out soon enough.

Back at the field, Jack ran to the phone. It was almost 7:00. He called Sheila's number. Harry Gebhardt answered the call. Jack tried his best to disguise his voice while asking if Sheila was home. When Harry said she wasn't, he figured he had not done a good enough job. He hung up. Jack walked outside and looked over to the Western Dusters hanger. All was quiet. No vehicles were around except for Harry's wrecked truck.

At the Gebhardt's house, Sheila had waited for the phone call. She was hoping to talk to her lover before Carter arrived. As fortune would have it, Carter showed up early.

"Well, look who's here," Harry said when Debbie had opened the front door. "Come on in, son." Turning to his wife he commanded, "Debbie, go tell Sheila, Carter is here." Returning his gaze to Carter he continued, "Going out tonight are we?"

"Yes sir," replied Carter. "Is Sheila ready? I'm a little early."

"She'll be out here in a minute. Have a seat. Can I get you a beer or something?"

"No thank you, I don't drink when I'm with your daughter," answered Carter.

Sheila had heard the doorbell. It was nearing 7:00 and Jack still had not called. This was not like him. Her mother knocked on the door of her room. "Come on in, Mother."

"Honey, Carter is here and says he has a date with you tonight. Is that right?"

"Yes Mother, we are going out to dinner or something," said Sheila buttoning her blouse.

Debbie was puzzled. "I don't understand honey," she lowered her voice to a whisper, I thought you and Jack...."

Sheila interrupted, "That's right Mom, we are."

This didn't make sense. Debbie raised an octave with her tone. "But...."

Interrupting again Sheila said, "I'll explain it all later, Mom. Can you go out there and give me a few minutes?"

"Sure, Honey," answered Debbie, starting to leave the room.

"Oh one other thing, Mom," Sheila remembered. "If the phone rings would you make sure you answer it?"

"Okay Honey," Debbie agreed. She didn't know what was going on, but wanted to help her only daughter as much as she could, regardless of the consequences.

Sheila waited, stalling as long as she could. Remaining in her room, she was ready but hoping the phone would ring. It was after 7:00. From the living room came the loud voice of her father. "Arn't you ready yet, Sheila?" he yelled. "Carter is waiting."

"I'll be right out, Daddy," Sheila yelled. She looked in the mirror, a beautiful, pretty girl stared back. Pretty enough for Jack, she thought. Sheila sighed and leaving the sanctuary of her bedroom, turned off the light.

"Well, it's about time," her father said as she entered the front room. Carter was sitting on the couch. At the other end, near the phone, was her mother.

Carter rose from his seat. "Ready to go?"

Sheila nodded. Carter escorted her to the door. Sheila looked back at her mother. Debbie nodded to her daughter. "Have a good time," her father said. "Not too late. Don't forget you both have to work tomorrow."

"Okay boss," said Carter, winking at Harry. "Have her home by midnight." They were soon headed downtown to eat.

Jack was still at the field wondering whether he should risk another call. Pat had landed and after parking his plane, checked the top of the damaged truck. Passing Jack leaning against the office doorway, all he said was, "See ya in the morning kid." Without speaking to anyone else, Pat left the field. Brownie and the last loader soon followed, leaving Jack alone in the office. He decided to try to call Sheila one last time before heading home.

The phone was on the end table next to Debbie. She was still sitting at the end of the couch. When it rang, she looked at her husband and picked it up. "Hello," she answered still looking at Harry. He was looking at the television listings in the paper for a program to watch.

Jack was relieved to hear Mrs. Gebhardt's voice. "May I speak to Sheila?" he asked.

Debbie recognized the voice and almost made a crucial mistake.

"I'm sorry Ja...uh, she's not here." Harry had not looked up from his paper. "Can I give her a message?"

"This is Jack, Mrs. Gebhardt, she wanted me to call her but I was running late today and just got in. Is she gone to the store? When will she be back?"

Harry looked up and stared at his wife. "Okay," Debbie said, "I'll tell her you called. Goodbye." She hung up the phone and rising, walked to the television. "Find something to watch dear." She turned the TV to the station Harry demanded and returned to her seat.

"Who was that?" he asked.

"Just one of Sheila's girlfriends," lied Debbie. "She'll call her at the office tomorrow." Debbie turned her attention to the program on television.

Sheila and Carter had just entered the restaurant. "Can I buy you a drink?" he asked his date.

"You know I'm underage," answered Sheila.

"Yea but, I know the bartender." Carter said, directing Sheila to the cocktail lounge of the restaurant. "He won't say anything. Trust me."

They sat down at a small, round table with only two chairs. The waitress came over to take their order. "Shirley Temple for me," Sheila told the waitress.

"Give me a Scotch and Soda," said Carter. Sheila looked around the dimly lit lounge. There were just a few tables and a booth in each corner that could seat four. At the bar there were a dozen chrome stools. The cushions covered with black vinyl. There the bartender waited on five customers. While waiting for the drinks Sheila and Carter didn't talk. The drinks were set on the table. "Put it on my dinner tab," Carter told the waitress.

He raised his drink and held it above the table. "Here's to a very pretty lady," he proposed the toast. Without saying anything, Sheila raised her drink, but the glasses never touched. She took a quick sip and set it down on the tiny table. She was not having a good time and wasn't going to try. Carter tried to converse with the girl but her answers were short and to the point. Sheila, facing the door to the outside, squinted when a figure she recognized entered. It was Jack's cousin Pat. Bar hopping no doubt. Looking for a date.

"Are you ready to eat? I'm hungry," asked Sheila.

"Already? You haven't even finished your drink," Carter answered. He noticed her looking over his shoulder. He turned and saw the man she was looking at. "That's the problem, huh? Don't want to be seen with me, is that it?"

"No Carter that's not it," replied the girl on the defensive. "I just don't want to start a lot of rumors."

"Rumors of you and Jack breaking up, you mean?" Carter leaned back, balancing the back legs of the stool on the carpet he alternately moved it back and forth. "I think that is pretty well said and done isn't it? According to your father anyway. That's what he thinks and you wouldn't want him to think any different...would you?"

Sheila had heard enough. "Carter, just take me home."

"What if I say no, what are you gonna do, ask old playboy over there for a ride?" laughed Carter loudly. "That'll start some rumors."

The bar patrons had turned to see why the couple was having so much fun. But only one of them seemed to be having a good time. Then Sheila removed the smirk of a smile from Carter's face. "Why don't I just make a phone call and tell the police how you ushered me in here against my will and bought me a drink."

But Carter's smile returned. "That's not a drink, there's no booze in that thing," he said pointing to her kid's drink.

Sheila looked down at the red colored fruity liquid in her glass. It was half consumed. She reached over to Carter's Scotch and Soda. She took his drink and filled her glass to the brim with the alcoholic cocktail. "It's a drink now." She took a sip and returned the glass to the table.

At the end of the bar, Pat Lawrence could see the couple but could not hear their conversation. After his eyes had adjusted to the darkness, even he had been a little shocked so see Jack's young girl, in one of his own favorite hangouts, having what seemed to be a good time. Pat asked the bartender for use of the phone. He called his cousin who was home waiting for Sheila to return his call.

"Jack this is Pat. You'll never guess who I'm looking at right now."

"Where you at? What are you talking about?" asked Jack.

"Your girl is down here at Sherlock's. Sitting in the bar with that Carter guy."

Jack couldn't believe it. "Your nuts, Pat. I just talked to her mom."

"Come on down and see for yourself," Pat advised. "Hey, I can break this up right now if you want."

"No, don't even think about it. Just stay there. Thanks Pat, I'm on my way down." Jack hung up the phone and rushed out of his house. He didn't know what he was going to do when he got there, but he knew there was going to be another confrontation.

Pat sipped on his beer. The couple he had been watching was preparing to leave. Instead of going out the door to the restaurant area, they left through the bar entrance. Pat didn't follow. His eyes returned to a lovely brunette with a low cut, strapless, dark blue dress, sitting at the opposite end of the bar. He rose from his stool. Walking coolly to the other end, he sat down next to her. His evening's fun was just beginning.

Outside, Carter and Sheila were standing between the parked cars. Carter was leaning against his own vehicle holding Sheila around the waist. He was apologizing again for what happened inside. Sheila stood, hands at her side, wanting to escape the grip of Carter. "What do you want Carter?" she pleaded.

"Just a make-up kiss," he answered.

"Will you take me right home after that?" she asked.

"Unless you'd like another one baby," he said confidently.

Sheila could feel Carter's hand tighten around her waist. "Okay, that's enough. You want that kiss or not?"

Carter smiled and pulled the girl to him. But Sheila was not yet ready. "One kiss and you take me home. You promise?" she asked.

"Okay, okay," he promised.

The restaurant parking lot was full. Across the street Jack had parked his car a moment earlier. He had started to get out to join his cousin in the lounge when Carter and Sheila had come out of the bar. He waited and when he had seen Carter put his hands around his girl, he fumed. Again he started to get out of his car. Then he saw the two embrace. He saw Sheila's silky blond hair stroked by Carter's hand as she tilted her head back and they kissed. When their lips had touched Jack started his car and drove away.

At the Gebhardt's, Harry had finished watching the TV program alone. Debbie had gone to the kitchen to clean up the evening's meal. Harry turned off the television and hobbled on his bad ankle to his office. Going over the past week's activities of his business, or lack of it, he decided to put Carter to the test, a test of his loyalty to Western Dusters. If he wanted to see Sheila again, Carter would have to succeed.

The couple returned earlier than Harry thought. When they walked in, Sheila had gone immediately to her room and closed the door. Carter went into his boss's home office.

"You're back early. Everything go alright?" asked Harry.

"Fine Sir," answered Carter. "Your daughter wasn't hungry and like you said, we both have to be at work early."

"That's good son," said Harry. "Come on in and close the door behind you. I think it's time we give some serious thought to the future of Western, and yours too."

Sheila came out of her room and went to the kitchen. There she joined her mom at the sink. "Any calls while I was gone?"

"Jack called," Debbie answered. "I think he called twice. Your dad answered the first time. I talked to him right after you left with Carter."

Sheila was worried why he hadn't called earlier. "Is he alright?"

"He's fine Honey, he just had to work late. We didn't talk too much because of your father, but I said you would call him. Why don't you use the phone in here? Your dad's busy in his office. I'll go out here and be right outside." Debbie dried her hands and left the kitchen. Sheila dialed the familiar number.

Jack had just returned home. Alan and Jack's stepmother were at an Elks Lodge dinner and would not be home until later. When the phone rang Jack had just sat down with a beer to ponder what to do next.

"Hi Jack, sorry I missed your call," said Sheila. "I had to go out for awhile."

"I know," said Jack. "Your mother told me. Have a nice time?"

The question confused Sheila. "What are you talking about, honey?"

"Do you call Carter honey, too?" Jack asked with an angry tone.

"Jack, you don't understand," Sheila pleaded. "I didn't have any choice."

Jack wouldn't listen. "At your age, you have a choice and after what I saw an hour ago you've made your choice. Goodbye Sheila."

"Wait Jack, don't hang up." Sheila heard the click at the other end. She called Jack's number again. There was no answer. Jack was already out the door, headed to Sherlock's to join his wild cousin Pat. Sheila tried once more with the same result. She left the kitchen and went to her room, closing the door behind her. Debbie, had noticed the tears starting as she rushed passed. She entered Sheila's bedroom. Closing and locking the door behind her, Debbie Gebhardt hugged and comforted her daughter the best she could.

Jack went to the bar but Pat was gone. The bartender said he had left with the brunette about ten minutes before. Jack had a beer and left. He drove to the airfield and parked. Entering the former Officer's Club, he laid down on one of the old sofas. For two hours he gazed at the ceiling thinking of the girl he thought he had loved, who he thought had loved him. The money he had spent on her family. But most of all he thought of the days to come.

CHAPTER SIXTEEN

The days passed. Jack spent most of his time at the airfield. After flying in the morning he would hang around with Brownie and the loaders playing ping-pong, pitching horseshoes out behind the hanger, or sitting in on a poker game in the Officers Club. Brownie knew something was wrong with Jack. He had seen Sheila's car at Western Dusters but she never called or stopped by anymore. Jack was quiet most of the time. The mechanic tried to keep the young man's spirits up, afraid that his depression might lead to a flying error or worse, an accident.

"Hey Jack," Brownie yelled across the hanger, "come over here."

Jack walked over to the mechanic. "Yea Brownie, need something?"

"We're playing a little poker in about an hour. I need you to help me play a joke on Tiny."

Tiny was a part time mechanic, full time loader, who had worked for Cal-Ag for a couple of years. A large man who was constantly eating donuts and sipping coffee with a little rum added for a kicker. Despite his size, he was very quick and agile. He once had a tryout for the Rams but a knee injury had ended his football career. Tiny was always good for a laugh, usually by a prank played on him by a fellow worker. He was terrified of snakes and spiders and jumped at unexpected events. Loaders hid in hoppers and as Tiny settled in the cockpit to check out the controls or instruments, the lid to the hopper in front of him would suddenly fly open and out pop a worker with a scream. Behind the plane, the rest of the crew would burst into hysterical laughter. "One of these days, you're gonna give me the big one," Tiny would say, holding his hand on his chest.

Brownie and Jack walked behind the tail section of a Stearman. Out of sight, Brownie reached in his pocket and pulled out a string of firecrackers. "Here, take these," handing them to Jack. "When we sit down to play I'll make sure Tiny has his back to the door. I'll turn the radio on to make some noise."

"Whaddya want me to do?" Jack asked.

"Give us about a half hour. Tiny will really be in the game by then. Just sneak up behind him and set these babies under his seat. All you have to do is light them and step back. Everyone will know what's going on except the big guy."

"Man Brownie, I don't know, these things are hot you know and illegal."

"Ah, come on Jack. It's not the worst we've done. Remember the snake?"

Jack thought back to the previous summer. Brownie had caught a garter snake near the tower at the field. He had put the snake in the glove box of the truck that he and Tiny were to drive to a landing strip. On the way, with Brownie driving, he had asked Tiny to check in the glove box for his grape knife. When he opened the small door, out came the snake. Tiny screamed and opened the passenger door. Brownie had to slam on the brakes to keep the big man from jumping out at 60 miles per hour.

After some thought, Jack agreed, "Okay, I guess. But he's gonna know I did it."

"We're all in on it. Don't worry, you can outrun him," laughed Brownie.

Jack put the firecrackers in his pocket and started to walk away. "We'll be over there in a little while," Brownie said, climbing on a ladder to check the spark plugs in the plane's engine.

Jack just shrugged. He went into the office and began going over the next day's field assignments. Easy going tomorrow. Everybody working. It was a typical crop dusting day in the middle of summer.

Later, the crew was sitting around a card table in the lounge. Jack quietly walked up the few steps to the screen door. It was just as Brownie had said. Tiny was sitting with his back to Jack and the doorway. Jack opened the screen. It squeaked as he eased it closed. Brownie glanced up from his hand for a moment and then immediately returned to the game. The hand finished and Bobby, the young loader, raked in the chips.

"Your deal, Tiny," said Bobby.

Jack watched as Tiny shuffled the cards. He reached in his pocket and felt the string of firecrackers. Leaning on the counter he picked up a book of matches lying near a display of cigarettes.

"Seven card stud," said Tiny as he dealt out the cards.

Jack waited until the betting had started. When the bets were placed and Tiny asked, "How many?" Jack moved behind the big man.

Squatting, he placed the string of firecrackers directly under Tiny's chair. In perfect timing, Brownie had engaged Tiny in conversation about his poker playing. Jack struck the match and lit the short fuse on the firecrackers. Stepping back, he had barely returned to the counter when the deafening popping sound began underneath Tiny. Everyone scattered, leaving Tiny scrambling and trying to get his large lower torso out from under the table to escape the chaos that was exploding below his butt. Finally, he just picked up the edge of the card table and tipped it over. Cards and drinks crashed to the floor. Tiny ran to the farthest wall and turned around. By now everything was quiet. Brownie had turned off the radio. Everyone, except Jack and Tiny, broke into raucous laughter. Bobby, holding his sides had fallen on the couch in hysterics. Tiny glared at the young pilot leaning on the counter. Jack just smiled and shrugged his shoulders.

"Man, that wasn't funny, I coulda been burned," he told Jack.

Jack grabbed a fire extinguisher hanging on the wall. "We woulda put you out, that is if this held enough."

"Come on guys, let's pick up the cards and finish the game," Brownie said, starting to do just that.

Tiny, still staring at Jack, returned the table to its upright position. "Just wait hotshot, you'll get yours. I'll make sure of that." The big man sat down. Brownie, still chuckling, handed him the deck of cards. "Don't blame Jack, big guy, it was my idea."

"That figures," Tiny confirmed. "But he lit the fuse," Tiny said, pointing his thumb over his shoulder without turning to look at Jack. "I won't forget the sneaky kid. You know, I don't know why I even stick around here."

"Cause you like us so much, doncha big fella?" Brownie said, patting the frustrated Tiny on the shoulder. "Now deal me a winner will ya?"

The cards were dealt and the gambling began again. Brownie looked at Jack and smiled. Jack just nodded and left the room, the screen door slamming shut behind him. "Damn kid," muttered Tiny as he looked at his poker hand. "Shit, I'll take four. Can't even deal myself a decent hand."

The day was finished for Jack. Nothing to do except go home, but he was bored at home. He couldn't listen to the hi-fi. All his records reminded him of Sheila. Sometimes he would take the family dog, Alpha, a Weimaraner hunting dog, for a ride and run, but it was now too hot in the afternoons for that. He drove through town and down the highway to Fresno. This is where he spent most evenings. If he wasn't bar hopping with his cousin Pat, he was walking the streets of Chinatown. On Inyo or Kern streets, he would stop and gaze at the Orientals who called these blocks west of the tracks, their home. Occasionally, a lady of the evening would propose a good time to Jack. He always declined the proposition. He had better things on which to spend his money, but this night was going to be different. He stopped in front of the old Lincoln Hotel. The building had seen better days. The cracked cement balconies of the second story could not be trusted to hold the weight of a guest or visitor. The vibrant colors of the Chinese artists who painted the building had faded to a dull hue. It was late. He debated on whether to return home or just check in to this hotel, getting an early start in the morning to be at the field on time. Jack walked into the lobby. He asked for a room. "That'll be ten bucks," said the desk clerk.

"Can I leave a wake up call for four?" asked Jack.

The clerk gave a hearty laugh. "Four o'clock! In the morning?"

"Is there a problem with that?" Jack asked again.

"No, not a problem." The little man at the hotel desk reached down and brought up an alarm clock. Setting it in front of Jack he said, "Here you go one wake up call. Just pay in advance. And leave this in the room with your key." The clerk struck the bells on top of the clock. "Now, you got ten bucks?"

Jack had the money but had changed his mind. It was only ten at night. He could cruise back to the field and sleep as before on the couch in the lounge. He pushed the alarm clock towards the clerk. "Thanks, but no thanks. Maybe next time." Jack walked out the wooden doors of the hotel and got in his car. He drove out of town to the west. He would take the long way home. Radio off, just coasting in his mind and on the back roads of the valley. He journeyed through the small westside towns, idling slowly down the main street of each hamlet. Every little community looked the same. A coffee shop, a five and dime store, a little theater with white marquee emblazoned with large black letters proclaiming the current movies that were playing the weekend matinees. For a quarter you could see a double feature and a cartoon. In Caruthers, the local constable followed Jack down the main road until he had left the city limits. It was past midnight now and he didn't want any trouble. Jack pushed the gas pedal a little farther toward the floor. He was 60 miles from home and had to fly in a few hours. Out of habit, in the warm summer night, he put his arm on the back of the seat, except this time there was no girl to pull toward him and hold against his side. No girl to lay her head on his shoulder; to close her eyes to a love song on the radio. He thought of her sleeping in her bedroom. He thought of the graduation night. He remembered the pasture, the warm nakedness of her body against his. Suddenly, a stop sign appeared. He pounced on the brake pedal. The tires squealed and he stopped almost in the middle of the intersection. Jack took a deep breath and raised his head from the steering wheel. There, across the road, nose down on the roof of a diner, was an airplane. A World War II T-6 Texan glistened in the glare of two lights on either side of its spread wings. Jack had never seen anything like this before. It looked like it had plummeted straight down from the sky to land fully intact nose first, damaging neither itself or the diner. Jack peered into the darkened coffee shop. There was no one inside. Suddenly the lights went off on the roof. The plane was now only illuminated by the evening moon. Even though there was not a hint of a breeze, a chill raised the hair on Jack's neck. He returned to his car and drove slowly away from the silver winged image radiating with rays from the evening's orb. An hour later, Jack was at the airfield. He stopped in front of the Officers Club. Without washing his face or removing any clothing he fell on the couch that would be his respite until morning.

    An hour later, still sound asleep in the Club, he wasn't aware of the shadowy figure passing by the front door heading toward the line up of Cal-Ag planes. Quietly, the figure climbed onto the wing and stepped into the cockpit. Silhouetted against the dark western sky by the green and white rotating beacon of the airfield, the figure continued onto the center of the top wing. The fuel cap was removed and the figure placed his finger in the opening. It came out wet. The tank was full. Still on the center top wing, the figure plugged the vent tube of the fuel tank with a cork that had been previously shaped to fit the opening. From his pocket he pulled a small bottle with a brush attached to the cap. From it, he applied clear liquid cement to the cork and vent tube. It dried almost immediately. Finally, he taped over the cement and cork. Climbing down off the wing he slid to the ground. Ducking underneath the bottom wing, he made his way to the rear of the hangers. He looked back at the duster and smiled. With the vent tube plugged air would not be allowed to replace the aviation gas in the tank as it was used. This would cause a vacuum and sooner or later the engine would stall. The figure moved under the tower and then disappeared in the darkness.

"Jack, let's go. Get a move on." Jack felt a hand shaking him. It was Brownie, "Come on man, the planes are running and Pappy is waitin' for you in the office."

Jack rolled to his feet and stood up. "Okay, I'll be right there. Let me wash my face."

"Just hurry up," said Brownie. "It's almost daylight."

Jack walked quickly to the restroom at the back of the building. He threw some water on his face and looked in the mirror. The stubble showed that he hadn't shaved for a couple of days. Jack debated on growing a beard. Thinking better of it, he vowed to shave after the day's flying. He slapped his cheeks, shook his head and yawned. "You idiot," he said to the image in the mirror, then headed to the office.

"Mornin' Dad," Jack said, sitting down in his usual chair.

"Well, you like you had a rough night," Alan said from behind his desk. "Out with your cousin again?"

"No just a late night. Mom wasn't worried or anything was she?"

"She didn't show it if she was," answered Jack's dad.

Jack looked out to the hanger area. "Where's Pat, anyway?"

"He won't be around for a couple of days," answered Alan.

"What!" Jack exclaimed. "This time of year. Is he sick or something?"

"No, he's grounded," answered the old man. "I know all about that little stunt he pulled on you coming back to the field. That was a dangerous maneuver. You both coulda been hurt. And besides, that truck repair is going to cost us. Actually it's going to cost your cousin."

"I guess that will mean extra flying for all of us huh?" asked Jack as he stood up to put on his gear.

"Extra flying and a change in planes." Jack turned around to face his father. "I'll use Pat's spray rig for the Pico Hills job," Alan continued. "You fly my duster today, Son. Brownie is repairing the 'tac' and manifold pressure gauges in yours."

Jack smiled. He was happy about flying his father's aircraft. It was the best maintained and handled beautifully in the air. "What's my assignment, Dad?"

"You get the McKinney vineyards today," said Alan rolling out a map on top of his desk. Jack came over and looked at the outline of the fields.

"You notice the power lines on the west and north?" Jack nodded. "Fly east and west, don't try to go under the lines. They're too low, especially since it's vines." Alan pointed to two spots on the map. "When you border the west side watch out for these two standpipes."

"No problem, Dad. Who'll be flagging?" asked Jack.

"Bobby," Alan answered. "The field is real close to the road you'll be loading off. I know you're a pilot now, but can you help Brownie load?"

"Sure, it'll be like old times."

"Take your time," Alan continued. "You should finish before it gets too hot. If it does, we'll go back and finish tonight or tomorrow." Alan looked out the window. The sky was beginning to brighten with the rise of the sun. "Well Son, they should be warmed up. See you back here this afternoon."

"Okay Dad," said Jack. He walked out of the office toward his father's duster. As he passed, Brownie yelled over the roar of the engine. "See you at the road, Brownie. Don't be late."

Brownie smiled and patted Jack on top of the helmet. "Don't wait for me. You know how to open the hopper door, Mr. Loader."

Remembering what his father had said about helping Brownie load the duster, Jack laughed out loud. Brownie walked to the waiting truck. It was the first time he had seen Jack laugh in quite a while.

CHAPTER SEVENTEEN

Jack landed his plane on the county road. On the shoulder were the rows of sulfur bags. He swung the wing over the top of the material and shut the engine down. He unbuckled the shoulder and seatbelt harness. Flipping the shoulder straps backward, they landed with a pop against the side of the metal fuselage. Brownie had not yet arrived. All was quiet. Jack, staring down the road, remained in the cockpit. A farmer on a tractor passed by and waved. Jack raised his hand in a salute to the man in overalls. Then he saw the familiar truck turn the corner and head towards him. He stood up in the cockpit and unlatched the hopper door. Brownie pulled up and jumped out. He handed Jack a grape knife.

"Ready to go kid?"

Jack nodded. "Start throwing them up here."

Soon, the mechanic was heaving the first of the fifty-pound bags onto the space between the cockpit and hopper. Jack ripped them open and dumped the ingredients into the abyss in front of him. When he couldn't get any more of the yellow powder in the hopper, he yelled at Brownie, "That'll do it, she's full."

Jack slammed the hopper door shut and dusted himself off. Brownie walked around to the prop. Jack sat down in the cockpit. The routine of commands were given. Brownie spun the prop and the already warm engine roared to life. Jack fastened his seatbelt and increased the RPM's of the engine. The power of the Pratt & Whitney was smooth and steady. Even with two thousands pounds of dust, there would be no problem getting airborne with this aircraft. He pointed the plane down the road, gave a nod to Brownie, pouring himself a cup of coffee from his thermos, and thundered down the road. He was soon in the air and headed for the McKinney vineyard a short distance away. Brownie would be able to see the passes from his vantage point in the bed of the truck or standing on the stack of sulfur.

Jack spotted Bobby immediately. The young man was waving a pole with a white flag attached. Jack lined up for his first pass. The plane crossed the road over the top of the flagger. The aircraft settled in just above the vineyard. The dust spewed out of the spreader below the plane, curling around and over the leaves of the grape vines. Jack kept the plane steady. With vineyard dusting there was no cushion of air between him and the ground this time. The end of the pass was near. Jack pushed the throttle forward and lifted the nose. The airplane's tires cleared the power lines with plenty to spare. His dad's airplane was flying magnificently. Jack made the turn, lined up with Bobby and brought the Stearman over the power lines. In the middle of the pass the engine coughed for an instant. "Hafta tell Brownie about that bad plug," Jack thought as he crossed the road. Another turn and he was headed west again, across the vines and toward the power lines. Near the end of the run he ran the throttle to full power again. But this time, the engine sputtered. Jack quickly glanced at his tachometer. The needle was erratic. He looked up to the power lines and a pole directly ahead. He had no choice. It was up and over or hit the pole. He pulled the stick back between his legs and made sure the throttle was on full power. The aircraft tried to raise its nose in response to Jack's movements but it was like a wounded bird. The last thing Jack saw was the cross-member of the power pole going underneath the propeller. The plane's undercarriage hit the wooden cross piece on top of the pole, ripping off the wires and insulators. Sparks flew everywhere. One of the wires became entangled in the still spinning propeller. The strand of electricity was whipped violently around the plane, slamming against the fuselage, the struts and the wings. The plane's nose suddenly pointed downward and in an instant buried itself in the ground. In the cockpit, Jack was still secured by the wide shoulder straps when the plane plummeted to the ground. When it hit, he felt the metal compartment surround and squeeze his legs as it compressed with the impact. He felt the sharp edges of steel pierce his skin and burrow deeply inside. Still conscious, he struggled with the safety harness. The electric lines were sparking against the fabric wings. With almost a full load of flammable sulfur and gasoline, he had to get out.

 At the loading sight, Brownie had seen the accident and was speeding to the crash. From the other end of the field, young Bobby was running through the vines as fast as he could. Halfway through the vineyard he saw the upper wing, near the center section, explode into flames. He could see Jack struggling to free himself from the confines of the wreckage.

"Jack, Jack," he yelled. "Get out, it's on fire!" Jack turned his head toward Bobby and pointed to his legs. The young flagger stood motionless as Brownie arrived in a cloud of dust.

"Quick Bobby, give me a hand," he screamed. "Get on the edge of the wing. We gotta pull him out."

Jack felt the heat of the flames near him. He leaned back and gasped for air. The smoke of burning sulfur was the only thing he inhaled. His throat burning, he coughed and gagged. Just before he reached him, Brownie could see Jack's head fall forward to be engulfed by the flames. Bobby was on the other side of the cockpit. The fire singed the hairs on both men as they tugged and pulled on the limp body in their arms. Finally, they managed to free the pilot from the hot and twisted confines of his entrapment. Brownie pulled the unconscious Jack to the ground and dragged him away from the wreckage. Bobby ran around to help. He started to pick up Jack's legs to help carry him but Brownie screamed at him, "Don't touch his legs, can't you see their broken?"

Bobby looked down at the bloody, twisted appendages being dragged across the dirt by Brownie. The young man turned away in horror.

"Get me some water out of the truck," yelled Brownie as he finally laid Jack down on the ground well away and upwind from what was left of the still burning aircraft. Bobby brought the cold water to Brownie. The mechanic removed Jack's helmet and goggles exposing the burned skin of his face. Bobby again turned away.

"Get in that truck and get to the McKinney house. Get some help here as fast as you can. Tell Billy to bring more water and his wife. Go...go, hurry up!"

Bobby ran to the truck and was soon speeding to the farmhouse a mile away. He did as Brownie had told him. When the ambulance arrived, the mechanic was still cradling the unconscious young pilot in his arms. The two ambulance personnel took over and Brownie, Bobby and the McKinneys were left watching the vehicle, siren screeching, speed away toward town and the hospital. They talked for a moment and Billy McKinney said if there was anything they could do to help to let them know. Brownie thanked them. The fire department had extinguished the flames and cut the circuit to the power lines. Brownie walked over to the smoldering wreckage.

Reaching out to the top wing he broke off the hollow vent tube. Then he and Bobby climbed into the truck and headed back to the airfield. Neither spoke to each other until they pulled up next to the hanger. The office was empty. Alan Lawrence and his crew were still flying. Brownie sent the shaken Bobby home with orders not to tell anyone. The mechanic went to the office and called the hospital. The staff would not say much, other than Jack was still in surgery. Brownie hung up and sat down in a chair to wait for Alan.

In a little while, he heard the familiar sound of one of his planes. The old man was returning. Brownie waited until Alan had taxied and parked the aircraft. He watched the senior pilot climb out of the cockpit and jump to the ground. Leaving the office, he met Jack's father half way between his plane and the hanger.

Across the field, Sheila and Carter were in the office. Sheila was doing some paperwork and Carter was leaning his chair back against the wall looking at the hard working girl. Suddenly, one of the Western loaders came running in the door.

"Did you hear about Cal-Ag?" he gasped. "One of their planes crashed. It was the old man's favorite duster."

Sheila dropped her pen and stood up. Carter leaned forward on his desk.

The loader continued, "Yea, it hit a power line on pull up and the wheels clipped the wires. There was a fire and everything. I saw it coming in. Pretty bad, I guess."

Carter was still at the desk. "So, how is the old man? Is he hurt or anything?"

"Looks okay to me," answered the loader, pointing out the window to across the field. "He's talking to Brownie right over there."

Carter was puzzled. Alan Lawrence must be a real lucky guy to have walked away from a burning duster. He looked at Brownie and Alan conversing. They finish and Carter sees Alan run to his car and head off the field to town. Brownie started walking immediately toward the Western Dusters office. At the door, he shoved the loader aside and entered. Approaching Carter, the Cal-Ag mechanic's dark brown eyes look at the man seated disdainfully at the desk. They are filled with a cold, hateful stare. Brownie threw the bent and burned vent tube on the desk in front of Carter. "If I ever find out that any of you were responsible for this accident. I'll ruin you. All of you." There was silence as the mechanic leaves, slamming the door almost off the hinges.

Sheila was right behind Brownie. She pulled at his arm but he kept walking without saying anything. The girl remembered seeing Alan Lawrence speed away from the field. She jumped in her car and headed to the hospital. When she got there, she parked near the emergency entrance. Running inside, she found Alan standing near the doorway that leads to the emergency operating room. He saw the young girl approach. A cold look greeted Sheila.

"Mr. Lawrence," she begins, "who was the pilot?"

"My son, Jack."

Sheila's knees buckle. She staggers to a nearby chair and begins to sob. Alan Lawrence pauses, then takes a few steps to lay his hand on her shoulder.

"You can stay here with me if you like," he told the weeping girl. "That way, we both can find out together. His stepmother is on the way, too."

Carter had followed Sheila to the hospital. Entering the doorway he found Sheila and Alan Lawrence embraced, trying to console each other.

"How's he doin'?" asked Carter.

"As if you care," answered Alan flatly. "If you really want to know, he's badly burned." Sheila, with the unexpected statement, looked up at Alan but maintained her embrace of the senior Lawrence as he continued. "He can't move his legs. Brownie says when he pulled him out of the flames they were caught in the smashed fuselage."

"Sounds like Brownie shouldn't have moved him," adds Carter. "Maybe he did all the damage to Jack's legs."

Standing up he yelled to Carter, "Get out of here!" Releasing the girl and doubling his fists he approaches his adversary, "Brownie saved my son's life." He pushed Carter toward the door. The nurse at the desk picked up the phone to call the police but the emergency room doctor looking over her shoulder gently took it from her hand and, shaking his head in silence, placed it back on the hook. Carter continued out the door with the help of Alan Lawrence who then returned to sit and wait quietly with Sheila.

CHAPTER EIGHTEEN

Gail Lawrence rushed to the hospital as soon as her husband called. She burst through the doors of the emergency room to find Alan and Sheila Gebhardt sitting next to each other. They both stood when she approached. Harry put his arms around his wife, telling her that they had heard nothing more than what he told her on the phone. The woman looked at the young girl standing close by.

"Hello, Mrs. Lawrence," said Sheila.

She stepped back from her husband. "Hello Sheila," Gail then paused for a moment before adding, "You've come to wait too, I see."

"Yes ma'am, I hope you don't mind?" Sheila asked, returning to her seat.

"Of course not," answered Gail, "Jack has told me all about you."

Alan Lawrence stepped away. "Here honey," he said, motioning to the chair he had been occupying, "sit here next to Sheila. I'm going outside to have a smoke." His wife watched him through the windows that filtered sun light into the somber emergency room. Her husband lit a cigarette and began pacing back and forth. Turning at the end of the walkway, he unknowingly retraced the same steps, back and fourth, until he finished his smoke. Jack's mother sat down next to her stepson's anxious girlfriend and waited. Together they tried to engage in conversation as their eyes remained on the area behind the nurse's desk and through the doorway to where Jack was being treated. They exchanged stories about the young man they have both grown to love in different ways.

Alan returned from outside and leaned against the wall. One foot crossed over the other, the sole of his boot was braced against the baseboard. His thoughts were on the crash and the description that Brownie had told of the scene. He also remembered the blackened vent tube his mechanic had showed him. He knows the accident was really no accident and it had been meant for him. But how could a fellow pilot like Harry Gebhardt become filled with so much hatred? Western Dusters was still a profitable business and there were plenty of acres in the area for both companies to keep busy. Was it all because of his stunt at the stage ranch where Harry had flipped his Stearman? Surely, he wouldn't put another man's life in jeopardy because of his own wrecked and already repaired airplane. From the evidence that Brownie had showed him it was obvious the plane had been sabotaged to crash. But who and why?

Finally, the doors to the treatment room opened and Jack's attending doctor walked out to the waiting area. "Let's go through here," he motioned, opening another door, "It'll be a little quieter." Alan and Gail Lawrence, with Sheila trailing behind, went through the door to a smaller waiting room with a couch and two comfortable padded chairs. The women sat down on the couch, the doctor in one of the chairs. Alan stood near the door. He started to ask the question but the physician spoke first.

"Your son is going to live," he said, looking alternately at Jack's father and mother. "He has just come through a very serious operation but his condition is stabilizing. He's a very lucky man. If he wasn't such a young man his body would not have survived what it has been through."

"Can we see him?" asked Gail.

"In a little while," the doctor answered. "We are moving him to the intensive care ward right now and getting him set up. He is still under sedation and probably will not even know you are there." Looking at Sheila, the doctor asked, "Is this his sister?"

The young girl looked at Mrs. Lawrence. "She is the girlfriend of my son," answers Gail.

The doctor paused he looks again at Sheila, "I think when it's time young lady, you should wait out here."

"No, no," Sheila responded, nearing tears, "I want to see him, I have to see him."

The doctor stood up and put his hand on Alan Lawrence's shoulder. "Can I see you out here for just a minute Mr. Lawrence? We'll be right back," he assured the women as the two men exited the small room.

Stopping in the hall, he began to explain to the elder Lawrence the condition of his son. "Mr. Lawrence," the doctor began.

"Please, call me Alan," interrupted Jack's father.

"Alright Alan," the physician continued, "I understand your son just began flying."

"He actually has been flying since junior high. He just recently received his Agriculture Rating. He has always loved the feel of flying."

"That's unfortunate," continued the doctor.

"What do you mean?" asked Alan, fearing the worst.

The doctor looks Alan in the eyes. "Your son's legs are badly broken. Shattered would be a better term for it. When the plane crashed it must have collapsed around his legs. Almost every bone is broken. His left foot may have to be amputated." The doctor stopped with that statement. He watched Alan carefully, trying to read the man's reaction before he continued. But the father just stared at the physician.

"What about his burns?" Alan asks.

"That is why I really don't think the young lady should see him right at this moment," the doctor put his hand on Alan's shoulder. "Your son's face was badly burned along with his upper body. The wounds will take a long time to heal and the scars may always be present on his face. Although, through skin grafts and operations there is hope of a somewhat normal appearance."

The doctor was now seeing something in Alan's facial expression in reaction to these words. He had seen it before. Anger mixed with hopelessness.

"Your son is going to need all the support you and the people that love him can give through these coming days, months and maybe years of rehabilitation." The doctor again looked directly into Alan's eyes. "Alan, you have to give him confidence. If he gives up mentally, he is through physically."

"Do you think he will ever be able to fly again doctor?" Alan asked.

"If his legs heal correctly. That will be the key."

"But what about his foot? You know, if you have to remove it?"

"I really don't think that will be a problem with the artificial prosthetics they have now. Doesn't it just push a pedal when you're flying?" the doctor asked.

"That's true," Alan answered, "but there is a certain feel of the controls."

"Well, to get his license back, that will be up to his instructor," the doctor smiled, "and I know his instructor will give him all the support and help the young man needs to fly again."

"I'll sure give it my best effort doctor."

"Patience and understanding will be the key, Alan. He already knows the skill it takes. He will have to learn the feel again or make allowances and find another way. But, let's get him walking first, then we'll see about flying."

"Yes, one thing at a time," responded Alan. "Now if you'll excuse me, I'll try to tell the ladies in there what you have said."

"I'll check and see how Jack is doing," the doctor began to leave, "I'll be back to get you in a few minutes."

"Thanks Doc," said Alan, pushing through the door to where Gail and Sheila were waiting.

Alan sat down next to the women and began to explain what the doctor told him. He came to where he has to speak of the burns and hesitated. He looked at Sheila and wondered just how strong her love was for his son. He continued, explaining that Jack's face may never be the same. His handsome features scarred forever, he will not be the same good looking man Sheila had previously loved.

"Mr. Lawrence," Sheila interrupted, "I love your son for the way he treated me. I don't care what he will look like when all this is finished. Please know that I will always love your son."

"That is very reassuring, but don't promise something before you have seen him or know exactly what years of treatment will bring. You are very young and are going to have to put up with a lot of pain and hurt. Jack will say things he probably doesn't really mean. Say things to you that are filled with hate and frustration over his legs and the way he looks. You, if you really love him as you say you do, will have to be strong. In the end, hopefully he will know that you, and all of us were there for him, through these hard times."

The doctor opened the door. "Okay, you can see your son now."

The three of them began to go down the hallway to the room where Jack rested. Before entering, the doctor asked again, "Young lady, are you sure you want to go in?"

"Yes sir, I am sure," answered Sheila.

The doctor nodded and opened the door to the room. Gail was first at Jack's bedside. Sheila moved to the other side. Alan stopped at the foot of the bed and looked down at his son. Both legs were in casts and elevated slightly. His upper torso was bandaged. Slight tinges of blood stained the white cloth wrappings. His head and face, except for narrow slits for Jack's eyes and mouth, was completely covered with gauze. Two bottles above his bed supplied vital fluids to his body through intravenous tubes in both arms. Monitors near his bedside electronically kept track of the young man's heart rhythm and breathing. The three people at his bedside said nothing. They just peer at the still figure in the bed. A figure that a few hours earlier had been full of vigor, enthusiasm and most of all, life. Alan, looking up at the two women on either side of the bed, watched them wipe tears from their faces. Alan is not showing it, but he is having a hard time with the situation too. He looked at his watch. "Are you two going to stay here?" he asked, "I hate to go but I have to get back to the field. Brownie should know, and the crew. We still have to fly tomorrow," he paused, then added, "somehow."

Gail looked up. "Go ahead dear, I'll stay until they run me out."

"Me too," added Sheila.

"What about your mother and father?" Alan asked.

"I'll call Mom and explain everything," answered Sheila. "Don't worry about me, she'll understand."

"What about Harry?" Alan wondered if Sheila thinks what happened to Jack was the result of her own father's revenge. Does she know, as he does, that the plane was rigged to crash?

"My father," answered Sheila, "He's too busy to worry about me. Besides, I was thinking about moving out anyway. It'll make it easier for me to help with Jack's rehabilitation." Sheila looked across the bed to Gail, "We'll stay here and wait for Jack to wake up."

"Go on Dear," added Gail. "We'll be fine, I'll call you if there is any change and when Jack wakes up." Alan's wife came around to the foot of the bed and kissed her husband on the cheek. "Now go on and do what has to be done."

Reluctantly, Alan Lawrence left the two women alone at his son's bedside. Almost unconsciously he drove to the airfield. He was thinking of his son but also of his wife and Sheila. This will be a long night, a long week, a long struggle, for all of them.

CHAPTER NINETEEN

At the airfield Brownie, Bobby, Tiny and the rest of the crew were waiting in the hanger. No work was being done, no games of ping-pong or horseshoes, just waiting. The phone rang. It is a farmer asking about the accident. After expressing his concern, the man wanted to know if his fields will be sprayed the next day. Brownie assured him that it will be taken care of. Shaking his head, Brownie returned to the crew in the hanger. Tiny had bought some beer and was sharing it with the waiting personnel. Brownie picked up a can and got a can opener from his toolbox.

"Pass me that church key," asked Tiny, reaching down for another beer out of the ice chest. Brownie tossed it to the big man. Tiny tried to catch it but dropped it into the half-melted ice of the container. He reached into the cold liquid and retrieved it. Punching two holes in his can, he tossed the opener back to Brownie. "Nice catch," said Tiny.

The senior mechanic looked at his crew gathered around him. "I hope everyone knows it will be business as usual tomorrow." Raising his beer can, he added, "Nobody be late or hung over."

"Who's gonna take Jack's place," Bobby asked.

"Gary and Pappy will do most of the flying. I'm sure Pat will show up too. The three of them can handle it. It'll be just like before Jack was flying."

The sound of a diesel engine signaled the approach of a large flatbed truck. On top was what was left of the plane Jack had been flying. Brownie left the hanger and stepped onto the cab of the truck. He told the driver to park the trailer alongside the hanger.

"The cops are right behind me," the driver advised Brownie. "They want to take some pictures and look it over."

"Okay, just unhook over there," the mechanic pointed to an area that paralleled the side of the hanger. "You can come get your trailer tomorrow. We'll have the wreck off by then. I'll have a check ready for you when you pick it up."

"That's alright," said the driver, "I work for the McKinneys. They said not to worry about it. If there is anything else give me a call or call Billy at the house."

Stepping down from cab, Brownie thanked the driver. He watched him back the trailer with ease to the exact spot where it would be uncoupled from the truck. As the driver was leaving, Brownie watched him stop in the middle of the road as a police car approached. He squinted as he saw the driver point in the direction of the trailer and then continue on toward the main road. The police cruiser, with two men inside, arrived and parked beside the trailer. The men got out. One of them was wearing a uniform and the other a suit. The man in the suit took off his jacket and jumped up onto the trailer. Starting at the front of the aircraft, he carefully started the inspection of the plane, occasionally stopping to write something on a notepad. Brownie approached and stood next to the uniformed officer. They watched the detective continue to inspect the length of the mangled wreckage. Finishing his inspection, he jumped down off the trailer and walked up to the two waiting men.

"Not much left of it," he said.

"Find anything you can use?" asked Brownie.

"Not much, the fire pretty much ruined any evidence. No use taking any fingerprints. Looks like engine failure to me."

"It was engine failure all right," Brownie assured the detective. "Planned engine failure."

"What do you mean?" asked the detective.

Brownie pulled the vent tube from his pocket. "Here's your evidence," he said handing it to the cop.

"What's this?" asked the detective, taking it between his thumb and forefinger and laying the twisted, burnt piece of metal on the edge of the trailer.

Just then, Tiny came around the corner of the hanger. "Find out anything about the wreck?" he asked the detective.

Brownie ignored Tiny's question and continued with the detective. "It's a plugged vent tube," he explained. "That is what caused the engine failure. You can still see the tape and the plug in the end of it."

Tiny looked at the tube on the edge of the trailer, "Let me see that." He grabbed the piece of metal. Turning it at different angles in his hand he added, "Just one little plug caused all that? Man what a mess." Tiny returned the tube to the trailer. Looking over Brownie's shoulder, he espied a familiar truck approaching. "Here comes the old man, Brownie."

Brownie turned to confirm the Cal-Ag vehicle. "He'll have news of Jack." Excusing himself, he told the detective, "I'll explain about that tube later. Right now, I've got to know about the pilot."

"Go ahead," the cop told him, "Come on down to the station later and give me a statement."

"Good," said Brownie, "I'll see you in the morning after flying if that's okay?"

"That'll be fine, I'll see you then." The detective and officer watched Brownie and Tiny return to the hanger.

There was silence from the crew as Alan Lawrence explained in general terms the situation at the hospital. He told his company personnel they can go home, but they stayed around the hanger talking softly and finishing off the beer that Tiny had brought. Alan told Brownie that they need to talk in the office. The door closed behind them. Inside, Brownie learned the horrible details of Jack's condition.

"I know who's responsible for Jack's injuries, Pappy," he told Alan.

"I know what you're thinking, Brownie," said Jack's father, "but we have no proof."

"I have all the proof I need with what I gave the detective," continued Brownie. "If it wasn't Harry Gebhardt then it was that asshole who works for him."

"I don't think it was Harry," Alan said, "I just can't see him doing that. And Carter wouldn't know how to do something like that."

"Unless someone told him how," continued Brownie. "You know, I think Harry found out that Jack was going with his daughter and I think he paid Carter a little extra just to get Sheila away from Jack."

"That's nonsense, Brownie," Alan exclaimed, thinking of the young girl waiting at the hospital. "She's old enough to make up her own mind."

"Not in that house, I don't think. You know, Pat saw Sheila and Carter together a couple of nights ago. They were having a pretty good time from what I hear."

"I didn't know that, but maybe Sheila didn't have a choice," Alan said, hoping that was the case.

"That's just what I'm getting at, Pappy. Her father rules that place like Hitler. From what I hear, he tells those girls exactly what he wants and expects nothing less. He certainly couldn't have the good-looking son of the competition's owner dating his daughter. I'm just guessing, but I think he set up Carter with Sheila and didn't give her a choice. But, when Jack refused to get out of the picture that's when he or Carter or the both of them decided to eliminate the competition. Not the flying competition, the competition for his daughter."

"Okay then, answer me this," demanded Alan, "how did they know Jack was going to fly my plane this morning. Just how did they know that without looking at the field and plane assignments on my desk in my office?"

Brownie paused, "That is a good question, Pappy. I can't answer that one, but I still think it was one or both of them. Who else could it have been? You tell me."

Alan Lawrence rose from behind his desk. "I don't know, maybe the cops can figure it out. I gotta see the chief tonight, maybe he can come up with something."

"I hafta go down to the station after we finish tomorrow," added Brownie, "I'll tell him what I know."

"They'll want to hear what you know, not what you think, Brownie," Alan told his trusted mechanic. "Let's keep it at that. For now, anyway."

"Okay, just for now," Brownie assured his boss.

Together, they returned to the hanger area. Alan told everyone they could stay as long as they wanted but to make sure they are here in the morning ready to work. The crew nodded their heads and told the senior pilot they will be ready to go bright and early the next day. Alan left the airfield and returned to his family and Sheila at the hospital. The crew, having finished all the beers that Tiny had brought, lingered a few minutes longer before leaving in their cars to town. Brownie locked up and just before leaving, called Pat. Depressed, he needed some company. Pat agreed to meet Brownie at Irene's Tavern for a drink.

Pat entered the dark tavern to see Brownie shooting a game of pool by himself. Choosing the easiest placed ball, the mechanic hit the cue ball hard with every shot.

"Who's winning?" Pat asked, approaching just as the clack of two balls sound loudly on the table.

"Nobody winning today, hey buddy?" Brownie stopped and laid the pool stick on the table. "Thanks for coming. Come on, I'll buy you a beer."

The two men stepped up to the empty bar and ordered a couple of drafts. Lifting his mug, Brownie turned to his friend, "Here's to Jack and a speedy recovery."

Pat tapped his glass on Brownie's and took a sip of the lager before asking, "I guess you've heard the latest?"

"Yea, your uncle just left the field," answered Brownie referring to Pappy.

"I just came from the hospital," said Pat. "Jack's a mess, it's gonna be a long time before he can get in a plane again, if ever. I can't understand it. He was a good pilot. Probably would have been the best around with a little time."

"You know Pat, that could have been you in that plane if Pappy wouldn't have grounded you for that stunt you pulled."

"Yea, I've thought about that," Pat said looking down into his half empty mug of beer. "I've thought about that a lot. If I wouldn't have done that stupid trick we all would have been better off."

"Hey now, it would have happened anyway. Only the pilot would have been different. It could have been you, the old man, or Gary. It was going to happen to one of you."

"I guess you're right," said Pat, emptying his glass of ale. "Bartender, bring us a couple of more, will ya?" He turned to Brownie, "Any ideas on what caused the crash?"

The bartender brought the two drinks and leaned on his side of the bar listening to the two men talk. "No ideas man, just proof," answered Brownie. "I know what caused it and who did it."

"Don't tell me," Pat paused, then continued, "the Gebhardts, right?"

"Yep, somehow or someway and that's exactly what I'm tellin' the cops."

The bartender interrupted, "You got proof of this Brownie."

"All the proof I need," said the mechanic. He told the bartender what he plans on telling the cops at the station the next day, all about the plane crash and the vent tube he had as evidence.

"Pretty convincing to me," replied the bartender after hearing

Brownie's story.

"They still gotta prove it in court," added Pat. "That'll be the hard part."

"I'll testify," assured Brownie, slamming his mug down on the bar. "Those guys are going down for what they did to Jack."

"I gotta git to the hospital to see if anyone needs anything," said Pat finishing his beer and getting up from his bar stool. "I'll see you in the morning buddy, take it easy."

Pat walked out the door, leaving Brownie and the bartender alone. Brownie finished his beer and ordered another one. "Hey Geno, how about some music?" he asked the bartender.

Geno threw a couple of quarters on the bar. "Play anything except 'B-14,'" he told Brownie. The mechanic walked over to the juke box and looked down at the song titles in front of him. "The Whiffenpoof Song" is B-14. An old tune sang by the Veteran pilots of World War II. Geno kept it around just for them but it was kind of sad when they all joined in the chorus; "we are poor lost sheep who have lost our way." Brownie skipped over it and just pushed some buttons. As he was returning to his stool and a full beer the door opened. Brownie didn't look up as he sat down in front of his drink. In the darkened tavern the new customer, his eyes still adjusting from the bright sun outside, did not notice the hunched over mechanic sipping on his beer. Carter sat down a couple of stools away. Geno came over. Carter ordered a drink of whiskey with a beer chaser. The bartender hesitated a moment before beginning to get Carter his drinks. "Come on Geno, I'm thirsty, I need a drink now," demanded Carter, looking up at the bartender.

Geno nodded toward the customer a couple of stools away. "Well, if it isn't the ace mechanic of the airfield," said Carter. Brownie recognized the voice but didn't look up from his beer.

"Take it easy, Carter," said Geno, "he's had a rough day."

"Rough day," repeated Carter loudly, "I guess so. Lose a pilot and your best plane. Hey Geno, you hear how it happened?"

Geno had just heard but wasn't telling, "No, but I heard it was bad."

"Yea, it was bad man," said Carter, turning toward Brownie. "Hey, ace mechanic, forget to check a plug or something? How did it happen?"

Brownie looked up from his beer with a cold stare. "You oughta know."

"Me, how am I supposed to know about something you forgot to do?" Carter looked back to Geno the bartender. "Yup, must have been a couple of faulty plugs. Now how 'bout that whiskey and beer?"

Geno returned with the drinks. Carter threw some bills down on the bar and once again mentioned to the bartender, "Yea, those plugs shoulda been checked before the plane took off."

Brownie had heard enough. He scooted off his stool and took the few steps to lean on the bar next to Carter. Grabbing the young man's full glass of beer he told Carter, "Here's your chaser for that whiskey." The angry mechanic tossed the cold ale into Carter's face then handed the bartender the glass. "I think this asshole has had enough don't you think, Geno?"

Geno nodded in agreement before Brownie continued, "And look at this mess. Why don't you go home and get cleaned up. You probably got a hot date tonight, don't ya?"

Carter, his eyes burning with alcohol, wiped his face with his shirt. "I'll get you for this Brownie, mark my words, I'll get you."

"Hey, I don't fly," Brownie said, grabbing the wet young man and pushing him toward the door. "Whaddya gonna do, sabotage my truck?"

Before walking out into the afternoon, Carter gave another warning to his adversary, "Don't worry, I'll find a way."

"Oh, I'm not worried," answered Brownie returning to his stool.

Carter stopped with the door half open as he leaves, "Hey Brownie, that hot date of mine you were talking about? Her name is Sheila." Carter finished his exit before Brownie could leap off his stool again.

"What a jerk," Geno told his only customer.

"Yea, a real punk," agreed Brownie, "I shoulda beat the crap out of him right here."

"Woulda been fine with me," said Geno. "Wanna another drink, my friend?"

"No, this'll do," answered Brownie. "I'm going by the hospital and then home. It's going to be hectic around the airfield until defoliation is finished." The mechanic emptied his last beer and pushed the mug toward the bartender. "Gotta go, thanks Geno, see ya later." Geno watched Brownie walk out the door, leaving the bartender alone to clean up the spilled beer while listening to the music still coming from the jukebox. When the last song ended, he poured himself a draft beer and took a dime from the till of the cash register. Before sitting on the last stool at the end of the bar, he put the dime in the slot of the music machine and pushed B-14.

CHAPTER TWENTY

The next day, at first glance, everything looked routine at the airfield. At the south end, Western Dusters was busy fueling and loading their planes for a job near the airport. Harry Gebhardt was smiling as he sat down in the seat of his duster. He was flying again. As soon as he was able to fly, he had returned to work and fired his long time pilot. The same pilot that had kept the business going while Harry was recuperating from his accident. On the ground, Carter was picking up the empty sulfur bags. He waved to Harry as the plane began to taxi into position for take off. In passing, Harry gave a thumbs up and soon was off to his dusting job.

On the other side of the field, Cal-Ag employees were scrambling to get their planes in the air. Instead of the jovial early morning talkative atmosphere that was normal, they went about their tasks in a somber quiet mood that reflected the previous day's occurrence. Brownie had arrived first and when Tiny showed up they checked and double checked all the planes for anything out of place. After starting the engines, Brownie took extra time listening to the sound of the motors. He checked the gauges, making sure they all were registering the correct amounts and indications. The pilots, Pappy, Gary Wilson and Pat, also took a little extra time at the warm up area before heading down the runway and into the air. The day's work finished without mishap.

When Harry landed he could see a police car in front of the Western office. After parking and shutting down his plane he walked calmly towards the office. Approaching the door he heard Carter and two policemen talking inside. He opened the door and joined in the conversation. Across the field, Brownie and Tiny were topping off the Cal-Ag planes with fuel. Both of them were watching the movement at the south end. After refueling the last plane Tiny parked the gas truck and returned to join Brownie, still watching and waiting outside the hanger. They both were leaning against the wing of a Stearman when the cops left the office and headed towards them. Tiny lit a cigarette as they approached.

"How's it goin' fellas?" said the detective in plain clothes.

Brownie ignored the opening question and asked, "Find out anything over there?"

"Not much," replied the detective. "They had all the right answers and we don't have much to go on."

"What about the vent tube I gave you yesterday?" asked Brownie.

"That's about all we have to go on, but it was so burned and crushed we couldn't get any prints or anything off of it. The same with the wrecked plane. Just too messed up for any evidence." The detective lowered his head. Pulling a cigarette from his pocket he put it to his lips. Tiny offered him a light with his Zippo lighter.

"Thanks," said the cop, "do you know anything about this?" he asked Tiny.

"Not me," answered Tiny. "The first I knew it happened was when the wreck was hauled back here."

"You still want my statement?" Brownie interrupted.

"Yea sure," the detective answered. "Why don't you come down to the station this afternoon like we had planned. It won't take long. Maybe by then we will have something to go on."

"I'll be there," assured Brownie. The mechanic walked away from the officers, followed by Tiny. The policemen returned to their car still parked in front of the Western office and left the airfield.

Inside, Harry and Carter watched them drive away. Harry opened the door of the small refrigerator in the office. Reaching inside, he pulled out two cans. "Here ya go my man," he said, tossing a beer to his young loader. "You did a fine job today. In fact, the last few days you have done an excellent job." Harry sat down at his desk. Carter sat down at the desk normally occupied by Sheila. Propping his feet up on the corner he raised his beer can to his boss, smiled, and then took a long drink.

At the hospital, both Sheila and Gail had fallen asleep in the family waiting room. The small town hospital had provided comfortable lounge chairs for the both of them. That morning, alone in his room, young Jack Lawrence awoke to the sounds of a Pratt and Whitney engine. He couldn't see very much or move without pain but he knew the unmistakable sound of the motor as a Stearman flew over the building. No doubt headed for a job. He was beginning to remember now. The crash, his trapped legs, now suspended at the foot of the bed. He remembered in his mind the pain of his crushed limbs. He looked up at his bandaged legs. He tried to feel them, to move his toes or feet. There was nothing. Jack remembered the searing heat on his face just before he blacked out. He slowly raised his hand to his face. He felt the thick bandages and tape that was holding what was left of his skin in place. He cursed. A nurse entered the room and began putting Jack's clothing in a bag. The patient wondered what she was doing but could not ask her any questions. The experienced nurse began to talk aloud.

"Good morning," she said cheerfully. "Just getting your things ready for when they come get you. Should be this afternoon or this evening."

"Come get me," Jack pondered. "And take me where?" he silently wondered.

"Nothing but the best for you honey," the nurse continued. "They have a fine burn center in the city. They can do wonders nowadays. With all the new ideas and procedures you'll be good as new with a little time."

Jack again felt the bandages on his face. He had a lot of questions to ask but his lips were also covered by the dressing. He saw the door of his room open again. It was his mother and his girlfriend. He turned his head away. Sheila stood at one side and he turned away to the other only to see his mother. Sheila gently laid her hand on his chest. Gail clutched his hand and squeezed slightly. Jack turned his head and looked up at the ceiling. Then the doctor came through the still open doorway.

"Good morning everyone," he said, "how's the patient this morning?"

"He's awake doctor," said Gail.

"That's good. Can you hear me son?" the physician asked. Jack nodded. "Good, now let me explain what has happened to you." The doctor told Jack about the treatment and operations that were done after the crash. He explained how Brownie and Bobby had pulled him, unconscious, from the wreckage and called for help. "That mechanic probably saved your life," he added. Jack again nodded in agreement.

"Everything is ready doctor," said the nurse.

"Thank you Mary. You may leave now." The doctor returned to

the foot of the bed as the cheerful nurse left the room.

"What did she mean by that?" asked a worried Sheila.

"We are transporting Jack to the burn center in Fresno as soon as possible. He'll get better treatment there than we can provide. They have an excellent staff and he will be well taken care of."

"How long will he have to stay there, when do you think he can come home?" asked Jack's mother.

"Oh, it will be quite a while before he comes home Mrs. Lawrence. The young man has had quite a trauma. His legs and face..." the doctor stopped in mid sentence. "Why don't you two wait outside for a moment while I check his vital signs and bandages?" The women left the room. The doctor closed the door behind them leaving him alone with his patient. He reached down and held Jack's hand. While pretending to take his patient's pulse he began to explain the weeks and months of effort and ordeal Jack was going to have to go through in his attempt to return to somewhat of a normal lifestyle. Jack just lay on his pillow looking at the ceiling. The doctor was encouraging, but his words were filled with the details of Jack's rehabilitation and recovery. Despite the blunt language, Jack felt the doctor was kind and caring. He told the young man that he would be transported by ambulance as soon as possible, assuring Jack that he would constantly be checking on his progress. Finishing, the doctor opened the door again and told the waiting ladies about the ambulance soon to arrive.

"Shouldn't you be getting to work Sheila?" asked Gail.

"Don't worry, I want to stay with Jack," answered the young girl. "I'm just gonna call Mom and let her know what is happening."

"Tell you what," announced Gail, "I'm going to follow the ambulance to the hospital. Why don't you ride down with me?" Gail reached out for Sheila's hand.

"Thank you, thank you so much Mrs. Lawrence."

"Fine, now go call your mother. I'll wait right here."

Sheila left the room to make the phone call. Gail returned to the bedside of her stepson. She leaned over as close as she could without touching the bandages on his face. "Everything is going to be fine," she whispered. "We both love you very much. Together we'll help you get through this, son." She stood up and looked at the young man she had helped raise since the age of seven. Jack shook his head.

Slowly rolling it back and forth on the pillow.

Sheila returned from making the call to her mother. Her eyes were red. In front of Jack she told Gail, "I can't go right now Mrs. Lawrence. I have to go to the office."

Jack's mother noticed that Sheila had been crying. "What's wrong honey, what happened?"

"Mother and Daddy had an awful fight last night after the police left. Mother wants me to go to the airfield and clean out my stuff from the office. She's packing at home and getting ready to leave. Oh Mrs. Lawrence I don't know where we'll stay?"

"Don't worry, I've got an idea." Gail, taking Sheila by the hand, opened the door to the hallway. Outside the room she told Sheila, "Jack was going to move into his own apartment you know."

"Yes, we had talked about sharing it together later after we got marr..." The young girl paused.

"Don't be afraid," assured Gail, "I know all about you two. Jack has been very honest in telling me about your love for each other."

"But, now I don't know," continued Sheila. "I don't know if he even wants me anymore. How do I tell him how I feel after this?" The girl was starting to sob again.

"That will come later," Gail assured. "Now, about you and your mother. Why don't you stay in Jack's apartment? The deposit and first month's rent is already paid and Jack certainly won't be using it for awhile. It's furnished and everything. And close to town."

Sheila looked at the lady in front of her. "You are so nice Mrs. Lawrence. I'll never be able to repay you."

Stepping forward to embrace the young girl, Gail Lawrence answered, "You already have, by loving my son."

Brownie was at the police station. He had finished giving his statement to the detective. It was of little help. Still, Brownie was adamant to the police about who he thought had done the evil deed.

"I'm sorry Brownie, but unless we come up with something else we'll have to drop the case," said the cop. "We just don't have enough evidence. In fact, we don't have any. Who else would know how to do make a plane go down like that?"

"Anybody that knows anything about airplanes or flying," answered Brownie.

"See, it coulda been anybody," said the cop.

"Yea, but we all know who was out to get Alan Lawrence. Gebhardt's been after him since his accident at the Stage strip. And that punk Carter is just the one who would do his dirty work. He's been after Jack's girl, Gebhardt's daughter, since he got here."

"But we can't prove it Brownie," stated the detective. "The DA would just throw it back in my face."

"Did you check everything?" asked the mechanic. "You know it was early and dark. The guy could have dropped something on the field, a tool, a piece of tape, something."

"Everything has been gone over," answered the officer. "Twice, three times, we looked at all the possibilities. Those guys both have alibis."

"Yea, I bet," Brownie angrily replied. "I'm sure they covered for each other."

The detective had heard enough. There was no need for further conversation. Standing up, he opened the door to the interrogation room. "Look Brownie, they were both at the Gebhardt residence that night. In fact according to Mrs. Gebhardt, Carter spent the night on the sofa."

Brownie stood up. "Fine, I'll settle this my own way."

"Now Brownie," added the detective, "there's already been enough tragedy around this town. Let's not get carried away."

"Don't worry," said the mechanic heading for the door. "I won't leave any evidence either."

"I'll remember that," yelled the detective as Brownie, leaving the room, slammed the door behind him.

Back at the field, the angry mechanic was busy checking his planes for the next morning assignments. He saw Sheila's car approach and stop in front of him. The tearful and afraid girl got out and asks him a favor. "Brownie, would you walk with me over to my office so I can get my things? I'm afraid if Carter is there or Daddy, something may happen."

Brownie was puzzled. "What's going to happen, Sheila?"

"I don't know, Mother just told me to get my stuff and get home."

Brownie finished tightening a screw on an inspection plate and put the screwdriver in his hip pocket. "Tell you what, I'll walk you over and wait by the door. If anything starts I'll be right outside."

"Thank you Brownie," said the girl. "Can we go now? I just

wanna get it over with."

"Sure, right now." The young girl and the mechanic walked across the tarmac to the Western office. Inside Harry and Carter had finished a six pack of beer. Three empty cans were on each desk. Sheila entered the office. Brownie, leaning on the fender of a Western Duster truck, waited outside.

"Hello Daddy," said Sheila nervously, "just came to get my stuff."

"Fine," replied Harry, "I suppose this is your mother's idea?"

"We talked, if that's what you mean." Sheila wanted to get in her desk drawer to get her personal belongings but Carter, sitting in her chair, still had his feet up on the corner.

Harry continued, "I suppose she told you her side."

"Daddy, do you want to tell me your side? I can't believe you slapped mother last night. Why, why would you do that?"

"She had it coming," Harry said rising from his desk. "When I ask her to do something I expect her to do it. Especially if the police are on their way to talk to us."

"What did you have to hide? Do you know something about the accident?" demanded Sheila.

"I don't know any more than you do," answered Harry. He looked at Carter. "Do you know anything, Carter?"

"Not me sir, I don't know a damn thing about that crash." Sheila pushed against Carter's legs trying to get to the drawers of her desk.

"Hey, I'm sitting here," exclaimed Carter. Sheila stepped back and looked outside at Brownie still leaning against the truck.

Harry grabbed another two beers from the cooler. "Aww, let the little girl have her things," he said to Carter. "I never needed her around here anyway." He tossed a cold can to Carter as he stood up. Sheila opened the center drawer and retrieved a few personal items from her former desk. Carter sat down on top of the desk and put his hand on Sheila's hair. Leaning forward he braced himself on the edge of the desk with one hand and with the other stroked her hair between his fingers. The girl jerked away.

"Arn't you gonna say thanks?" he asked coyly.

The fingers of his hand resting on the desk dangled over the edge at the opening of the center drawer. Sheila saw the digits curling over the edge. "Thanks," she said and with all her might she slammed the drawer of the desk against Carter's fingers.

"God damn it," screamed Carter pulling his fingers away. A thin bloody gash ran evenly across each finger. He wrapped a shop towel around his hand. "You fucking bitch," he said in pain. Sheila backed away toward the door. With the suddenly loud and foul language, Brownie had started toward the office door. Harry could see the mechanic approaching.

"Let her go, Carter," he said. "We've got better things to do. Get home to your momma little girl. I'll talk to the both of you later."

Sheila started to state what her mother had said about moving out but thought better of it. Brownie arrived at the door just in time to open it for the young girl leaving with her things. He took her bag and escorted her back across the field, leaving a bleeding Carter and a chuckling Harry together to finish their drinking.

Before leaving she thanked Brownie for his help.

"Are you going to be alright?" he asked.

"I'll be fine," she answered. "It's Jack I'm worried about."

"We all are babe, it's gonna be a long time before he can fly again."

"Do you think he ever will again, Brownie?" asked a doubtful Sheila.

"If I know that kid like I think I do, he'll be back in the air as soon as he can."

"But the burns and his legs, how's he gonna look?" she asked again.

"Look, do you love him or what he looked like? Jack's going to be the same person. The same person you loved. If his feelings change, or his attitude towards you or flying, it won't be because he has lost his love for flying or you." Brownie grabbed the girl by the shoulders with a firm grasp. "Look, if you don't think you can handle the way he will look or be there when he needs you the best thing to do is get out of his life forever and right now. Don't give Jack any false hopes."

Sheila was shaking. "Oh Brownie I love him so much, but...but I don't know."

"Well, you better figure it out real soon young lady, 'cause he's gonna need all the support he can get. If you want to give him one less thing to live for that's up to you. But, I can tell you one thing, that man loves you and always will." The mechanic let go of the girl and opened the car door for her. She started to give Brownie a hug or a kiss on the cheek. But she just said, "Thanks, thanks for everything," and drove off toward town and her waiting mother.

CHAPTER TWENTY-ONE

A week later, Brownie, Bobby and Tiny had driven to City Hospital and visited Jack. The young man was still in bed, recuperating. Except for Brownie the conversation was restricted and strained. Brownie was able to make Jack smile with a couple of jokes and a tale of yet another prank played on the unsuspecting Tiny. Upon leaving the hospital, Brownie could see that Bobby was shaken by the appearance of Jack. Tiny was subdued.

"How about a beer, you guys?" he asked his two riders. "I know a good spot we can get a cold one. Even you kid," he added, looking at Bobby.

"Sure why not," agreed Tiny, "I think we all could use one right now."

Brownie pulled into the parking lot of the Hacienda Hotel. "This place has a bar below the pool where you can watch people swimming through a big window. Who knows Bobby, you might get lucky and see a pretty girl lose her suit."

They walked into the cocktail lounge and ordered three beers. It was just as Brownie had said. The young Bobby sat at the bar, his eyes transfixed on the large window behind the bartender. A few tourists, passing through town, were cooling themselves in the hotel's swimming pool. Their ages revealing various shapes and sizes of humans like different species of fish in an aquarium.

"It looks like Jack has a long way to go," Brownie said raising his glass. "But at least he's alive."

"Yes alive," responded Tiny, "that's the most important thing." Turning to look at Brownie he added, "Thanks to you we can say that."

"Man, you woulda done the same thing," said Brownie.

"Yea, I guess I would have," acknowledged Tiny.

The three of them sat quietly at the bar. After another round Brownie got up from his stool. "Better hit the road guys. Come on Tiny, let's get the kid home."

Back at the airfield, Brownie dropped Bobby off in front of the hanger. The youngster was soon headed home in his jalopy to be greeted by his parents with beer on his breath. Brownie parked the car in front of the Cal-Ag hanger. "See ya tomorrow big guy," he said to Tiny. But the large man followed Brownie into the hanger. "Hey, you can call it a day. I'm just going in here to check tomorrow's assignments." But Tiny continued to follow the mechanic into the office.

Brownie, ignoring the person following him, began to look at the paper work on the boss's desk.

"Brownie, I need to talk to you," said Tiny.

"Listen, if you need tomorrow off I can give you half a day but that's all," Brownie said in anticipation of Tiny's question.

"No that's not it." The big man was starting to sweat. "I need to sit down." He sat down opposite the desk. Brownie moved the maps and paper to one side. He planted his buttocks on the desktop.

"Well, if you don't want the day off what is it?" Brownie asked.

"I don't know how to tell you," answered Tiny. He wiped his brow and back of his neck. The man facing Brownie looked down at the floor. "It's just when I saw Jack today...saw how bad he was," he stopped. Then started again. "Brownie, I'm the one responsible for Jack. I did it. I made the crash happen. I didn't want it to happen like that. Just to run out of gas on the runway or sooner. I didn't know it would take so long."

Brownie was stunned. He stood up from the desk. "I can't believe that Tiny. Who are you protecting?"

"Nobody man, I did it on my own," Tiny answered.

Brownie continued, "How much did Gebhardt or Carter pay you?"

"They didn't. It was on my own. After that firecracker trick when we were playing cards, I was so mad I just wanted to get back at him. To embarrass him. Really Brownie, I didn't know this was gonna happen."

A still disbelieving Brownie asked, "How did you know which plane Jack was going to fly that day? How did you know the old man was going to switch planes?"

Tiny pointed to the desk and the paperwork. "I checked the assignments that night before I left. Pappy had it all set up for the morning. He musta made up his mind the day before and waited to tell Jack while the planes were warming up."

Brownie clinched his fists and started toward the big man still sitting with his head down. He stopped in front of Tiny. "Get up, get up God dammit." Brownie raised his hand, "I oughta..." Tiny raised his open hands to protect himself. The former boxer returned his arm to his side. His fists still clenched.

"Sit down," he pushed Tiny backward into the chair. "Now, this is the way it's going to be. Just like I say. Do you understand?"

Tiny nodded in agreement with whatever Brownie was going to say.

"Not a word of this to anyone...unless you want to go to prison for a very long time. You got me?" Tiny nodded. "You have no reason to tell anyone what you told me. Understand?"

"Yes Brownie, but the cops, they'll be around asking more questions." The man in the chair wiped the sweat from his face and neck again.

"We'll take care of that right now too," responded Brownie. "You still livin' on your own, right? Nobody here in town? No relatives?"

"That's right, just me," answered Tiny.

"Good! Now your finished with Cal-Ag." Brownie reached down and pulled the large man out of the chair. "Get out of town now, and get out for good. If I ever see your face around here again you won't have to worry about going to prison. Now clean out your locker. You better be out of this town by tomorrow. You're a big guy to try to hide in a small town."

Tiny left the room. He removed his things from his assigned locker as Brownie watched. When finished, he walked to his car with Brownie following. Then the mechanic added, "Don't forget, not a word. If anyone asks, you've got family problems and don't know when you'll be back. Is that clear?"

"Yea Brownie," Tiny answered. "Don't worry I won't be back."

"That's right, you won't be," Brownie assured. Tiny left the field in a hurry. A dust cloud trailed behind him almost to the highway.

"Shit," said Brownie, returning to the office. He went over the assignments and checked to make sure all the planes were ready for the next day. Then he decided to head for Irene's Tavern.

"Hey Geno, a cold one please," he told the well-known bartender. "What a day. Seen Pat around?"

"No, I think he went down to see Jack," replied Geno.

"Hmm, musta passed each other. I just came from the hospital."

Geno was naturally curious on the condition of the young pilot he had seen grow up through the years. "How's the kid doin'? Is he gonna fly again?"

"Oh yea," said a hopeful Brownie. "The kids got a lotta guts. It'll be awhile but I can see him in the cockpit again. Maybe not ag flying, but charters and you know things like that."

"Any word from the cops?" Geno asked. "They got any leads?"

"Oh yea, just like the rest of us, they know who did it. They just can't prove it. I tell ya Geno, Harry Gebhardt and his goon Carter knew how to rig it. They left no clue, nothing to lead the cops. Gebhardt even got his wife to say they were both at home that night and had Carter spending the night on the couch at his house. Where the hell was Sheila? I know she wasn't out with Jack. They had just had an argument."

"How's Sheila doing, anyway?" asked the bartender.

"Oh, she'll be alright. One thing for certain she won't be living at home with her dad any more. I think her and her mom are moving out real soon." Brownie sipped on his beer. Three more town's people and a rancher came into the darkened lounge for drinks. The mechanic continued his story about the sabotage and crash. Placing the blame on Harry Gebhardt and Carter. Raising his voice he said, "Well, gotta go." He paid for his drink and began to leave. Noticing a long time rancher at the end of the bar, Brownie turned back toward Geno and added, "You know, if I was a crop owner around here I wouldn't let a guy who tried to kill another pilot fly my fields."

At the next bar the mechanic related the same story. Stopping for dinner at the Town House restaurant he walked into the lounge. Seeing yet another farmer he sat down beside him. "Hey John, how's it going? Can I buy you a drink?" Not waiting for an answer he ordered the man a drink. Soon he was telling how the plane had been rigged to crash and whom he knew for sure had done the deed.

By the next morning, when Harry Gebhardt came to work the office phone was ringing. His customers and clients were canceling their dusting and spraying orders. Some just said they didn't want Western doing their fields. Others were more specific. "Can't wreck your own planes enough, gotta wreck Cal-Ag's too, is that it Harry?"

said one valued customer. He was losing business, all of it. In town it was even worse for him and Carter.

"Hey Geno, give me a beer," said Carter, walking into Irene's. The people at the tables and on the barstools just glared silently at the young man as he sat down.

"Not today, Carter," replied Geno.

"Whaddya mean man? I want a beer!" demanded Carter.

"Like I said," repeated Geno, "not today, not ever. Take your business somewhere else. We don't serve plane wreckers around here."

It was the same for Harry Gebhardt. His service club black balled him. He tried to join another, but they too refused him admittance. The local country club removed him from membership. At home he was alone. His wife and daughter had moved into Jack's apartment. Carter, at his own apartment, had been told by the manager that he had ten days to vacate. He had already begun to get things ready in anticipation of returning to college but he had promised Harry he would stay for defoliation season.

Cotton defoliation was a complete failure for Western Dusters. The income and money was running out. Unbeknownst to Harry, when Jack's checks quit arriving at the chemical company, the Gebhardt's credit ended. At places of business, it was "cash only" for Western Dusters. Harry was laying off employees. Meanwhile, Cal-Ag pilots and crews were working overtime. Harry had also lost his best loader, who was now working for the competition, taking Tiny's position and duties at Cal-Ag. It was nearing fall and the slack time. Only grain spray lay ahead until the following spring. Harry Gebhardt and Western Dusters had managed to stay in business, but just barely. Carter was still trying to see Sheila. The young girl spent most of her time at the hospital with Jack. When she did see Carter around town the girl ignored him completely, even though Carter had explained many times to her where he was the night before the accident. How he had slept on the couch at her house and had left early the next morning before she woke. She didn't believe a word of it. The young girl had not spoken to her father since the scene at the office. Only her mother had talked on the phone to Harry and the conversations had not been pleasant. They would start with Harry pleading for his wife to return to their home, telling her he was a changed man, a kind and understanding person. But Debbie would always refuse, making Harry angry. Sheila could hear his voice yelling through the phone until Debbie, in disgust, would hang up.

CHAPTER TWENTY-TWO

    Brownie stood alone in the hanger doorway sipping from his cup of hot coffee. The foggy mist that shrouded the airfield was almost a light rain. Everything was damp. There would be no flying today. Inside the hanger, on sawhorses, lay wing sections that were going to be covered with fabric. A large crate held a new Pratt and Whitney engine that would be installed before the next season. Soon the pilots, Alan, Pat and Gary would join the mechanic. Together they would be salvaging what they could from Jack's crashed duster. Parts of the steel tubing of the fuselage, wing struts, tail section parts, even nuts and bolts were separated and placed into bins. All would aid in rebuilding the Stearman and test flying it before spring.
    At the hospital, Jack was still in rehabilitation. The doctors had managed to save his foot. His young bones had healed quickly and everyday it seemed he could manage a few more steps. He was regaining the feeling in his legs and with the help of a therapist soon would be able to walk without crutches. But there was one thing no therapist could help. Jack's mental attitude was a constant state of depression. The burns that he suffered to his face and upper body had left a deep scarring. Not only on his body but also on his mind. His clothing would cover his torso but the scorched and shriveled skin of his once handsome face haunted him every minute. When the doctors first removed the bandages he had looked across the room to a mirror and saw himself. Jack, for a moment said nothing, then he screamed and cursed at the doctor and nurses. Yelling at them to get out and leave him alone. From that moment on he gave strict orders that his family and especially Sheila was not to come to his room. But his father would have nothing to do with that.
    One morning, after a rather rough physical therapy session, Jack was sitting up on the edge of his bed. Gazing out the window at the valley fog that hid the view of the city he wished that there could be a shroud, like the morning haze, that could hide his scars. By mid-morning he would be able to see the tall buildings of downtown. He thought of Chinatown, across the highway, just to the west of those towering concrete structures. That night before the crash he should

have stayed in that hotel. If only he would have been late for work. Who would have flown the plane that fateful morning? Then he remembered that late night drive on the lonely road returning to the airfield. The old plane, on the roof of the café, its tail pointing straight up, its nose seemingly crashing directly downward through the top of the building. Just like it had hooked some wires or mysterious barrier, turning it immediately perpendicular to the earth.

Suddenly the door of his room opened. "Howya do'in Son?" said his father. Jack turned away from Alan.

"Get me a nurse," he yelled. "I told them not to let anyone in here."

"Jack, I'm your old man. They're not going to keep me out of here. Besides it's not their fault. I demanded it."

Jack, his back still turned away, shouted at his father, "Just get outta here, Dad. I don't want to see you or anybody. Not now, not ever."

Alan approached his son. Placing his hand on Jack's shoulder he explained, "Son, the scars and stuff doesn't matter to us. We love you. We want the best for you. For you to get out of here. Return to flying and to lead a normal life again."

Jack turned around. Showing his face to his father. "Oh yea, lead a fucking normal life. With a face like this."

Alan Lawrence had seen the scars on his son many times before while Jack had been under sedation. It had been no shock to him. In the war he had seen many such burns on bomber crews and airmen. "Look Son, they have many new developments now. Plastic surgery can do wonders. Just have a little patience and we can get through this thing. People, your friends, will get used to it and every time they see you after another procedure you'll look better."

"Just get out of here, Dad," cried Jack. "Just leave me alone."

"Your mom and Sheila are outside. They want to see you, Son."

"Damn it Dad, why'd they come here?" Jack was getting agitated and nervous. "Get out of here. Get outta here now." Jack slammed his fist down on the table near his bed. Just then the door to his room opened again.

Gail was first into the room followed by Sheila. Jack turned away again. "Hi honey," said his mother.

"Hi Jack," said Sheila. "Look, I brought you a chocolate shake from our favorite drive-in."

"Shit!" yelled Jack. "Can't you see I don't want any of you here?"

Alan could see that his son was angry and furious. He stepped toward the doorway. Motioning to his wife and Sheila he suggested, "Why don't you two wait outside for a moment?"

Jack, now standing near the window at the table next to his bed, yelled again, "God dammit just leave! All of you! Just leave me alone."

Sheila approached him from behind. "Jack here's your milkshake. Don't you want it? I even brought two straws so we can share." Jack did not turn around as Sheila held out the ice cream drink.

"I don't want anything from you," he shouted again. "Nothing from any of you! Just leave me alone."

"I'll just set it down here honey," Sheila told him. She put the milkshake down on the tray setting on the table. From behind she put her arms gently around Jack. "Oh Jack, I love you so much."

Jack, feeling her hands join together at his stomach, reached down and pulled them apart. He threw them away and suddenly turned around to face the three in the room. Pushing Sheila away he screamed, "Can you love this, little girl?"

Sheila, startled by Jack's sudden movement and shove, had almost fallen. Alan had caught her and helped balance the young girl as she stumbled backwards. Jack's loud yelling and screaming had brought a nurse and a male attendant through the doorway. Now the room was crowded with people. Jack was still yelling at everyone to get out. Sheila, with tears starting to stream down her red cheeks, made another effort. "Jack," she said starting to approach the angry young man again, "Oh Jack please, I just want to be here with you. Be here for you."

Jack turned to the tray on the table. Picking it up he screamed again, "All of you, get the hell outta here right now." He flung the tray, with a pitcher of water, a glass, and the milkshake, toward the doorway and the people. After bouncing off the end rail of the bed it crashed loudly to the floor, mixing water, the milkshake and broken glass together in a mess of liquid and shards. Alan and the attendant went toward Jack. Each large man grabbed an arm while the nurse reached in her pocket and pulled out a syringe.

"Calm down Son," said Alan as he and the attendant wrestled

Jack back onto the bed.

"Leave me alone," Jack blurted as he struggled to get free. "Fuck all of you. Get outta here."

The two large men held Jack down while the nurse administered the shot of a sedative that soon was having an effect on the hostile and dangerous patient. A few minutes passed and the room fell silent. Alan and the other man released Jack from their grasp. He was quiet. His eyes closed and his breathing had returned to normal. Sheila was crying. Gail put her arm around the young girl and together they left the room.

Looking at the nurse, Alan told her, "It'll be okay now. Thank you. I'll stay a few minutes more if you don't mind." The nurse nodded and left the room. Alan looked at his only son and held the young man's hand. The veteran pilot remembered when he first put his son in an open cockpit airplane. Jack had sat on his father's lap as Alan pulled the shoulder straps and waist belt over the both of them. After taking off, he lowered his hand on the stick and placed the small fingers of his child on the top of the control. The young boy began to pull and tug on the stick as if he was actually flying the old biplane. Afterwards, the boy had jumped out of the cockpit and ran over to Brownie who was placing the wheel chocks at the tires, yelled in laughter at the mechanic, "I flew, Daddy let me fly the plane." That was many years ago. Those had been hard times for both Alan and Jack. Alan's first wife, Jack's real mother, had died after suffering for a long time. Jack had just began school and didn't understand why he was living with his grandparents while his father spent so much time at work. A year later, a young beautiful red haired lady had entered their lives. Jack, at first, shied away from his new mother. But with time and her love for him this wondrous and beautiful lady soon was raising him through his formative years. Now Alan looked down at his only son. He stroked the hair that had grown back on Jack's head. He squeezed the hand of his son gently and let go. Before leaving the room he looked at himself in the mirror. Grabbing a dry washcloth big Alan Lawrence, veteran bomber pilot, business owner, crop duster, wiped the tears from his eyes before he walked out of the room to join his wife and Sheila.

In the hallway he told the waiting girls, "Jack's resting. Maybe we can try again tomorrow." He motioned the ladies toward the exit.

"It's best we just leave. There's not much we can do until his attitude changes." He looked at Sheila. "Do you need a ride Sheila?"

"No thanks," she answered. "I have my own car. I plan on going to the field. Do you need me to do anything in the office?"

"No thanks Honey," Alan answered. "Everything is okay for now. Maybe tomorrow I may need to send you to Stockton to pick up some wing struts. That is if you don't mind going."

"Of course not, Mr. Lawrence," the young girl answered with appreciation. "You and Gail have helped me and Mom so much over the last few weeks. Giving me a job and us a place to stay. I'm really thankful."

"Honey, we appreciate how you have stayed with Jack through all of this," Gail acknowledged. "And it looks like we will all have to be there for Jack when and if he decides to need us."

Alan opened the exit door for the girls. He and Gail, with Sheila walked to their cars. The Lawrences got in their car as Sheila walked toward her vehicle farther away in the parking area. As Alan and Gail drove by her they waved to the walking girl. Returning the wave, she opened the door of her car and sat down inside. But she didn't start the engine. Watching the Lawrence car leave the hospital grounds, she waited until it was completely out of sight. Then she lingered a few minutes longer before getting out of her car. She closed the door and walked back into the hospital. At the nurse's station she stopped and told the lady in white, "I forgot something in the room, I won't be long." The nurse nodded and made a note of the time. Entering the room, Sheila approached her still sedated and sleeping lover. The young girl looked down at the red blotches and burnt tissue of Jack's face. With a trembling hand she softly felt the ridges and roughness of the skin. Jack didn't move. His breathing remained the same. Sheila's gaze was fixed upon his face. She was thinking of that night after graduation. The grassy field, the warm summer evening. Her lover's tenderness as they were wrapped in the passion of their lovemaking. She had been a willing concubine to this romantic, amorous and handsome suitor. That night she had truly fallen in love with the man now laying in this hospital bed. Sheila leaned forward and whispered in Jack's ear. "I love you Jack, I'll always love you Jack." She moved her lips from his ear to his face and kissed the sleeping man on his chapped and cracked lips. After a moment, the girl raised and stood up. Still near the bedside she clutched Jack's hand in hers. Sighing, Sheila said aloud, "Goodbye Jack, I won't ever forget the way you were."

Jack was dreaming. Dreaming of that cushion of air that all pilots feel under the wings of the aircraft while flying low over row crops like cotton. That cushion of comfort and safety. He could feel the soft warm summer breeze on his cheeks and lips as the wind rushed over and around the cockpit. He could feel his hand wrapped around the joystick of the plane. But it was soft and seemed to control his every movement. Each pass was low and perfect, each turn was precision. His flying had never been better. But then, it was just a dream.

At the airfield, Brownie with Pat and Gary had finished the work on the new wings. Tomorrow they would fit them in place. "Wanna go get a beer?" Pat asked the other two.

"Nah, I'm going home," replied Gary. "See you guys tomorrow."

"Well Brownie, it's you and me I guess," Pat continued. "Come on."

"Okay, I guess," Brownie answered. "But just one. I wanna get home early tonight."

"Okay, I'll meet you at Lee's," said Pat. "That's closer."

"See ya there," said Brownie watching the young pilot drive away.

Brownie got in the company truck and started down the road away from the field. He saw Sheila's car approaching from the other direction and slowed to a halt. He held his arm out the window and motioned for her to stop along side his truck. He leaned out the window and told her no one was at the field.

"Can you give Alan a message for me?" Sheila asked the mechanic.

"Sure, what is it Sheila?"

"Tell him I won't be able to go to Stockton tomorrow to get those parts he wanted," Sheila told him.

"Is something wrong?" Brownie asked.

"No, nothing's wrong," answered Sheila looking at another car approaching in her direction. "I better go now Brownie. Thanks a lot."

"Okay little girl, I'll tell Pappy." Brownie also saw the vehicle approaching on the narrow road. "Better get outta this guy's way. Don't worry we'll manage. I'll see you later."

"Goodbye Brownie," said Sheila putting the car in gear. They parted in opposite directions. At Lee's Bar, as Brownie was walking to the door he saw Sheila had made a U-turn and was leaving the field. He waved as she passed but it was not returned. He watched her cross the busy highway and drive down a farm road out into the country. Brownie shrugged his shoulders and entered the dark cocktail lounge. He sat down next to Pat, his young pilot friend, and ordered a cold beer.

CHAPTER TWENTY-THREE

It had not been a joyous holiday season for the Lawrences or the Gebhardts. Jack had been allowed to leave the hospital just before Thanksgiving. Gail had prepared a grand meal to celebrate his return home. Jack's mother had invited his uncle and aunt, grandparents and Sheila. Gail had not seen Sheila since that awful day at the hospital. Many weeks had passed. Gail had talked to Debbie Gebhardt at their apartment but Sheila had gone up north to the bay area. It really didn't matter. During Thanksgiving, Jack had not left his room. Gail and Alan begged him to come out and join the family, as they got together, but he refused. Instead he busied himself listening to the radio. Changing stations frequently, he spent the days cataloging songs he heard. Listing title and singer and rearranging them in alphabetical order. Every once in a while, Gail would hear the radio be turned off and a crash come from his room. She never asked why or if anything was wrong. During Christmas, the same took place. Sheila and her mother were again invited for the big Christmas meal. The Lawrence family was there but not Sheila or her mom. Jack again remained in his room.

Harry Gebhardt also spent the holidays alone. Christmas and New Years found him at a downtown Fresno bar. Just him and the bartender swapping tales of loneliness and failed businesses. In her apartment, Debbie Gebhardt was also alone. It was New Years day. After watching the parades on television she had tried to read a book but it wouldn't hold her interest. Then she heard someone at the door. It opened and there stood her daughter looking disheveled and tired. Dropping the book she leaped forward to hug her offspring.

"Honey, are you alright? Where have you been?" asked Debbie. "It's been so long."

"I'm fine Mother," answered Sheila taking off her coat. "I went to see about registering for school in Berkeley."

"At Cal," exclaimed Debbie, "that's where Carter goes."

"Yea, I know. I saw him there. He showed me around campus."

"But, but what about you and Jack? I thought..." Debbie hesitated.

"That's why I'm back, Mother. How is Jack doing?" Sheila asked.

Debbie explained that Jack was home but did not leave his room except for therapy. She also mentioned that he was still not seeing anyone other than Alan and Gail.

"That's too bad," Sheila said rather coarsely. "How have you been?"

Her mother was taken aback by the change of subject but answered, "I've been fine honey. I got a job working at the grocery store."

"How's Daddy?" asked Sheila. "Have you seen him lately?"

"Okay, I guess. I see him around town sometimes but we don't speak. The divorce will be final in a couple of weeks. Are you here to stay?" she asked her daughter.

"Yep! For awhile anyway. I still have a bed don't I?"

Debbie came forward and hugged her daughter again. "Of course, Honey. I've missed you while you've been away."

After the holidays, the weeks went by fast. At the field the crews of Cal-Ag and Western were busy getting everything ready for the next season. Alan had finally talked his son into coming out to the field with him one morning. It was all smiles on Brownie and the rest of the employees. Jack smiled back but didn't say much except to Brownie.

"Where's Tiny," he asked the mechanic.

"He had to leave town in a hurry," answered Brownie. "Something about a new job. Somewhere down south, I think."

"Come on Jack," said Alan, grabbing his son by the arm, "let's see if you still got it." He began walking his son to the row of Stearman biplanes parked neatly wing to wing.

Jack pulled away from his father's grip. "I don't think so Dad," Jack said. "My leg hurts a little this morning."

"Okay," agreed Alan. "Then how about riding co-pilot while I take the 'bonanza' up for a check ride?"

"Alright, I guess so," Jack replied nervously.

They climbed into the four passenger plane that Cal-Ag used for charter flights. Soon they were in the air. Alan looked over at his son. Jack had his hands in his lap. He was looking straight ahead. "Engine sounds good, huh Son?"

"Yea, pretty good I guess," answered Jack.

"Brownie can really fix 'em."

"Yea, he's a good mechanic," agreed Jack.

Alan set the trim of the aircraft. "Wanna take her, Son? Everything's set. It'll be good for you to take the yoke again."

Jack, his palms sweaty, nervously grabbed both sides of the steering yoke in front of him.

"That's it, Son," encouraged Alan, "get the old feel back."

"It feels okay." Alan could see his tense son leaning forward in the co-pilot's seat. "Why don't you see if you can get her back to the field. I'm sure you can find your way," laughed Alan.

Jack didn't respond but instead banked the plane in a wide circle to return to the airfield. Fifteen minutes later they were on the downwind approach to the runway.

"Take her on in, Son. You can do it. Just like before."

Jack was quiet as the runway passed by on his left. He turned the ninety degrees and soon was on his final approach. But he was not getting lower.

"Lower, Son," Alan told Jack. "You're going to overshoot."

Jack kept the nose and wings level as the beginning of the runway came closer. "Down Jack," Alan demanded. Jack lowered the nose a little. The ground and the cotton field below the plane got closer. Alan looked at his son. Sweat was running down his forehead and face. He could see the salty fluid stinging the tender scars and sensitive skin. Jack looked down at the approaching ground and pulled the nose up suddenly, almost stalling the aircraft above the runway. "I'll take it, Son," said Alan grabbing the steering wheel on his side. He leveled the plane and added power. The plane cruised smoothly a hundred feet above the runway. Pulling up at the end, Alan again began the downwind approach for landing.

"Want to try it again, Son?" asked Alan in a calm voice. "It's alright, I understand. It's been awhile. Come on now, we've got plenty of time. Whaddya say?"

"Go ahead, Dad," replied Jack. "Just get it down so I can get out of here."

Alan expertly touched the plane down onto the runway and taxied to the parking spot. As soon as the propeller stopped, Jack crawled out and jumped to the ground. Without saying a word to anyone he got in his truck and drove home.

Brownie watched the truck leave a trail of dust down the road.

"Didn't go too well I take it?" he asked Alan as he checked the prop and engine.

"Oh, okay I guess for the first time," answered the chief pilot. "He has this fear of low level flying. From the crash I guess. He was fine until we started our final approach. Then he suddenly panicked. He pulled up way too quick." Alan patted his mechanic on the shoulder and laughed. "One thing Brownie, I know the stall buzzer works."

Brownie smiled. Inside, he was hoping that Jack would overcome his fear. He only had a month to get back in the air. Cal-Ag was going to be very busy this spring and summer.

Jack had weekly visits to the therapists for his legs. He also was visiting a plastic surgeon on a regular basis. The doctor kept encouraging the young man by saying, "Years from now, hardly anyone would be able to tell that you had been in that terrible accident." All Jack heard was "years from now" and "hardly" anyone. The only thing he thought of was he was not going to wait for those "years," or "anyone" to notice.

A couple of weeks later, Alan was still pressing his son little by little. He was patient, but he knew time was running out. In the Bonanza, he now had Jack in the pilot's seat. They would cruise around the valley. Flying above large open fields, with no power lines, Alan would encourage his son to fly lower and lower. He could get down to a little below a hundred feet before he would pull up again. Each time Alan would congratulate him. After a relatively long day they were approaching the field. "It's all yours, Son," Alan told Jack as he turned on his final approach. "I'm not touching it this time."

Jack was quiet but looked straight ahead. He added flaps and, over the threshold of the runway, cut the power. The V-tailed bonanza settled gently down on the paved surface. "That a way Jack," Alan yelled. "I knew you could do it."

Jack was sweating as he turned the plane toward the hanger. "Yea, that felt pretty good."

As they passed the row of Stearman dusters and sprayers his dad proudly told him, "We'll have you back in one of those real soon now."

"Yea, sure Dad," was Jack's only answer.

The next morning the fog cleared early. Jack limped around the hanger. His walk was getting better everyday. During this time it was usually just he and Brownie working. Pat and Gary would check in every once in awhile to see if any charter flights were available. Brownie was almost finished with the rebuilt Stearman. He and Jack leaned against the workbench at the rear of the hanger.

"Pretty good lookin' bird if I say so myself, huh Jack?"

"Yea, it looks real nice," Jack answered.

"Bet you can hardly wait to get back in the cockpit, eh my man?" asked Brownie slapping Jack on the shoulder.

Jack lowered his head. "I've been meaning to talk to you about that Brownie."

Just then Alan pulled up in front of the hanger. Getting out he walked by the freshly painted biplane. "Looks good Brownie, but can she fly?" Alan chuckled.

"A couple of more days and we'll find out Pappy," Brownie laughed. Knowing that everything would go well on the initial flight. He had done this many times before.

Alan looked at Jack. "Well Son, nice morning, let's say we get you in a Stearman and let you get the feel of a duster again."

"I'm not sure Dad, I don't think I'm ready yet. Besides my leg is bothering me a little more today." Jack was thinking of excuses as fast as he could. But Alan wouldn't hear of it.

"Brownie, is three-seven ready to go?"

"Sure thing Pappy. I'll go out with you and help crank her up."

Alan and Brownie, with Jack trailing behind, walked out of the hanger toward the waiting duster. Alan climbed up on the black step of the lower left wing. He motioned to his son to climb up and get in the cockpit. Jack hesitated. He looked at Brownie walking around to the front of the plane. He began turning the prop to get the oil into the cylinders.

"Come on, Son," encouraged Alan, "you'll do fine."

"Come on Jack," said Brownie from the front. "I'm not going to turn this blade all day. It'll be just like the old times. Climb in the seat and call 'contact' when you're ready."

Jack lifted his bad leg up on to the step alongside the fuselage. He grabbed the edge of the cockpit and pulled himself onto the wing. He looked at his father standing along side of him. "Need some help climbing in, Son?" asked Alan.

"No, I can do it Dad." Jack swung his leg into the seat and then pulled himself in. He sat down on the cushion.

Alan put his hand on Jack's shoulder. "How's it feel, Son?"

Jack looked at the controls, the joystick between his legs, the "money handle" that controlled the spreader, the throttle control, the magneto switch. He placed his feet on the pedals and pushed them alternately back and forth.

"Go ahead Son, turn the switch," encouraged his father.

"Contact," yelled Brownie from in front.

Jack put his shaking hand on the switch then hesitated. He was sweating in the cold morning. "Contact," Brownie repeated, his hands gripping the top of edge of the large metal blade.

Finally, Jack's fingers moved the switch. He leaned over the edge of the cockpit. "Contact," he answered to the mechanic.

Brownie swung the propeller blade. The engine coughed once then sputtered and stopped. "Off," said Brownie.

Jack turned the switch to off and confirmed it to Brownie. The mechanic moved the propeller into position for another pull. "Give it some throttle this time, Jack. She'll go."

Once again Brownie pulled down hard on the blade of the prop. Jack eased in the throttle and the engine roared to life. He looked at his father still on the wing. Alan, his black hair blowing and tangled with the wind from the propeller, patted his son on the shoulder and jumped down. Brownie came around to the far edge of the wing. He gave a thumbs up to the young man and stepped back. Alan joined him. Together they watched Jack slowly pull the shoulder harness over his back. Jack, held the brakes while his shaking hands tried to buckle the belt. He looked at his father and Brownie standing nearby. He tried again but there was no latching the three belts. The wind from the prop and the cold sweat was stinging his face. Jack reached up and turned off the engine. In the quiet aftermath, both Brownie and Alan looked at each and then approached the plane. Jack climbed out without saying anything.

"What's wrong, Son?" Alan asked.

"Are you alright kid?" asked a concerned Brownie.

Jack looked at the both of them. "Dad, I can't do it, Okay? I tried. Isn't that good enough for either of you?" He turned and walked away toward his car at the hanger. Alan started after him but

Brownie grabbed him by the arm.

"Let him go, Pappy. He'll be alright," he told the pilot.

"But, he's my son," replied Alan.

"That's why you need to let him go. Give him some time," continued Brownie. "With the season coming, we've all been pushing him. Maybe he needs to regroup. Let him think about it. We can give it another shot in a couple of days."

Alan watched his son drive away. Maybe Brownie was right. But maybe, thought Alan, emotionally and mentally Jack would never be a pilot again.

Two more days passed and Brownie had the rebuilt duster ready for a test flight. Everyone was at the field that day. Brownie, Pat and Gary pushed the plane out of the hanger. The fog had cleared and the new gold paint on the wings glistened in the bright winter sun. Pat climbed into the cockpit.

"Nice feel, I'm gonna like flyin' this beauty," he said.

"Better not pull any more crazy stunts or you won't be flying at all," quipped Gary, who, when it came to the number of flying hours, was actually the number two pilot behind Alan.

Emerging from the hanger, Alan was adjusting the chin strap of his helmet. "Alright hotshot," he yelled at Pat, "Outta that cockpit." Pat sighed and climbed out and down to the ground. There, he joined the crew and pilots of Cal-Ag and the townspeople who had come out to watch the test flight.

Passing his uncle, he chuckled, "Just checking the controls Uncle Alan."

"I'll let you know how they feel after I land," replied Alan, climbing into the plane.

Alan taxied the new biplane to the end of the runway. He ran up the engine. Increasing the RPM's, he checked the gauges and controls. As the pilots and crews watched, Alan turned the plane into the wind and was soon airborne.

From his office window, Harry Gebhardt saw the plane lift off the asphalt and climb smoothly to gain altitude. He sat down at his desk. On top of it were a few papers and even less work orders for the spring. Down to one plane and a crew of three, he knew this was going to be his last season at this field. He reached down and pulled open the lower right desk drawer. Pulling up a half empty bottle of

Jack Daniel's whiskey, he poured himself a small glass. Downing it, he looked at the bottle and again removing the top, took a swig directly from the container. Wiping the alcohol from his lips, he heard the Cal-Ag Stearman roar across the field in front of the crowd. He tossed the bottle back in the desk drawer. Picking up the phone, Harry called a friend and airport manager in a small town in Arizona. By the end of summer he would be out of town forever.

Alan put the Stearman through maneuvers. The biplane easily handled the stress of aerobatics. The skilled pilot banked it steeply. He stalled it on purpose, regaining the power when he put it into a dive. In a simulated crop dusting maneuver he came in low over the field and then pulled up sharply and banked the plane to the left. After an hour of flying and stunts he landed the Stearman, touching all three wheels on the ground at the same time. Taxiing by the people that had gathered he gave Brownie a thumbs up. When he climbed down, Alan removed his helmet and briskly shook the mechanic's hand.

"Great job, Brownie," Alan told him. "Fly's like an angel. Where's Jack? I want to see what he thinks."

Jack had been watching from behind the crew and pilots. He stepped out from the group. "Looked good, Dad."

"It's a real good plane Jack," said Alan. "Why don't you just take her up for a couple of touch and go's?" Jack hesitated. Would it be so hard to just take off, make a couple of turns, return to the field and practice a couple of landings? He grabbed his father's helmet and goggles. His father nodded and Jack walked to the formerly burned and mangled plane, now rebuilt, sparkling in the springtime sun. He slowly climbed in the cockpit. Settling into the seat, he looked at Brownie.

"Contact," he said to the mechanic.

Brownie smiled and trotted over to the front of the plane. "Contact," he replied and pulled down on the propeller. The still warm engine sprang to life with a roar. Pulling the chocks from in front of the wheels, Brownie swung his arm and pointed toward the runway. Jack, head down, began to taxi the plane to the run-up area. The mechanic, Alan and the other pilots watched the black and gold duster come to a halt. They waited for the increased roar of the Pratt and Whitney engine. Suddenly, the plane turned and headed back towards them. Jack pulled the plane in front of the hanger and silenced the engine. Alan met him when he climbed down.

"What's wrong, Son? Something foul with the plane? Engine trouble?" he asked.

"The only things that's wrong is you got the wrong guy in the seat," replied a sullen Jack. He started to walk to his car but Alan grabbed his shoulder.

"It's okay, Son, we'll give it another chance."

Jack wrenched away and getting in his car replied, "Nice try Dad, I'm finished okay? It's all over." Jack drove away and headed toward Irene's. He hadn't been out in public since the accident, but now he didn't care. He wasn't going to be around here long anyway.

Back at the field Alan was distraught. He thought he had been easy on his son. Letting him take his time in returning to flying. He talked to Brownie and the mechanic agreed that everything was going along as planned until now. Alan sighed and decided to talk to his son that evening at dinner when Gail would be present. The other pilots had left and the crowd had returned to town. Alan left for home, slowly driving away from the field. Brownie checked his planes, closed and locked the hanger doors and headed out to have a beer.

At their apartment Sheila was explaining to her mom about what happened when she visited Berkeley. At this point, Debbie Gebhardt was going to let her daughter make up her own mind without being an influence. Sheila was having a rough time with any decision. She told her mother she loved Jack but she had such a good time in the bay area that she wanted to make that her home. Carter would be able to provide a good income and nice home. He had all but proposed to her on her last visit. Debbie Gebhardt sat quietly while Sheila let it all out. Afterward, the two girls, mother and daughter, sat down together and talked briefly. At the end of the evening, in her room, Sheila lay back on the pillows on her bed. She stared up at the ceiling. Tomorrow, she decided, she would tell her mom of her decision.

When he entered Irene's, Brownie was surprised to see Jack sitting at the end of the bar sipping on a beer. He was looking down, subconsciously hiding his facial scars from the people that were patronizing the darkened lounge.

"Howzit goin' Jack?" asked Brownie, sitting down next to him.
"Okay, I guess," the young man answered.
"You're doin' okay in the plane too ya know," said Brownie with encouragement.
"Ah it sucks, Brownie. You heard me at the field. I'm through. Through flying, through with Sheila." Jack raised his glass to Geno, the bartender, signaling he wanted another beer. "I can barely handle the Bonanza. But, get me in that open cockpit of a Stearman and all I see are those power lines and the flames. I get to the run up area, look down the runway for takeoff and my hands start shaking. Shit, I can't even keep the ailerons level."
Brownie tapped Jack's beer mug. "Hang in there, you'll get it. When was the last time you saw Sheila? I heard she had gone to San Francisco."
"A long time, I was still in the hospital," answered Jack. "I thought I saw her driving through town the other day so I turned down a side street."
"Why didn't you stop and see if it was her?"
"Oh yea, she's going to want to see me," Jack answered, then pointing to his face he continued, "and see this!"
"Hey," exclaimed Brownie, "that's looking better all the time. You're still getting treatment right?" Jack nodded. "Fine, then don't be so hard on yourself."
"Even if we got back together," he told Brownie, "how am I supposed to support her? All I know is flying and now I can't even do that."
"Tell you what, Jack," said Brownie putting his arm on the back of the young man, "in a couple of days, you give it one more shot."
"I can't Brownie, it's useless."
"Hey, I've practically raised you in that cockpit," Brownie said raising his voice. "Give it one more chance. Just for this old mechanic." Jack looked at the man with whom he had shared so many experiences, the man that had saved his life that terrible day.
He lowered his head. "I don't know, Brownie. You don't have any idea what it's like in that cockpit."
But Brownie was firm. "Just give it one more shot. If you can't do it, I'll understand and won't push you anymore. Hell, then I'll make a mechanic out of you," he laughed.

"Okay, one more time," agreed Jack. "Just for you and if it doesn't work I'll be leaving for good. I couldn't work around planes without being able to fly them."

"That's great," said a smiling Brownie. "Finish your beer. Let's get outta here. Geno, I got these." Jack, his head down, walked out the back door of Irene's to his car.

"Geno," said Brownie, "give me one more. And can I use the phone in your office?"

"Sure Brownie," Geno answered. "The door's open. Just close it behind you if you want a little quiet."

"Thanks," said Brownie. He went in the office. Closed the door and dialed a number he had memorized before.

Sheila had been startled by the call. She had just dozed off when she heard her mom answer the ring. "Sheila? Why yes Brownie, she's here. I'll get her for you."

Sheila was already out the door of her room. "Who is it Mom, Carter?"

"No, it's Brownie," Debbie answered.

"Brownie?" said a puzzled Sheila, "what does he want I wonder?" She picked up the receiver and said, "Hello."

The next five minutes Debbie Gebhardt listened to a one way conversation. She watched as her daughter nodded her head several times. Every minute or so she would acknowledge what had been said by Brownie on the other end by just saying, "yea," or "okay." Finally, she told Brownie thanks and goodbye and hung up the phone.

"What was that all about?" asked her mother.

"It was a warning from Brownie," Sheila answered.

"Warning? Warning about what?"

"About Carter," Sheila replied. "It seems the police have found some evidence about the crash of Jack's plane and want to question him again. Brownie said they may arrest him."

"Arrest him!" exclaimed Debbie. "Maybe you oughta call him honey?"

"Mom, I'll be leaving soon to go up there," explained Sheila. "I'll let him know then. I just can't believe he didn't tell me. You don't think he actually caused that plane wreck, do you Mom?"

"I don't know what to think anymore honey," answered Debbie.

She returned to her seat and looked at Sheila. "All I know is, I want what is best for you. I'm going to be fine after your father leaves for Arizona. You've got your whole future, your whole life ahead of you." Debbie stood up and hugged her daughter. "No matter who it is with, don't make the same mistakes I have."

Two days later at the airport, it was almost the same scene as before. But this time, with the plane having been proven airworthy, the only people watching were the Cal-Ag crew and pilots. This time Brownie was with Jack in the hanger as he slipped on his flying gear. He handed Jack his crash helmet.

"This is it kid," said Brownie. "This one's for me."

"Yea sure," Jack said, beginning to walk slowly to Brownie's rebuilt bi-plane.

Alan Lawrence stood silently as the two passed. Leaning on the wing tip, he watched Jack climb up on the wing and into the cockpit. Brownie jumped up on the wing walk. He leaned over and pulled the safety belts over Jack's shoulders. The shaking pilot managed to latch the belts at his waist. Brownie patted him on the helmet and jumped to the ground. Jack looked at his Dad, shrugged his shoulders and lowered his goggles. The plane started on the first effort and was soon headed down the taxi way toward the warm up area at the start of the runway.

As the plane coasted down the asphalt, Jack's fears were running rampant through his mind. This was useless, he thought. The cockpit check, the taxiing down the runway, the run up to check gauges, all of that was habit. But, with each routine he became more nervous. Now, he turned the plane into the wind. Pointing it down the runway. There he sat. Engine idling. Minutes passed. The wind from the propwash stung his cheeks. This was stupid. Why not just turn around and go back? His Dad would understand. Brownie, always encouraging, would tell him nice try. All he would have to do is get in his car and leave the field, never to return. Jack could see his dad and Brownie, along with his cousin Pat and Gary with the rest of the crew standing near the hanger. Brownie was waving, "come on," motioning with his arm to take off.

Jack eased in a little throttle to get the plane to start rolling. "Fuck this shit," he said to himself. "I don't need this." He pushed hard on one brake, forcing the plane to begin a turn around. As he had almost completed the turn to head back to the hanger Jack noticed a car racing down the taxiway towards him. He stopped the plane from turning anymore. Who the hell was this, he thought, cars weren't allowed on the runways. The car stopped along side Jack's plane. Inside Jack could see it was Sheila. He crouched down in the cockpit, trying to hide his face. Sheila leaned out the window. Jack could see her lips but the roar of the engine muffled any sound. The plane started to roll again, still headed back toward the hanger area. Sheila was banging on the side of the car with her hand as she leaned out the window. Jack finally sat up in the cockpit. She smiled at him. He pulled his goggles up onto his helmet exposing his full face to her eyes. He watched her as she settled back in her seat. He could read her lips as she looked right at him and said, "I love you." She motioned with her arm out the window to follow him and sped off to the far end of the runway. Jack, looked over his shoulder, as she stopped at the opposite end. Sheila got out of the car and held her arms out as if Jack was right in front of her. The young pilot turned the plane around again and lowering his goggles, pushed the throttle to the maximum. The smooth sounding engine roared as the RPM's increased. Jack leaned over the side of the cockpit, watching the girl with open arms at the far end. When there was enough speed the tail wheel raised and Jack could now see Sheila over the cockpit, jumping up and down as the plane came closer. Nearing the rotation speed to become airborne Jack noticed that his face and hands were no longer sweaty. It was probably all the wind created by the prop and airspeed. But, no matter, it was time to make a decision. He pulled back on the stick and the beautiful black and gold biplane lifted off the ground. Jack looked down at Sheila as he passed overhead. The girl blew him a kiss before dust from the wind of the prop forced her to cover her eyes. Jack made a crop dusting turn and headed back toward his girl. He lowered the nose and swooped over her head again. At the hanger, Brownie placed his hand on Alan's shoulder.

"Looks like you just lost your new plane Pappy," laughed the mechanic.

Alan just smiled. Jack had made another turn and was now flying down the runway, just feet off the ground. He pulled up over the top of Sheila. Leaning over the edge of the cockpit, he took one hand off the throttle and waved to the smiling, laughing girl on the ground. Jack buzzed the Cal-Ag crew. Passing over the hanger he dipped his wings to the waving pilots. The sun was setting on the horizon. Jack, after one more pass over Sheila, brought the duster in for a landing. The flight had been over quickly. But, he was ready now. Ready for the season to begin. It would be the best of seasons for Cal-Ag.